The Townsend Legacy
HEAVENLY PLACES II

*To Jessie, God bless you.
Love your radiant smile,*

Arvil Jones

Ernestine Smith and **Dr. Arvil Jones**

Ernestine Smith

Wasteland Press
www.wastelandpress.net
Shelbyville, KY USA

The Townsend Legacy: Heavenly Places II
by Ernestine Smith and Dr. Arvil Jones

Copyright © 2014 Ernestine Smith and Dr. Arvil Jones
ALL RIGHTS RESERVED

First Printing – December 2014
ISBN: 978-1-68111-006-6

This is a work of fiction. Names, characters, places and incidents either are the product of the author's imagination or are used fictitiously, and any resemblance to any actual persons, living or dead, events, or locales is entirely coincidental.

NO PART OF THIS BOOK MAY BE REPRODUCED IN ANY FORM, BY PHOTOCOPYING OR BY ANY ELECTRONIC OR MECHANICAL MEANS, INCLUDING INFORMATION STORAGE OR RETRIEVAL SYSTEMS, WITHOUT PERMISSION IN WRITING FROM THE COPYRIGHT OWNER/AUTHOR

Printed in the U.S.A.

0 1 2 3 4

Introduction

The Townsend family, guided by the strong hand and stalwart disposition and character of the Reverend Jeff Townsend, along with the gentle and gracious love of their mother Becky, continues to live and thrive in spite of the harsh environment, the economic conditions, and the racial and religious prejudices of the post-Civil War era. From the majestic mountains of West Virginia to the rolling hills of Kentucky and Tennessee, the saga of the Townsend and Tillotson families continues to unfold with stories of unflinching courage, unfailing faith, and undying love. But there are also the harsh realities of human failure, human weakness, broken hearts, broken lives, and broken families, all of which are healed and made whole again by unconditional forgiveness.

It has often been said that love conquers all, meaning, of course, that no object, no person, no condition, and no circumstance can overcome, or defeat the power of a constant, consistent, sincere and heart-felt love that exists between a soul and the living God, and neither can these forces defeat or diminish the love of a man and woman who are totally committed to God and to one another. The Townsend and Tillotson families, now separated by hundreds of miles and hundreds of mountains, are again drawn together by unforseen circumstances. Jeff Townsend and Tom Tillotson, born years apart, brought up under quite dissimilar circumstances, and endowed with virtually opposite temperaments, were destined to become the best of friends, each man, in his own way, demonstrating the indisputable truth that, "if God brings you to it, He will bring you through it."

The Townsend Legacy
Heavenly Places II

The train that would carry Jeff, Becky, and the two children back to West Virginia didn't run on Sunday, so Jeff and Becky had to stay another two nights in Cleveland Tennessee. Jeff, knowing this in advance of their trip to Tennessee, had made arrangements for Deacon Joseph Parks to conduct the Sunday service at the Jenkins Memorial Baptist Church. And in order to give the newlyweds (Daniel Ray and Sarah) their privacy on their honeymoon, Tom and Pearly Mae insisted that Jeff and Becky spend at least one of those nights with them. Tom, of course, had an ulterior motive - wanting his congregation to hear Jeff preach on Sunday morning. Tom's parents, Mary and Avery, went home with Tom and Pearly Mae Saturday night also. It was a time of both celebration and reflection for three families, all of whom had been brought together by the most unforeseeable of circumstances, or, as Jeff and Becky commented later that night, by the sovereign will of God.

After Samuel, Ollie Marie, Mollie, Carter and Thomas Clark were put to bed, the three couples spent about four hours catching up on thirty years of their respective histories. By that time (which was nearly midnight) everyone was very tired, and ready for bed. But just before leaving to go back to their own home across town, Avery, seeing the little portrait of Mary on the mantle over the fireplace, looked at Tom with an inquisitive squint in his eye, inquiring, "By the way young man, just out of curiosity, would you have any idea where my whip and Bowie knife might be? They seem to have just disappeared about thirty years ago." Tom quickly assured him, "They're both in a safe place Sir." For reasons known only to himself, Tom couldn't tell his father the whole truth about the location of the whip and Bowie knife in the presence of Jeff and Becky. Avery gave Tom that hesitant, momentary stare that said that he would accept his answer for now, but that he was by no means satisfied with it. Tom understood that stare, for he had seen it before, while he was growing up under his father's stern military discipline.

As Jeff and Becky lay in bed that night, very few words were spoken. They were both very tired from all the activities of the last few days, and neither of them wanted to admit to the other that, in spite of the fact that they had thoroughly enjoyed themselves, they were both terribly homesick. They missed the twins, the farm, the church, the little town of Bruceton Mills, and the lifestyle of which they had become very fond. They were both thinking, "there's no place like home."

Jeff was also silently praying about tomorrow's sermon. His silence was, to Becky, what Avery's stare was to Tom, it was clearly understood. Becky could tell by the expression on Jeff's face when he was going over a sermon in his mind, and she simply left him to his thoughts, praying silently with him, and for him. And as tired as they were, it was still difficult to fall asleep in a bed that was not their own.

Becky fell asleep perhaps an hour before Jeff could. In spite of the fact that he knew they would be leaving around 2:00 a.m. Monday morning, and that tomorrow's sermon might be the only sermon that he would ever preach at the Copper Springs Baptist Church, Jeff refused to look past his sermon to the next day. Every message he had ever delivered, he had done so with all of his heart and soul, knowing that every message might be the last one he would ever deliver. He also knew his next sermon might be the very instrument that God would use to draw some poor lost soul to Christ. He took nothing for granted when it came to his preaching. He dared not fall asleep without asking God to give him the very message that was needed for tomorrow morning. Before he fell asleep, he was certain that God had answered his, and Becky's prayer.

Sunday morning, June 4th, 1876, Copper Springs Baptist Church, Cleveland Tennessee.

The Copper Springs Baptist Church was somewhat larger than the Jenkins Memorial Baptist Church, both the building and the congregation. Both Jeff and Becky were so thankful that God had given Tom such a great opportunity in the sprawling community of Cleveland Tennessee. A great work had already been done, and an even greater work lay ahead. Many of the congregation had already met Jeff and Becky and Mary and Avery at the wedding, but for the sake of those who had not attended the wedding, Tom introduced them to the whole congregation again on Sunday morning.

After nearly every person in the church had shaken hands with Jeff and Becky, one elderly gentleman came forward, walking very slowly, with the aid of a homemade cane. His back was bent, and Jeff could readily see that the old gentleman was in pain. Jeff didn't wait for the old man to reach him, he walked toward the old man. As Jeff closed the gap between them, the elderly gentleman raised his head, looking upward into Jeff's face. His voice trembled slightly as he cautiously moved the cane from his right hand to his left, reaching out his hand to Jeff.

"Reverend Townsend, do you remember me?" he asked.

As Jeff looked closely at the old man's wrinkled face, tears filled his eyes, his own voice trembling, as he recognized the preacher who had led him to the Lord when he was ten years old. It was Preacher Cloyd Smith, the man who had baptized Jeff, and ordained him to the ministry many years ago.

"My, My, Brother Smith, it's really you!," Jeff replied, as he tenderly embraced the aged preacher. A beaming smile came across the elder minister's face as Jeff helped him into the pew.

"I've been hearing a mighty good report about you young man," Rev. Smith commented, and when I heard you were going to be preaching here today, I just had to find a way to come and hear you, just to see if what I have been hearing is true."

Jeff beamed with joy and pride just to think that the dear old preacher who had baptized him long ago would make the painful effort to come so far just to hear him preach.

"Well Sir, Jeff replied reverently, I sure hope you will not be disappointed. And I appreciate your coming more than words can say."

It was time for the worship service to begin, and Reverend Smith gave Jeff the same nod of approval he had given him years ago, when Jeff had preached his first sermon at the Caleb's Creek Baptist Church in Henry County.

As Jeff stepped behind the pulpit, a reverent silence fell upon the whole crowd of about 200 persons. Jeff cleared his throat, and, to the surprise and pleasure of Pastor Tom Tillotson, asked the folks to turn in their Bibles to the third chapter of Hebrews, verse one. The whole congregation stood with their Bibles open, as he read the words - Wherefore holy brethren, partakers of the heavenly calling, consider the Apostle and High Priest of our profession, Christ Jesus.

Jeff immediately saw the big grin on Tom's face, knowing that Tom remembered that he himself had preached from this very verse the first time he had stood to preach. But Jeff also noticed something else. All the children, including his children, were being very quiet, and even seemed to be listening intently to his every word. He also noticed that Brother Cloyd Smith was listening just as intently. He simply had to introduce Brother Smith to the congregation before he could proceed.

"Ladies and gentlemen, he began, today I have the distinct honor and pleasure to introduce to all of you the man who delivered the message the day that I was saved. He is also the man who baptized me, and later ordained me to the ministry. He is here with us today, the Reverend Cloyd Smith." Brother Smith rose slowly from his seat, as the entire audience stood with him, clapping their hands in unison in his honor.

After everyone was seated again, Jeff began the sermon.

"Several years ago my wife and I, along with a congregation about the same size as this, had the pleasure of hearing a fine young minister preach a great sermon from this verse that I just read to you. That young minister was your Pastor, Brother Tom Tillotson. Our Lord blessed that sermon to the salvation of about fifteen souls. If the Lord will help me today, I would simply like to pick up that message where brother Tillotson left off, and extend it just a bit further, and ask you to pray with me that our Lord will do the same today, and bless this message to the salvation of souls."

"In his message that day long ago, brother Tillotson emphasized four reasons why that every man, woman and child should earnestly consider the Lord Jesus Christ as their own personal Savior. Having prayed earnestly for the proper message for you folks this morning, the Holy Spirit has led me to add perhaps one or two more reasons why all of the descendants of Adam should consider Christ as Savior and Lord before leaving this world. In his message, the four reasons brother Tillotson cited for considering Christ were as follows, firstly, because the Bible says so, secondly, because of who He is, thirdly, because of what He can do for you, and fourthly, because you must face Him someday."

Listening to Jeff's booming and anointed voice, Tom, Pearly Mae, and the whole congregation shivered with excitement as the Holy Spirit took full control of Jeff's mind and mouth. Both Tom and Pearly Mae beamed with pride to think that Jeff had remembered Tom's every word from a message he had delivered so long ago. Jeff continued, "Another good reason you should earnestly consider Jesus Christ is simply this, that, the difference between considering Him and not considering Him, is the difference between Heaven and Hell. After all, has He not given you ample time and opportunity to consider Him? And has He not given you sufficient reason to consider Him, having provided all things that are profitable and pleasing to human existence? And has He ever said or done anything to you that was so repulsive to you that you were left with a reasonable excuse for refusing to consider Him? And can you sit here today, and convince yourself that you would rather burn in an eternal Hell than give Him a reasonable hearing and consideration?"

As Jeff's voice rose and fell, and as he moved from one side of the pulpit to the other, powerfully stressing each point, he could see the message was already producing its desired effect upon many in the congregation. His own heart pounded in earnest prayer as he looked out over the congregation, knowing the convicting power of Christ had already begun to do His work, drawing precious souls to Christ. In Jeff's entire ministry, he had never extended any message beyond what the Holy Spirit wanted him to say, but neither did he ever shorten a sermon by a single word the Holy Spirit wanted him to say. He continued.

"Now if the difference between considering Christ and not considering Him is, as I have said, the difference between Heaven and Hell, then it behooves us to know what it means to "consider Him". To consider Him is to hear and to weigh the historical evidence that attests and affirms His identity - the fact that He is God in flesh. And there was one thing, and one thing only, that Jesus Christ had to do to prove to the world that he is God - He had to rise bodily from the grave. Has He done so? Yes, He has. And how do we know that He has risen from the grave? Because He is speaking to your hearts this very moment through the Word that I have preached to you with the anointing of the Holy Spirit."

Jeff hesitated only for a brief moment, scanning the faces of the crowd. It was time for his last point to be made, and he wasted no time in making it. "And yet another reason everyone should earnestly consider Jesus Christ is the fact that there is no one else to consider, if you want to go to Heaven. This fact, of course, is confirmed by the words of Christ Himself. In the fourteenth chapter of John, in verse six, Jesus said to Thomas in particular, and to the rest of the disciples in general, "I am the way, the truth, and the life: no man cometh unto the Father but by me. Will you please notice He did not say that He is one of many ways to the Father, but that He is "the way", the only way, to the exclusion and prohibition of all other ways. If, then, we would see the Father, we must come through His Son, Jesus Christ. This eliminates all other names, all other means, and all other methods by which men attempt to gain access to God, eternal life, and Heaven. It eliminates our works as a means of salvation, it prohibits us from calling upon any other name, and it forbids us from claiming any merit of our own as grounds for receiving His grace, for if our merit could obtain salvation, then grace would be unnecessary."

"We have yet another sure word and witness from one of His own disciples, the Apostle Peter, who said - "Neither is there salvation in any other: for there is none other name under heaven given among men, whereby we must be saved (Acts 4:12)." Again, this excludes the names of all other gods and goddesses, all other men and women, and the names of all human organizations, institutions and religions. And all of this is as much as to say that, all who have ever been saved, and all who will ever be saved, must be saved the same way - that way being Jesus Christ, plus nothing else."

Jeff had been a preacher long enough to know when to bring the sermon to a close, and to extend the invitation, and that time was now. And no sooner had he asked the people to stand than his own son, Samuel, (with Becky one step behind him,) came running down the aisle toward him with arms outstretched.

"Papa, Papa, I am saved, I am saved!" he cried.

In an instant, Jeff knew why his heart had been pounding so hard while delivering this message, and he knew there had been more than one reason for their trip to Cleveland Tennessee. As Samuel threw his arms around Jeff, Becky and several others, including Tom, Pearly Mae, Sarah, Daniel Ray, and all their children, all gathered around the altar, hugging Samuel, while some others shouted.

"Hallelujah, bless the Lord!"

Tears of joy streamed from Jeff's and Becky's eyes as they stood there together, their arms around their firstborn son. In all his years of preaching, Jeff could not recall a moment that was more gratifying than this moment. God had heard and honored his and Becky's prayers, and had rewarded their faithfulness in the salvation of their son.

The joy of being used of God to win his own son to Christ was beyond words for Jeff Townsend. Seldom did he ever get so choked up he couldn't speak, but this was one of those rare occasions upon which the tears in his eyes and the glow on his face said far more than mere words could ever express. The same was true for Becky. Being there when one's first child is saved is something that defies description for a Mother who has prayed for him from the day he was conceived in her womb. It is a matter of the heart, so touching, and so humbling.

Samuel was only nine years old, but no one would have guessed it from the mature and articulate way in which he made his own profession of faith that day. He stood boldly in front of his Mother and Father, and a crowd of 200, and openly confessed Jesus Christ as his personal Savior, without any help or coaxing from anyone, and asked to be baptized that very day. And the Copper Springs Baptist Church, like so many other Baptist Churches of that day, was deliberately situated near a creek, river, or other body of water large enough in which to immerse a new convert.

Samuel, followed by the whole congregation, was taken to the little creek that flowed about a hundred yards from the Church, and was baptized by his Father. Pastor Tom Tillotson helped Reverend Smith into his buggy, and drove him down to the creek to witness the baptism.

After the baptizing, Reverend Smith made his way slowly to where Jeff and Samuel stood on the bank of the creek. With tears of joy on his cheeks, the elderly minister shook hands, first with Samuel, and then with Jeff.

"Well, Brother Townsend, I can testify that the work I spent on you years ago was not wasted. You are what you profess to be, and I am proud of you. The good report that I have heard of you is true. Keep up the good work son, and may God continue to bless you and your family. And if we never meet again Brother

Townsend, I'll be waiting for you up yonder, and I have a feeling it won't be long for me."

A big lump formed in Jeff's throat again, as tears flooded his own eyes. He didn't have to say a word, because both he and Reverend Smith knew what was going on in the other's heart at that moment. Both Samuel and Jeff wore their wet clothes back to Tom and Pearly Mae's home, where they changed into dry ones.

But there was yet another pleasant surprise in store for Jeff before that glorious day was ended, and this time, Becky herself was the perpetrator. After celebrating Samuel's conversion over a good hot meal and lively conversation, Becky asked Tom and Pearly Mae if they would mind watching the children for a while so that she and Jeff could have some quiet time alone. Samuel and Ollie, of course, were thrilled to spend some more time with Uncle Tom and Aunt Pearl, knowing they would soon have to say goodbye to them. Becky quickly ushered Pearly Mae into the kitchen, whispering something in her ear. Pearly Mae smiled, and quickly packed a few things into a picnic basket for her. Becky carried the picnic basket into the living room, and just as quickly, ushered Jeff out to the front yard where the horse and buggy were already waiting.

"Where are we going sweet lady?" Jeff questioned with a big grin, as if he almost knew the answer already. Becky just smiled.

"You just drive where I tell you to go, handsome."

"Yes Ma'am," Jeff nodded as he gently slapped the reins.

Becky placed the basket underneath the seat, and moved as close to Jeff as she could get, laying her head against his strong shoulder, silently thanking God above for making her the happiest woman in the world. Everything was so beautiful, the blue sky above, the birds chirping merrily, wild flowers in full bloom, and it was June 4th, the day that Jeff and Becky had first met, sixteen years ago.

Everything was beautiful, and everything was perfect. The setting could not have been more perfect for what Becky had in mind. She and Jeff had not had the privilege of having a lot of time to themselves for a long time, and now that they had a few precious hours, she intended to make the most of them. Even the little horse seemed to know where the couple wanted to go, and stopped within a few yards of the very spot where Becky Davis and Jeff Townsend had met on that blessed day, long ago. Jeff instantly recognized the spot. Sixteen years had not changed this place at all. Even the same old oak picnic table was still sitting in the same spot underneath the wooden shelter. On any other occasion, Becky would have waited for Jeff to step out of the buggy, and come around and lift her down, but not this time. As soon as the buggy stopped, she grabbed the picnic basket from under the seat, slid out of the buggy, and ran toward the wooded area, telling Jeff to close his eyes, and no peeking till she came back. Jeff had no idea what Becky was up to. He closed his eyes, and waited. Five minutes later, Becky returned.

When Becky softly whispered, "You may open your eyes now Mr. Townsend"

Jeff's heart leaped into his throat. There stood the barefoot Becky Davis, wearing the same beautiful blue dress she had worn the day they met. She had kept it all these years, and had brought it with her from home, just for this occasion. She had put it in the bottom of the picnic basket, under the sandwiches. Suddenly, sixteen years just melted away, as time turned backward. She was a heavenly vision to behold. The dress, which, although faded from time, still fit her shapely figure perfectly. Fourteen years of marriage, hard work, four children, and countless hardships had failed to mar her beauty.

She held out her hand, whispering, "Hello, I'm Becky Davis, from Bradley County."

The lump in his throat that had nearly strangled him sixteen years ago suddenly returned, as he took her hand, barely managing to get out the words.

"Hello, I'm Jeff Townsend, would you like to go for a walk?"

The same passion that had mounted in their hearts sixteen years ago now burned again. In fact, it had never diminished. If anything had changed since the day they first met, it was the fact that they now loved each other more than ever. Theirs was a love that could not be described nor defined by the pen of any poet or scribe, a love that neither time nor tragedy could touch. The bond that held them together had been forged by an unseen hand, the same hand that had guided them through every trial and test, together. Not a ghost of a thought of ever loving another person the way they loved each other had ever crossed either of their pure minds. As they held each other close under the shade of that old oak tree once again, their hearts pounded wildly as their eyes closed, and their lips met. One thing was different. their kiss lasted much longer than that first one had, sixteen years ago. If it is possible for time to stand still, it happened on June 4th, 1876, on the outskirts of Cleveland Tennessee, just over the hill from the picnic area of the Copper Springs Baptist Church, beneath an old oak tree, as Heaven smiled down upon a man and wife, who loved each other more than they loved their own lives. After several hours of walking and kissing and holding hands, they drove back to Daniel Ray's house, where they spent Sunday night.

Sunday, June 4th, 1876, Jenkins Memorial Baptist Church, Preston County, West Virginia

But time does not stand still, it moves intricately, with each tick of the clock. And although it may have seemed that time was standing still for Jeff and Becky Townsend, kissing underneath a huge oak tree, it was meticulously moving at its prescribed rate for Dr. Joseph Parks and the congregation of the Jenkins Memorial Baptist Church. While Jeff had been preaching to the folks at the Copper Springs Baptist Church, Dr. Joseph Parks was delivering a message to the folks at the Jenkins Memorial Baptist Church, four hundred miles away. And what the Holy Spirit was doing at the Copper Springs Baptist Church in Tennessee, He was also doing at the Jenkins Memorial Baptist Church in West Virginia, He was convicting souls, and drawing them to Jesus Christ. And in the same way that Jeff Townsend could not drift off to sleep on Saturday night, neither could Dr. Joseph Parks. Several things were gnawing at Dr. Parks' brain as he lay awake, praying and pondering over what he had been entrusted to do tomorrow. He smiled in the darkness as he pondered how Jeff had so easily left him, a black man, in charge of the Sunday service in a church that had, since the day it was founded, been exclusively white. Dr. Parks knew there were other men, both black and white men, in the church who, in his estimation, were as well qualified to deliver a message as himself. No black man, (preacher or deacon,) had ever delivered a message from the pulpit of the Valley Grove Baptist Church, which, of course, had been re-named the Jenkins Memorial Baptist Church.

Also like Jeff, Dr. Parks understood the magnitude and the gravity of the responsibility that had been placed upon him. Not only was he about to stand as a representative of the great God of Heaven, and deliver a message that would affect the lives of other men (the greatest responsibility that could be placed upon any man,) he was also about to fill the shoes of a man who was highly respected, widely known, and deeply loved by thousands of folks from several states. He thought to himself, "Pastor Townsend must have a great deal of trust and confidence in me. I pray I will not disappoint him."

But his concern over not disappointing Pastor Townsend was paled in comparison to his fear of disappointing or misrepresenting his Lord and Savior Jesus Christ. Before he finally fell asleep that night, Dr. Parks knelt beside his bed with his wife Carolyn, praying earnestly.

"Dear God, will you please grant me the grace and wisdom to deliver a message that will honor you, and minister grace to those who hear me, in Jesus' name, Amen."

Carolyn, with her arm around his shoulder, added, "You will do just fine Joseph. You are a good man, and you have a good God who will be your help."

She laid her hand upon her stomach, adding, "I pray this time the good Lord will give us a son, and that he will grow up to be just like you."

"I like the way you think sweet lady," Dr. Parks whispered, taking her into his arms. They embraced in a long passionate kiss, and drifted off to sleep.

The Jenkins Memorial Baptist Church was filled with faithful members. Nearly every member of the church came to every worship service, Sunday morning, Wednesday night, and Sunday night. Hardly anyone ever missed a service, except for reasons beyond their control. Everyone enjoyed the sweet fellowship, the relaxed atmosphere, and the solid, Scriptural, anointed teaching and preaching they received every time they attended. In other words, when they met, the Lord met with them, and the reputation of the church and its leadership was quickly spreading far and wide. The news that a black man was going to be preaching in a predominantly white church spread even faster. Before Jeff and Becky had left for Tennessee, Jeff had announced to the whole church that Dr. Joseph Parks would be delivering the message on June 4th. It was a rare occasion. So rare, in fact, that it soon reached the ears of the news media. The same three newsmen who had attended Dr. Parks'

Tom Tillotson's ordination deliberately asked their superiors that they be assigned to cover the rare event, which, of course, was bound to make headlines.

When the newsmen arrived at the church, there was standing room only. Even with all the extra chairs being placed at the ends of the pews, there was not an empty seat to be found. The journalists joined the scores of others who lined up around the four walls of the church, from front to back. The house was abuzz with whispering as the beautiful Carolyn Parks took her place at the piano. Dr. Parks swallowed hard as he stood with his hymn book, seeing the huge crowd in front of him. He glanced toward Carolyn, who smiled at him with total confidence, nodding for him to start the singing, as she softly touched the keys for the old hymn - Rock of Ages.

As Dr. Parks' deep bass voice resonated, and the sweet low tenor of Carolyn Parks joined in, one by one, folks began to stand, adding their own voices to the great old hymn. It seemed that all of Heaven had joined in the singing. Suddenly, Dr. Parks lost all his inhibition and nervousness. He was totally immersed, and totally comfortable in the sweetness of the singing, and the beaming smiles on the faces of the congregation. As he continued to sing, he silently prayed.

"Thank you sweet Jesus!"

The anointed and exuberant singing itself had already affected the crowd powerfully before Dr. Parks stood to preach. Many in the crowd were still wiping tears of joy from their faces as Dr. Parks stepped behind the pulpit with his Bible open. Before he spoke a single word, he couldn't help but notice four young men who appeared to be in their mid-twenties, standing against the back wall of the church. They were all dressed in fine suits and shiny shoes, and were all well-groomed. Somehow, they all looked vaguely familiar. But it was time to preach, and he couldn't stare at them any longer. Following Pastor Townsend's example, he smiled at the audience, asking them to stand for the reading of the Scripture. He read a single verse, from Luke 5:20 - And when he saw their faith, he said unto him, Man, thy sins are forgiven thee.

"You may be seated," Dr. Parks began.

"Now for those of you who are serious students of the Scriptures, you know who spoke these words, and you know the man to whom they were spoken. But for those of you who may not be familiar with the passage, the man who spoke these words was none other than the Lord Jesus Christ. And the man to whom they were spoken was the paralytic, who was carried by four friends up to the rooftop, and was let down through a hole in the roof, a hole which they themselves created in order to get their helpless friend into the presence of the Great Physician."

"As most of you know, and as a few of you can testify from personal experience, I am a trained surgeon." Before Dr. Parks could say another word, Rufus Rutherford, and several others upon whom Dr. Parks had performed major surgery, were on their feet, with their hands in the air, testifying, "Amen Doctor, Amen." Dr. Parks smiled his approval, glancing toward Carolyn, who smiled back at him, nodding her own approval. He continued, "and being a trained surgeon, and having operated on several of you in this and other communities, my scalpel has revealed to me the physical condition of your inner organs and tissues. My stethoscope has allowed me to listen to your hearts and lungs. I have looked down your throats and into your eyes and ears, and have by thorough examination discovered what was ailing you, and, in most cases, was able to diagnose and treat the ailments, and to help you toward full recovery."

Again there were loud "amens" from nearly every pew. Dr. Parks hesitated momentarily, stepping out to one side of the pulpit, rubbing his belly, adding, "and I and Mrs. Parks want you all to know that we both greatly appreciate all the pheasants, chickens, eggs, fruits and vegetables that all of you have so generously bestowed upon us as compensation for our services." The whole crowd burst into spontaneous laughter. Carolyn Parks smiled and blushed at the same time, putting her hand over her mouth to prevent herself from laughing out loud. Stepping back behind the podium, Dr. Parks continued in a more serious tone.

"But with all of my training, and with all of my years of experience, and with all of my medical instruments and medicines, there is one thing inside every one of us that neither my scalpel nor my stethoscope have been able to reveal, and that my medicines have failed to cure, and that thing is sin, the most dreadful and deadly of all diseases - a disease that affects both body and spirit."

A deep and reverent silence fell upon the crowd, as the truth of what Dr. Parks had just said began to hit home, driven by the power and conviction of the Holy Spirit. Dr. Parks scanned the faces of the crowd, noticing that many heads were bowed. He continued, "According to the eyewitness account of Luke, whom we all know was himself a physician, the man who was paralyzed had no hope of recovery by any human means. Doctor Luke could not cure him, and Doctor Luke knew that he could not cure him, and made no attempt to cure him, for his condition was beyond the reach of all medical knowledge of that day.

But what does our Lord, the Great Physician, say to him? He says, thy sins are forgiven thee."

"May I humbly submit to you this morning that, even though there were many in the crowd that day, including Doctor Luke, who could easily have diagnosed this man's physical condition, (for it was obvious to all that he was paralyzed,) there was only one man in the crowd who knew what his real problem was, and that man was Jesus. Now don't get me wrong folks, this man's physical malady was very real, and I will not attempt to convince any of you that his physical condition was the direct result of his spiritual condition. But I must, and I will venture to say that, very much like this man, all of mankind would feel so much better physically, if only their spiritual condition was first improved. I will go so far as to proclaim that, in my educated opinion, about ninety percent of all physical ailments could be cured, or at least lessened in severity, if only the soul and spirit could first be relieved of the inner guilt of sin."

"And that is why we are here today, to refer you to the one and only Physician who is able to heal both body and soul. I refer you all to the one Doctor whose eyes alone are the only stethoscope that is needed, and His Word the only scalpel that is needed, for His eyes are able to see what no surgical instrument can reveal, and His Word is quick and powerful, and sharper than any two-edged sword, piercing even to the dividing asunder of soul and spirit, and of the joints and marrow, and is a discerner of the thoughts and intents of the heart. Neither is there any creature that is not manifest in his sight: but all things are naked and opened unto the eyes of him with whom we have to do (Hebrews 4:13&13). And His blood is the medicine that is able to cure the most fatal of all diseases, the disease of sin in the human soul. And His Holy Spirit is the nursemaid who comforts and nurtures. Look around you dear neighbors, and see the living witnesses here in your very presence, all of whom can testify that their lives have been changed and made better by a simple faith in the shed blood and bodily resurrection of the Son of God. In closing, may I add that I myself, and my dear wife over here, have ourselves been cleansed by that same blood, and can therefore recommend it to you as the only remedy for the condition of your souls. Let us stand please, as the choir comes with a hymn of invitation. With your heads bowed and your eyes closed, are there any here today who, by an uplifted hand, will acknowledge that you stand in need of spiritual healing?"

As the choir assembled, Dr. Parks noticed that scores of hands were raised. He moved out to the front of the pulpit area, in the center of the aisle. As the choir began singing "Just as I am," eight men and three women made their way to the front. Dr. Parks immediately recognized Judge Elias W. Bracken and his wife Nola, who were walking beside one of the journalists. Dr. Parks stepped to one side, as the eight men and three women knelt at the altar. Seven of the men were pouring out their hearts to God, asking Jesus to come into their hearts, while Judge Bracken and his wife Nola knelt beside one of the journalists, with their hands upon the young man's shoulder, praying with him. As they stepped past Dr. Parks, both he and Carolyn Parks suddenly recognized all the other seven men also. Three were the journalists who had come to get a story. The other four were Jason and Travis Phelps, along with Joshua and Gideon Bowen, the four young men out of whose buttocks Dr. Parks had plucked several buckshot on Halloween night, nearly six years ago.

Dr. Parks waited for just a few more minutes, hoping others might come forward. When no one else had responded after about four minutes, he knelt at the altar with the men who were still kneeling there. One by one, the men stood, each one professing that he had been saved, and wanted to be baptized. The first one to speak was one of the journalists, who, as it turned out, was none other than Elias W. Bracken III, the grandson of Judge Elias W. Bracken. The other two journalists were Trevor Hollister and Randall Sexton. The ladies who had come with the other four young men were their mothers. Caroline Phelps, the mother of Jason and Travis, and Minerva Bowen, the mother of Joshua and Gideon Bowen.

After the seven men had made their professions of faith, and were accepted as candidates for baptism (which was scheduled for the following Sunday,) and several testimonies were given, the worship service was dismissed in prayer. The Bowen family, the Bracken family, and the Phelps family, along with the other two journalists, Trevor Hollister and Randall Sexton, all crowded around Dr. and Mrs. Parks, congratulating Dr. Parks on his powerful delivery of the sermon, and Carolyn for her beautiful singing and piano playing. Dr. Parks admitted that he was somewhat shocked, but well-pleased, to see all of them there. Judge Bracken and Nola were simply overjoyed over their grandson being saved, as were Mrs. Phelps and Mrs. Bowen for their sons.

Dr. Parks shook hands with Mrs. Phelps and Mrs. Bowen as their sons introduced their mothers respectively.

Dr. Parks commented, "I never thought I'd see the four of you again. Where have you been keeping yourselves?"

Gideon Bowen became the spokesman for the four, replying, "Well, Doctor Parks, we never thought we'd see you again either, but when we heard that you were going to be preaching here today, we all remembered the kindness and respect you and your wife showed us six years ago, and we just had to come and see you, and tell you that you and your wife were a profound influence upon us, and we just wanted to thank you. As you can see, we have all matured a great deal since then, and we have even started our own businesses. Joshua and I have opened our own hotel just outside Morgantown, and Jason and Travis here are partners in a blacksmith shop just up the road from our hotel."

"Well, that is so good to hear Brother Bowen," Dr. Parks replied, shaking his hand again. "We are very proud of you, and thankful that we could be just a small part of your lives. We'll be looking forward to the baptizing next Sunday." The boys mothers hugged Dr. and Mrs. Parks, thanking them for being such a positive influence upon their sons. As the crowd slowly dispersed, Judge Bracken invited Dr. and Mrs. Parks to lunch at the Judge's new home, which he had built on the shore of Cheat Lake, about half way between Bruceton Mills and Morgantown. Dr. Parks graciously accepted the invitation. Dr. Parks was in for another pleasant surprise after they arrived and Judge Bracken's home. As he and the Judge caught up on old times, Nola and Carolyn were in the kitchen, where Nola was preparing Dr. Parks' favorite entree`, roast pheasant.

On Monday morning, June 5th, the headlines in three newspapers read:

Local Baptist Church thrives amid persecution.

The articles underneath the three headlines were nearly identical. The article written by Elias W. Bracken III read:

"Yesterday, I and two of my colleagues visited the Jenkins Memorial Baptist Church in Preston County, where we were sent to observe the proceedings, and to investigate rumors that have surrounded this thriving church since the day it was built. After having visited this church twice, this reporter can state unequivocally that the rumors and negative publicity which this church and its Pastor, Rev. Jeff Townsend have received, are unwarranted, unkind, and untrue. In fact, this article is now long overdue. I, for one, wish to express my sincere apology to Rev. Townsend and the church for any adverse manner in which I may have contributed to the negative publicity afore mentioned. But that is not enough. I also wish to go on record as saying that I have never met a kinder gentler man than Reverend Jeff Townsend, a man who, by both his words and actions, has shown that his beliefs and convictions are real. In spite of ongoing persecution, antagonism and negative publicity from nearly every quarter, the church continues to prosper, and to grow exceedingly. The Jenkins Memorial Baptist Church is a serene sanctuary, where men and women of all races and backgrounds may meet together with their families, and worship the one true and living God in peace and harmony. It is with a softened heart that I can now write to all who may read this paper, that I myself have received the Lord Jesus Christ as my personal Savior. And as shocking as it may be to some who do not share my newfound faith, I must add that my conversion yesterday was due in part to the preaching of one Dr. Joseph Parks, the well-known black surgeon from Bruceton Mills, who in spite of severe persecution and harassment, yet remains faithful to his duty as a servant of the people, and a steward of his Lord. By Elias W. Bracken III.

The next day (Tuesday,) the daily articles of Elias W. Bracken III no longer appeared in the newspaper for which he had written for ten years. In its place was an article by the editor, which read:

"It is not the policy of this newspaper nor any of its affiliates to endorse any particular religious group or denomination. The ownership of this newspaper wishes to apologize for any article or articles that its readers may have seen that seem to be in favor of one denomination or church, to the exclusion of all other worthy denominations and groups. Such articles will no longer appear in this paper. The ownership furthermore wishes to emphasize that this paper does not favor or exalt any particular race above another race to any degree whatsoever, regardless of whatever profession in which such persons of any color may be engaged. It is the contention of this paper that, while we find it highly commendable that a person of color may attain to a noble position such as a physician or surgeon, we in no way want our readers to conclude that it is more commendable for such a person of color to reach that status than for a person of another race or color to do so.

Needless to say, Elias W. Bracken III was released from his duties as a journalist for that particular newspaper. With unbroken stride, however, he immediately contacted his father, Elias W. Bracken II, a Law Professor at a nearby University, who immediately enrolled his son in Law School. Years later, Elias W. Bracken III would become Chief Justice of the State Supreme Court. The newspaper from which he was released slowly went bankrupt because of a lack of subscribers, and a series of bad investments by the owners.

June 5th 1876

Back in Cleveland Tennessee, it was nearing midnight, and Becky knew she would be leaving her father's home, and would be returning back to West Virginia this very night. Her heart was so heavy. The wedding had been beautiful, and the reunions that had taken place there in that church could only have been put together by the hand of God. She had enjoyed seeing her brothers and sisters, and her sweet niece and nephew Abby and Alexander. Becky was trying so hard to be as happy as possible for her father Daniel and her best friend Sarah, but the memories of her mother were so alive and seemed to surround her completely. It was all she could do to muster up the strength and courage just to keep a smile on her face. Becky knew in her heart that Sarah deserved all the happiness she could find. Clark's unforeseen death had been so hard on Sarah and the children. Despite all the tragedy, Carter had grown into a very handsome young man, and Mollie was a beautiful young lady.

Becky and Jeff were staying in her father's house this last night before they headed home. Becky was restless, and wanted to get back home to the twins, Elick and Erica. She missed them so much, even though she knew they were in good hands with Claudette, Rufus and Becky Sarah. There was something Becky simply had to do before leaving. She had deliberately delayed the dreaded trip to visit her mother's grave. Even on the return trips back here before, she had not had the courage to go there on that little quiet knoll where her mother's body lay resting in heavenly peace. She longed to see her mother so bad she knew when she finally did visit the grave that she would fall apart. Her father had encouraged her to go there and see the place for herself, but until now, Becky had not been able to. She felt that as long as she didn't see a grave she could somehow keep her mother alive, at least in her heart.

As she lay there beside Jeff, watching him sleep, her mind wandered back to the events of this trip, the train ride, the excitement the children had in taking their first train ride, the romantic picnic she and Jeff had there, in the very same place that they had met so many years ago, and the joy of renewing the love they had for each other. Her mind recalled the emotions that had overcome her at the glimpse of her father's home again. She half expected to see her mother come running through the yard to meet them, with her beautiful smile. She had mixed emotions from the wedding, sadness, joy, resentment, and questions on top of questions. The glorious reunion of Tom and his parents would be forever engraved in her memory. With all of this rolling through her mind she grew so restless she could lie there no longer. She got up and quietly slipped out of bed so as not to awaken Jeff. He stirred softly as she gently placed the covers around his shoulders.

Becky tiptoed into the kitchen where she quickly put on her shoes, wrapping herself in her mother's shawl. The night air was cool for this time of the year. The heavy fog had rolled over the mountain tops and settled down in the narrow valleys. As she walked out the kitchen door, trying to be as quiet as possible, she eased the door shut, preventing it from making a banging as it closed, the big grandfather clock struck midnight! Becky nearly jumped out of her skin! Just two hours till they would be leaving to catch the train and she had not been asleep yet.

The big golden moon hanging in the heavens was shining so bright that no light was needed as she walked down the narrow path which lead to her mother's grave. A small white picket fence surrounded the two graves, one belonging to her little sister Elva Jean, the other to her beautiful mother Ellen. Becky could not stop the tears. The last two days had been so emotional for her, now that she was finally here near her mother's grave, there was no holding back. So many lives had been changed by so many circumstances, and she knew she would have to change with them. She only wished she could see her mother and talk with her one more time.

Becky sank to the ground with her heart feeling as though it would explode. Unashamed she cried.

"Mama! my sweet Mama, why? Oh why did you have to leave so soon? I wish someone could tell me how to get past all this. How do I accept my father and my best friend as husband and wife? It should be you here with us Mama! Clark should be here with Sarah. He was such a good man. You would have liked him Mama, Oh God help me." Burying her face in her hands she nearly screamed out the words, "I just can't leave this place without seeing your face again. I wish you could hold me in your arms and tell me that everything will be alright again."

Becky sobbed uncontrollably for what seemed like hours. Then she remembered something Jeff had told her many times before when she had been nearly overcome with grief.

"Talk to the Father" was his prescription.

Becky had learned that, in times like this, He was the only one to whom she could go for the comfort she needed. No one else could help her at this moment, not even her sweet, wonderful understanding Jeff, or her earthly father. She had wept for so long her tears were dried up, there were no more.

Becky looked up toward heaven, crying in a broken voice, "Dear God, I don't know why you took my mother so soon, she was too young, we had so much to do. I know I am not supposed to question you, but I need your guidance. I don't understand why a crazy man's bullet had to take Sarah's Clark when he was needed so much in the church and by his family. Please God give me some understanding so that I can go back home with peace in my heart. I hate this thing called death, and I can't get past this, but I know that I must. Please Father, give me the peace that I need, to go on and put all this behind me. If I need to find forgiveness in my heart then please forgive me, so that I can forgive others. I am so sorry for the bitterness I feel for the sickness that took my mother, and for the bitterness I feel toward the men that took Clark's life."

Becky's voice melted down to a whisper, as she lay down beside the grave, unaware of the beauty of the place. Beautiful red and white roses had been planted along the picket fence. Blue Spruce Pines towered over the back of the small cemetery, like sentinels standing guard against the outer world. From sheer exhaustion Becky fell asleep. As she slept, the most pleasant dream came to her. She dreamed she was a little girl in the kitchen with her mother, cooking and baking as they did so many times. She could hear her mother's sweet powerful voice singing "Love lifted me" as she smiled at her little girl, standing up in a chair with her hands in the flour bowl. Becky's dream faded as she fell into a deep sleep. She was suddenly awakened by the barking of a dog far off in the mountains behind her. As she sat up and slowly got to her feet, dusting herself off she looked up toward Heaven with a smile, whispering, "Thank you Father."

With one final look at the resting place of her loved ones, she knew in her heart all was well, and all the bitterness and pain she had felt was gone. God had so graciously let her see and hear her mother in a sweet dream. Now she could go back home with peace in her heart, and continue her wonderful life with her own little family. As Becky made her way back to the house she saw Jeff standing on the porch waiting for her. Just one look at her face and he knew where she had been, and he felt her pain. As she walked into his arms, he held her as she buried her tear stained face into his chest, telling him of the dream and how God had given her peace at last. And even though death was still so hard for her to understand, now she fully understood - it was part of life, and a gateway to her eternal home.

They made a pot of coffee, and sat on the porch, enjoying each other's company before they woke the children up for the long journey home. She quickly packed their things and tidied up her father's home while Jeff fed the animals. She woke up Samuel and Ollie, and prepared them breakfast. They were so excited just to know they'd soon be riding the train again. Tom was taking them to the station.

Tom arrived just as they were finishing up with the chores and packing. He jumped down from the wagon and gave Jeff a big bear hug. Then he grabbed Ollie up, swinging her around in circles as she giggled and begged him to do it again.

Ruffling Samuel's hair with his big callused hand Tom asked, "Would ya like ta drive the team to the station young man?"

Samuel beamed with joy. "Could I uncle Tom? Really? Ya mean it.?"

Samuel looked to his father for approval. Jeff grinned and consented.

"Shore ya can son." Both Jeff and Tom reached at the same time to give Samuel a boost up to the driver's seat, but they couldn't get their hands on him, he had already scrambled up into the driver's seat, taking the reins in his hands.

Becky walked out of the house and greeted Tom with a hug, reminding him to please give Pearly Mae and Thomas Clark a big hug and kiss from her. Tom assured her that he had special orders from his sweet Pearl to give them all a goodbye hug also. After all the hugging and farewells, they were all loaded in the wagon, Jeff, Tom and Samuel up front, Becky and Ollie in the back. As they drove away from the farm Becky glanced back for one last look, feeling a sense of sweet peace for which she had been searching ever since she had arrived here on Friday night. With a smile she turned her thoughts and mind toward home and the twins. She was excited to be going back to the church and all the family and friends who were waiting for their return.

Jeff, Becky and the children arrived at the train station near Albright at approximately 2:45 p.m. on Monday, June 5th. The whole trip took almost twelve hours. Rufus and Claudette, each holding one of the twins in their arms, were there waiting for them with the wagon. When the twins saw Becky and Jeff, Claudette and Rufus couldn't hold them any longer. They screamed and squirmed so much they had to put them down. They ran toward Jeff and

Becky as Jeff and Becky ran toward them with outstretched arms. The twins were both screaming, "Mama, Papa."

Tears of pure joy ran down Jeff's and Becky's faces as they scooped them up into their arms. Elick jumped into Jeff's arms while Erica jumped into Becky's arms. Their little hands clasped tightly around their parent's necks, as they hugged and kissed as if they had been gone for months instead of just four days. With the exception of the time that Becky had spent helping with the delivery of Claudette's baby, or when Jeff was preaching a revival in some distant county or state, this was the longest amount of time either of them had ever spent away from any of the children. Each of the twins looked sternly into the eyes of their mother and father, shaking their tiny fingers in their faces, while issuing the ultimatum.

"You caint never weave agin."

Becky held her little girl tightly, promising, "I promise honey, Mama and Papa will never let you out of our sight again."

Jeff held Erica in his lap while Becky clung to Elick the whole six miles to their home. The twins, now feeling the love and safety of Mama and Papa, soon drifted off to sleep. Samuel and Ollie each wanted to take turns driving the team of horses. The road that led from the train station was deeply rutted from many a wagon, so that the wagon practically guided itself in the ruts. But holding the reins of the team of big horses gave the children a sense of command and accomplishment. Rufus handed the reins to Samuel first. Ollie folded her arms and sat silently for about two minutes, glancing from Samuel to Rufus.

"Is it my turn yet Uncle Rufus?" Ollie questioned, with excitement in her eyes.

"Just another minute or two darlin," Rufus promised.

Ollie folded her arms again, counting off the seconds. Finally, after what seemed an eternity to Ollie, Samuel was tired of holding the reins, and handed them to her. The beaming smile of the face of the little girl was so touching, Rufus almost laughed out loud.

Her little hands raised the reins upward and then downward with a snap, as she called out to the horses.

"Giddy-up Mr. Beecher, Giddy-up Stardust!"

After less than a mile of having command of two powerful horses and a wagon load of people, Ollie also tired of the driving, and handed the reins back to Rufus, politely saying.

"Thank you Uncle Rufus."

She climbed over the seat into the back of the wagon, and soon fell asleep beside Samuel. Rufus and Claudette and Jeff and Becky spoke in whispers the rest of the way home, with Becky giving Claudette every detail of the wedding, while Rufus explained to Jeff that everything had gone well in his absence, with seven men being saved at the church on Sunday.

As the wagon rolled lazily through town, about two dozen folks from the church and businesses, including Dr. and Mrs. Parks, came out from their homes and places of business just to welcome Jeff and Becky back home, exclaiming with big beaming smiles.

"Welcome home Pastor, welcome home Mrs. Townsend, we sure missed you folks something terrible."

As Jeff and Becky leaned over to shake their hands, many followed the wagon all the way through town, telling Jeff and Becky how glad they were to have them back. Jeff and Becky beamed with appreciation at the heart-felt welcome they were receiving, as if they had been gone for months. Jeff asked Rufus to stop the wagon long enough for him to congratulate Dr. Parks and Carolyn for the fine job they had done in his and Becky's absence. Dr. Parks nodded, removing his pipe from his mouth, replying, "Any time Pastor, any time."

Jeff and Becky couldn't help but notice all the wagons, horses, mules, buggies and carriages hitched to the hitching posts on all sides around the town's new restaurant.

"What's going on in there?" Jeff inquired.

Dr. Parks quickly informed him, "You'll have to go inside and see for yourself Pastor. They've hired a new - shall I say - well-endowed waitress named Margie, and every warm-blooded young male in the county has heard about her. The owner says his business has tripled since he hired Margie!"

Jeff shot a quick glance toward Becky, clearing his throat, replying.

"Hmmm, well, maybe some other time Doc, but not today."

Becky grinned, elbowing Jeff in the ribs, adding, "I better not catch you in there gawking at a young waitress Preacher Townsend!"

Jeff laughed, answering, "Not to worry sweetheart, I have all the woman I'll every want right here beside me."

As they were about to drive away, they heard a loud burst of laughter coming from inside the restaurant.

Jeff remarked, "Well, they all seem to be having a good time."

Then there was total silence. Jeff and Dr. Parks looked at each other inquisitively, saying nothing, as they shook hands again, and Jeff motioned for Rufus to take them on home.

Inside the restaurant, a red-faced young man had just learned the meaning of the word *respect*. Margie, the new waitress, was a beautiful, brown-eyed brunette, in her late twenties. Raised on a farm just outside Albright, she was used to hard work. With the effects of the Long Depression affecting virtually every business and farm in the state, many young women began to seek employment outside the home in order to help sustain their families. Margie laid aside her gingham dress, pulled on a pair of her brother's blue jeans, and rode her horse to Bruceton Mills, looking for a job. One look at Margie in those jeans was all that was needed. She was hired immediately. Business at the restaurant began to increase on her first day of employment, and increased steadily every day thereafter.

As Margie brought three plates of hot food to a table, one of the three young men decided he was going to *flirt* with the new waitress, and at the same time, show himself to be manly. He stared at Margie's curvaceous figure for a few moments too long.

"My, My madam, they shore ain't no room for nuthin else in them britches."

Margie calmly sat the food down on the table, looked him straight in the eye.

"That's right fella, not even for a little boy like you."

The whole restaurant heard the exchange between Margie and the young man, and burst out in laughter and applause. From that day forward, Margie was treated with the utmost respect.

Jeff had been away from his home a lot because of his ministry, and he was always extremely glad to get back to Becky and the farm, but even more so now that they had the children. The trip to Tennessee for the wedding had taken both of them away from the twins and the farm for four days, and never in their lives had either of them been more happy to see the front door of their little home than today. Rufus and Claudette helped them carry the sleeping children and the suitcases into the house, and quickly said their goodbyes, knowing the whole family was bone tired from the long trip. As soon as all the children were tucked in, Jeff and Becky knelt beside their own bed, thanking God for a safe journey, for good and faithful friends like the Rutherfords and the Parks, and for seven more souls that had been added to the church in their absence.

While Jeff and Becky Townsend prayed beside their bed, the folks who lived in the near vicinity of the Moundsville Penitentiary were praying for their own safety. Wesley Phelps and William (Bill) Bowen, whose brothers, Orville Phelps and Reese Bowen had been hanged back in 1866, had less than a month to serve of their ten-year sentences. But neither of them could take any more of the prison. It had turned into a brutal hell hole, with men being killed by other inmates nearly every week. The prison had now earned the reputation of being one of the most violent prisons in the country. Some even claimed the prison was haunted by the ghosts of inmates who had been murdered there. The prisoners were allowed one hour out of twenty four each day to mingle in the prison yard. Those who had tobacco rations rolled cigarettes and smoked them quickly, before those who had no tobacco either stole it, or beat the one who had it to death with his fist.

The prison was woefully understaffed, and since Warden Bickford had retired, and Warden Slocum had taken his place, the security had become woefully inadequate, making an escape inevitable. Wesley and William had gotten their heads together during one of the hour-long outings, and devised a plan to escape. They deliberately started a fight among themselves and the other inmates, calling them dirty names. Fists started flying, and a melee soon erupted. While the meager band of guards were doing their best to quell the violence, Wesley and William slipped from among the heap, and were over the fence and into the woods. One of the guards saw them as they cleared the fence, but was too busy defending himself to even care about two escapees. Once they were across the railroad tracks and into the woods, they stopped running just long enough to tell each other goodbye.

Wesley asked William, "Where you goin pal?"

With all the bitter hatred that had built up in his soul for nine years, William stared into Wesley's eyes, replying instantly, "I'm gonna kill me a preacher man."

Wesley stood stone still and silent as William Bowen gave him one last stern glance, warning him.

"Don't follow me Wesley. And don't tell nary soul which way I went, or I'll hunt you down and kill you too."

Wesley Phelps nodded to William, turned his back, and ran as fast as his legs would carry him, north, toward the panhandle. William Bowen headed south, toward Preston County.

Going in a semi-circle, he soon came back to where the railroad tracks stretched south. He sat down in the bushes, and waited for the next train. As the locomotive disappeared around the bend, he ran alongside the train, grabbing onto the iron ladder of one of the freight cars, swinging himself upward onto the train. Two hours later, he jumped from the train, and ran into the woods of Preston County. As darkness fell, he made his way to the back of the General Store, which was situated in the fork of two roads, one that led from Bruceton Mills toward Kingwood, and the other that led up the valley toward Jeff Townsend's farm.

He couldn't risk breaking the glass of one of the windows with a rock, which would make too much noise, and wake up someone who lived nearby. He pressed his forearm against the wooden joints that divided the panes of the window, applying just enough pressure to slowly crack the glass without completely breaking it. Slowly the glass gave way to the constant pressure, and broke. The glass that fell inward made some noise, but luckily for William, not enough to awaken anyone. He climbed slowly and carefully through the window, feeling his way around the shelves and cases. He couldn't see well enough to find all that he wanted, so he sat down between the shelves, and waited for just enough daylight to find a pistol, some cartridges, a Bowie knife, some writing paper, a pencil, two blankets, a pair of binoculars, a canteen, a pocket watch, a pair of jeans, a shirt, a hat, a new pair of boots, and enough beef jerky to last him three days.

Before Dan Martin, the owner of the General Store opened the store, William had changed clothes, thrown his prison garb into Big Sandy Creek, and was gone back into the woods, headed northwest, up the valley that led to Jeff's house. When Mr. Martin opened the store at 7:00 a.m., he saw the broken window, and noticed that several items were missing from the shelves and cases.

When his first customer, Carolyn Parks, came in at 7:30 a.m. to look at some material, Mr. Martin told her about the robbery, and every item that had been taken, and asked her to tell everyone she knew about it also, so that they could be on the lookout for the thief, and for each other. Every customer who came into the store was informed about the robbery, and was asked to spread the news to his or her neighbors. Before the day was over, virtually everyone within the city limits of Bruceton Mills, and some who lived beyond the city limits, had heard about the robbery. Jeff's farm was about a mile from the General Store and Bruceton Mills, and after one day, the news of the robbery had not yet reached Jeff and Becky. That was long enough for William Bowen to find a spot on the western ridge overlooking Jeff's house, and to watch every move that Jeff and every other member of his family made.

For three days William Bowen watched the house through the binoculars. He noted the exact time that Jeff and Becky emerged from the house. He noted the time they went back into the house. He noted how Samuel and Ollie helped with small chores, while staying close to their parents and each other. He noticed the twins were never far apart. He scanned every inch of the house, the barn, the corral, the smokehouse, the outhouse and the fences. His evil mind was concocting a devious plan on how to get close enough to Jeff to kill him. There was only one way to do that, he would get to Jeff through one of the children.

It was now Thursday, June 8th, Jeff's and Becky's anniversary. William Bowen, of course, didn't know that, but it still worked to his advantage. He took out a piece of paper, and wrote a note to Jeff Townsend. Stuffing the note in his shirt pocket, he checked his pistol to make certain that every chamber was loaded, then eased his way down the slope to a clump of hazelnut bushes, just inside the thick woods, and waited.

The news of the robbery had reached everyone except Jeff and Becky, and it bothered Mrs. Parks that no one had taken the news to them. She asked Dr. Parks if it would be alright for her to take the buggy and drive the one mile trip to inform them, just in case. So far, the news of the prison break in Moundsville hadn't gone beyond the walls of the prison. No one outside the prison knew that two dangerous criminals were on the loose. While Dr. Parks was lifting

Carolyn into the buggy, Jeff, Becky, and the children were sitting down to breakfast.

Samuel was now nine years old, Ollie was seven, and the twins, Erica and Elick, were five, and bursting with energy and curiosity. And if there was one thing every mother and father in the state of West Virginia taught their children more than any other, it was that they were to watch out for each other, and protect each other at all times. There were simply too many dangers, seen and unseen dangers, that could harm, or, God forbid, kill an un-protected child. The woods were full of poisonous snakes, bears, and mountain lions, and the creeks teemed with cottonmouth. Every child that was old enough to understand was taught how to identify poisonous and non-poisonous snakes, and poisonous and non-poisonous plants, berries and bushes. They were also taught to beware of strangers.

Jeff had deliberately fenced in his house and yard within an area that was large enough for children to romp and play, yet small enough to keep them within eyesight and earshot, and every child knew that the fence was the outer limit of their playground, a detail that William Bowen had noted to his own advantage. To the northwest of Jeff's house, he had removed the gate of the yard fence that marked the edge of the yard, so that he and Becky and Tom and Pearly Mae would not have to stop and open a gate every time they visited each other. Since Tom and Pearl had moved away, Jeff simply had not found the time to put the gate back in place, and really didn't see any need of doing so. But an opening in a fence is an open invitation for two five year old children to go beyond the boundary. It was also an opportunity for William Bowen to set his wicked plan in motion. While the family was eating breakfast, he had made his way to the thick grove of poplars just back of the Tillotson's cabin. After breakfast was over, and the morning chores were done, Jeff went out to the barn to let the horses out into the pasture. Becky was still in the kitchen, preparing an anniversary surprise for Jeff. The children were playing hide-and-seek.

William Bowen had now crept his way from the back of the Tillotson's cabin to the front fence. He saw Jeff go into the barn, and Becky was in the house. He hunkered down behind some rose bushes that Pearly Mae had planted just inside the fence. That was where Elick and Erica had chosen to hide while Samuel had his eyes closed, counting to ten. Ollie had already hidden behind the smokehouse.

When Jeff stepped inside the barn, and let the horses out, he held the big barn door in his right hand. He had built the barn himself, and had opened and closed that door thousands of times. He had become so accustomed to the feel and weight of the door as it swung on its hinges that the slightest difference would be noticeable. This morning, the barn door felt just a bit heavier than before. Jeff glanced at the inside of the door. Hanging on a big spike were Tom Tillotson's gun belt, whip, and Bowie knife, with a note tied around the shaft of the knife.

While Jeff untied the string from around the note, Elick and Erica had run through the opening in the fence, and darted behind the rose bushes. William Bowen grabbed them both, throwing them to the ground, clasping his big hands over their mouths to prevent them from screaming.

He quickly explained to Erica, "Now you listen real good missy, I'm gonna give you this here note, and you're gonna take it to your Papa. I'm gonna take your little brother with me. And if you don't do exactly as I tell you, you will never see him alive again. Do you understand?"

Her little heart was pounding wildly with fear. Tears filled her eyes as she listened to the rough hateful words of the big man.

Elick tried to get loose from William's grasp, but the harder he kicked and squirmed, the more pressure William put on his mouth.

The note that Tom had left for Jeff read: *"Dear Jeff, I won't be needing these things anymore, and I have you and Becky to thank for that. I don't know if you will every have any use for them, but I just wanted you to have them as a reminder of our long and lasting friendship, just in case we don't get to see each other again. You have been the best friend I have in this world, and I will never forget all that you and Becky did for me. Take care big man, and God bless you and your family, Love, Tom."*

As William Bowen released his hand from Erica's mouth, he slapped her hard in the face, leaving the print of his hand upon her cheek. commanding

"You better not scream or say a word young lady, till you hand this note to your Papa."

The little girl nodded submissively, and ran with the note as fast as her little legs would carry her. Before she had run fifty yards, William Bowen was already into the woods, carrying Elick with him, his big hand still clasped tightly over Elick's mouth.

Jeff held Tom's note briefly, then tucked it into his shirt pocket, smiling, remembering so many scenes from his and Tom's past. He took the Colt from its holster, quickly getting the feel of its weight and balance, twirling it around his trigger finger. There was only one secret in Jeff Townsend's life which he had kept so well-hidden that not even Becky knew about it, because Jeff didn't want anyone knowing about it. That secret was the fact that there was not a man alive faster on the draw, or more accurate with a pistol than Rev. Jeff Townsend. He had never worn a gun in his life, but he always carried one in his saddle bag whenever he went on long trips. In the 1800's, every man knew the day might come when he would be forced to use a gun. The only things Jeff had ever killed with a gun were the animals he killed for food, or snakes that had threatened him or his family. While he worked in the fields, he always kept a gun belt hanging on one of the fence posts, just in case a wild animal or poisonous snake appeared unexpectedly. He had never pointed a gun at any man, but that was about to change in a few short minutes.

Samuel had finished counting, and was searching for the hidden children. Ollie was crouched behind the smokehouse. When Erica came running across the open space between the fence and the house, Jeff stepped out of the barn. He saw his little girl running hard, with something in her hand, waving it. He turned and hung the gun belt back on the big spike, and ran toward Erica. She was panting for breath, so scared she couldn't speak. She handed the note to Jeff, pointing toward the woods on the western slope. Jeff stooped down, lifting her into his arms, holding her gently, calming her fear till she could speak. He noticed the redness of her little cheek where William had slapped her. His own face turned fiery red with rage.

Erica regained enough composure to whimper, "The big man Papa, the big man, he hurt me Papa, an he got Elick."

She buried her head in Jeff's chest, weeping uncontrollably. Jeff opened the piece of paper, and read: **"Preacher, I have your son. Meet me half way up the western hill before sunset, or I will kill him. Come alone. William Bowen."**

The Townsend Legacy: Heavenly Places II

Carolyn Parks arrived at the front gate of the Townsend house. Hearing Cricket barking, Becky came out to help Carolyn down from the buggy, wondering what Carolyn could possibly be doing here in her condition, and alone. By the time she and Carolyn walked from the buggy to the front porch, Jeff had come around the corner of the house, carrying the weeping Erica in his arms, followed by Samuel and Ollie, who were both holding onto his pant legs, crying.

Becky glanced from Carolyn to Jeff. She had never seen that expression on Jeff's face before. She knew something was dreadfully wrong. When Carolyn started to explain that there had been a robbery at the General Store three days ago, Jeff handed the note to Becky. She sank to her knees immediately, pale as a ghost, gasping for breath, as she handed the note to Carolyn Parks.

Carolyn read the note quickly, exclaiming, "Oh my dear God, I must get back to town and tell everyone!"

Jeff stopped her, shaking his head. "No Carolyn, I must go alone, or this man will kill our son. It was my testimony that sent him to prison nine years ago, and my testimony that sent his brother to the gallows. It's me he wants, and he's using my son to get to me. Please don't tell anyone about this till I go up there and get my son."

Becky was still on her knees, sobbing. "But Jeff, he'll kill both of you if you go up there."

"I don't think so Becky, Jeff tried to assure her. If he gets me, maybe he will let Elick live. It's a chance I have to take. You stay here. I'll be back before sunset, with our son."

Becky knew there was no stopping Jeff now, and she also knew he was right. It was the only chance of saving Elick's life, and Jeff was willing to take that chance. He quickly kissed her cheek, and ran to the barn, strapping on the gun belt. As he stepped out of the barn wearing the Colt at his side, Becky almost fainted. She had never seen Jeff with a gun on his hip. As Jeff leaped astride Mr. Beecher, Becky was torn apart inside, not knowing if she would ever see her son or her husband alive again.

Like all murderers and other criminals, William Bowen had made several mistakes. The first one was heading south toward Preston County after escaping from the prison. The second mistake was robbing the General Store; the third mistake was that he had failed to notice that the pistol he had stolen was a single-action revolver. In order to fire it, the hammer had to be pulled back before pulling the trigger. The fourth mistake was throwing his prison clothes into Big Sandy Creek without making sure they would never be seen again. His fifth mistake was slapping Jeff Townsend's little girl; and the sixth, and worst mistake he ever made in his entire life, was kidnapping the son of Jeff Townsend.

William Bowen was a huge man, strong as an ox, and as mean as a rattlesnake, but he was about to face a man like no other he had faced before, a man who loved his children more than his own life, and a man who feared nothing and no one, not even death itself. Jeff rode hard and fast toward the western slope, fully aware that Mr. Bowen could probably kill him at any moment from wherever he was, up on the hillside. But he also knew that Mr. Bowen wanted to look him in the eye before killing him, to make him sweat, using his son as a shield. At the edge of the woods he dismounted, knowing that William could see his every move. He prayed silently as he made his way up the steep slope, pulling himself upward by grabbing onto small trees or bushes.

As Jeff reached for a young sapling about half way up the slope, pulling himself up onto a level spot about forty feet wide, William Bowen stepped out from behind a huge boulder with his left arm around Elick, his hand still over Elick's mouth. The pistol was pointed at Elick's head. He removed his hand from Elick's mouth, gripping Elick's neck, grinning devilishly at Jeff, growling out his words.

"Howdy preacher, remember me? I'm shore you do. Of course I'm nine years older now, but then, you know that too don't you reverend?"

Elick kicked William's shins as hard as he could kick, screaming.

"You leave my Papa alone mister, my Papa can beat you any time."

William squeezed Elick's neck harder, causing him to scream in pain.

"Well now, I see the little squirt has some grit, unlike his Pa here, a dirty rotten bible thumpin coward."

"Let my son go Mr. Bowen, Jeff demanded.

"I'm the one you want, so let's not drag this out any further. Do with me what you will, just let my son go."

"Yeah, you shore would like that, wouldn't you nigguh luvah? William grunted, But not just yet. I jist want to see you sweat and tremble, like my brother done afore he wuz hanged. I want ta hear you beg and plead like the coward you are. Now, drop the gun belt, or I blow his head off."

Jeff eyed the man with a steely gaze, looking straight into his eyes, replying, "I'm afraid I can't do that mister. Now you've got to the count of three to let my son go."

William Bowen had faced a lot of men in his life, but none of them had shown the fearlessness of this man. There was not the slightest tremble in Jeff's voice, and he never blinked as he pulled back the tail of his coat, watching for the slightest movement of William's thumb on the hammer of the pistol. He counted - "one...two"... William shoved Elick away from himself, turning the pistol toward Jeff. Before he could pull back the hammer, the Colt was in Jeff's hand as quick as greased lightning. In less than two seconds, he had fired three shots. His first shot went into William's wrist, rendering him unable to pull the hammer back on his pistol. The next shot penetrated his heart. As he was grabbing his chest with his left hand, a third shot got him between his eyes. He was dead before he hit the ground.

Jeff quickly holstered the Colt, as Elick leaped into his arms,.

"Papa, Papa." he sobbed.

Never in his life had Jeff Townsend experienced the mixture of emotions that now flooded his soul. The sheer joy and relief of knowing that his son, who had moments before been threatened by death, was now safe in his arms, was somewhat clouded by the dark fact that he had just killed a man. Suddenly, and unexpectedly, his mind flashed back to that day ten years ago, when he had knocked Tom Tillotson unconscious. He recalled that, in the heat of that moment, he had momentarily thought about killing Tom with his own pistol. And now, ten years later, he had used that same pistol to end the life of another man who had threatened the life of one of his family. Holding onto his little boy, he lifted his eyes toward Heaven, thanking God for the safety of his son, and at the same time, asking forgiveness for having killed Bill Bowen. He also prayed that Elick's young mind would soon forget what he had just seen on the slope of that hillside. He knew that Becky and the children were at home, terrified. He had to get William's body onto the back of his horse, and get away from this horrible place immediately. He put Elick down, and whistled for Mr. Beecher. Mr. Beecher obeyed, making his way slowly and cautiously up the slope. When the horse got close enough, Jeff stopped him in a spot just wide enough for him to roll William's dead body down the slope, over a ledge of rock, and across the horse's back. He picked Elick up in one arm, and led the horse diagonally down the slope, to the edge of the grove of poplars.

Becky's heart seemed to stop as she heard three shots ring out from the mountainside. She grabbed Samuel and the shotgun. Carolyn had heard the shots also. Becky quickly ushered the children inside the house. Carolyn got busy cleaning the little girl's cuts she had gotten when she fell. Becky was beside herself, not knowing whether to run after Jeff or stay put.

Samuel grabbed the rifle from over the mantle.

"Samuel Jeffery Townsend! You put that rifle back this minute," Becky heard herself almost scream at him. Samuel would not hear of it. He had never disobeyed his parents before, but now he was standing his ground.

"Mama, I have to go help Papa, I can shoot Mama, please let me go.?"

Becky took the rifle gently from Samuel's hands, explaining to him about this man that had taken his little brother, and just how mean and dangerous he was. Samuel finally agreed that he would wait, but if his father didn't come back soon, he was going to help him. Becky knew she would have to keep her eyes on him or he would slip away when she wasn't looking.

The waiting was torture for both Becky and Carolyn, while trying to keep Samuel in eyesight, as well as keeping Ollie and Erica in the house and away from the windows. The two of them prayed silently. A thousand chilling thoughts ran quickly through her mind. Would this mean, crazed madman destroy her family by killing her son and her husband? She began to imagine what might be going on up there on that mountainside, what her sweet baby boy must be going through in the hands of this man. She prayed and cried at the same time, just trying to stay sane, and in control of herself. In a matter of moments she went through a funeral. She saw it all - the cold forms of her baby and husband. She saw the people, the beautiful flowers, and felt the pain of her broken heart. She found herself crying uncontrollably with her friend Carolyn holding her hands as she cried with her.

"Mama, please don't cry, Papa will get Elick back, you'll see Mama," Samuel's sweet voice pleaded, as he gently put his arms around her neck.

"I know sweetheart, and you are right, Papa and Elick will be alright," Becky answered, as she wiped the tears and held her son, trying to regain control of herself. She asked Carolyn if she would stay in the house with Ollie and Erica while she and Samuel went to the barn. Carolyn quickly agreed, assuring her that she and the children would be fine, but for her and Samuel to please be careful.

Becky, carrying a shotgun in one hand, and half dragging Samuel with the other, ran to the barn, where she could get a better view of the western ridge. She wanted to wait here to watch for the return of her husband and Elick. And if by an awful fate someone else, namely, Mr. Bowen should come down that ridge, she would be ready. She had never killed a living creature, and never wanted to, but to protect her family she knew she would. She placed the shotgun up on a shelf where she could easily reach it, telling Samuel he was not to touch it. Becky looked around the barn for any clues that might be there to help her understand this whole thing. Was the man ever in the barn, watching them as they did their chores? She could just imagine him there, planning out this evil deed as they went about their daily duties, unaware of the danger that was lurking on their farm, perhaps here inside this barn. She and Samuel searched every nook and cranny, all the while keeping an eye on the mountainside, watching for whoever came down the hill, praying it would be Jeff, carrying Elick.

Time seemed to stand still for Becky, standing there with a weapon in her hand. Then she and Samuel heard a rider approaching the house at a very fast speed. It was doctor Parks. He too had heard the three shots from a distance. He had followed Carolyn to make sure that she was safe. Since the robbery at the store he had gotten worried, since she had been gone for hours. He jumped from his horse and ran up onto the porch. Carolyn ran outside as Becky and Samuel ran from the barn to meet him explaining to him what had happened, handing him the note that William Bowen had written. Samuel went inside to check on his sisters. Becky told him to stay there until she knew it was safe for him to come out.

Dr. Parks, and the two women stood there with their eyes glued toward the ridge where Jeff was last seen riding at a very fast speed. They kept their voices down to whispers, listening for any sound. Dr. Parks was getting restless, pacing from one corner of the yard to the other. Then looking up toward the western ridge, they all saw Jeff leading his horse with a body lying across its back. The most precious sight Becky's eyes ever saw was her husband, walking with their son Elick in his arms. Becky and Carolyn cried and rejoiced in each other's arms. Samuel had heard the shouts of joy, and despite the orders to stay in the bedroom, he, Ollie Marie and Erica came running onto the porch. Samuel bolted past Becky, running full speed to meet his Papa, passing Dr. Parks like a young deer. Becky watched as Elick saw Samuel, and jumped down from his father's arms. He and Samuel ran ahead toward the house, straight into Becky's arms. She held him so tight he moaned, "Mama, I can't breathe."

His sweet smile and small voice was all she needed to see and hear to know he was alright. She gathered Samuel, Elick, Ollie and Erica all in her arms as she thanked God for his watchful eye that had kept them all safe. She opened her eyes to see Jeff and Joseph heading toward the barn with the horse and the dead man. She and Carolyn took the children inside the house. Becky didn't want them to see the scene that was taking place inside the barn. She wanted to take Jeff in her arms, but she knew he was safe now, and would tell her the whole story later.

Dr. Parks had never seen this somber expression on Jeff's face before. He knew that Jeff was a man of great integrity, humility and compassion, but he also knew Jeff was a man of strong convictions, who, since he had known him, had never had to explain or apologize to anyone for his words or actions. But now it seemed that Jeff was reluctant to even look him in the eye. His gaze seemed to be fastened on the dead body of William Bowen, as if he almost wished he could turn back the clock, and somehow erase the last few hours of his life, and William would be still alive somehow, and none of this whole sordid affair would have happened. Being a man of deep discernment himself, Dr. Parks recognized that his friend and Pastor, at this moment, needed one thing, he needed a friend who understood what was going on inside his heart. For a brief moment, Dr. Parks and Jeff Townsend embraced in a manly hug.

Dr. Parks reassuring Jeff, "It's alright Pastor, I know the truth, I read the note."

He could see the tears in Jeff's eyes, tears he didn't even try to hide. No words needed to be spoken as Dr. Parks saw the deep pain in Jeff's countenance. He knelt beside the body, examining the bullet wounds one by one. He looked up at Jeff just as Jeff unbuckled the gun belt, and hung it back on the spike where Tom had left it. Jeff asked Dr. Parks if he would ride into town and get Sheriff Murphy. He wanted Sheriff Murphy to see the body and the note, and to hear his own story of what had happened up on the hillside.

The news of the prison break had now leaked out, and had been spread far and wide by telegraph, newspapers, and word of mouth. Sheriff Clarence Murphy, having known about the robbery of the General Store from the first day it had happened, had put two and two together, and immediately put out Wanted posters on both of the escapees, Dead or Alive!. A bounty of $1,000 each was on their heads. When Dr. Parks rode up to his office, Sheriff Murphy knew something was terribly wrong.

Dr. Parks didn't even dismount, he just yelled out, "Sheriff, come quick.!"

Sheriff Murphy reached up and took the note from Dr. Parks, read it quickly, and mounted his own horse, as the two of them spurred their horses up the valley.

Ten minutes later, they dismounted in the barn yard, where Jeff stood alone, waiting for them. Becky, Carolyn, and the children were still inside the house, waiting for Jeff and Dr. Parks to come in. Sheriff Murphy examined the dead body carefully, noting the location of each bullet wound. He listened intently as Jeff explained in detail what had happened. Sheriff Murphy, who had himself become a member of the Jenkins Memorial Baptist Church, knew that Jeff Townsend did not lie. But there was one thing about the whole matter that troubled him, and being the inquisitive investigator and lawman he was, he simply had to ask Jeff some pointed questions.

He began, "Pastor, I've known you a long time, and I ain't never questioned your integrity for a single minute. And I can see all the evidence right here in front of me, but there's one thing I just can't make any sense of. You see Jeff, when the County elected me as Sheriff, they didn't elect me simply because of my experience and knowledge of the law, they also elected me because I'm the fastest man in these parts with a gun. I just can't for the life of me see how a country preacher could possibly put three shots in a man when that man already had the drop on him. That's gonna take some more explaining Pastor, not only for my own satisfaction, but for everybody else who will wonder about it."

Jeff knew he was between a rock and a hard place, and that his story did seem a bit far fetched to anyone who knew him. No one had ever seen Jeff Townsend with a gun on his hip, much less with a gun in his hand. His story would indeed seem incredible to anyone who had ever fired a gun. There was only one way for him to convince Sheriff Murphy of the truthfulness of his story, and that was to beat him in a mock gunfight. Without another word, he reached for the gun belt, and strapped it on his waist. He removed the three remaining cartridges from the chambers, stepping off twenty paces from Sheriff Murphy. Sheriff Murphy removed all six cartridges from his own pistol, and waited. Dr. Parks was asked to count to three. On the count of three, Sheriff Murphy went for his gun. Before he got the pistol half way out of the holster, Jeff had already cleared leather, and fanned the hammer of the Colt three times.

Sheriff Murphy and Dr. Parks gasped at the lightning speed of Jeff's draw. Neither of them had ever seen anything like it in their lives. Sheriff Murphy's face turned beet red, as he stood there speechless, his gun still half way out of the holster. He shoved the pistol back into the holster slowly, a little embarrassed, more surprised, but even more relieved, remarking, "Pastor, I ain't never seen a draw that fast in my life. I'm convinced. But for your own safety, my safety, and the safety of everyone in the County, I think we better keep this to ourselves." Both Jeff and Dr. Parks agreed quickly, knowing that if the news ever got out that there was a faster gun than Sheriff Murphy, every gun slinger in the State would come looking for that man, wanting to prove he was faster.

The three of them loaded the body into Jeff's wagon, covering the body with a blanket, and the entire wagon with a canvas. They hitched Sheriff Murphy's and Dr. Park's horses to the wagon. Jeff turned toward the house, where Becky and Carolyn were watching from a window, waiting for him to give them a signal that it was alright for them to come out. He motioned for them to come outside. The children were told to stay inside. Becky and Carolyn came out to the porch, where Jeff and Dr. Parks met them, explaining that the three of them were going to take the body into town to the Coroner's office. Carolyn gave Becky a quick goodbye hug, as Dr. Parks lifted her gently into the buggy. She drove slowly in front of the wagon all the way into town. Jeff followed close behind, riding Mr. Beecher.

After unloading the body at the Coroner's office, Dr. Parks and Sheriff Murphy insisted that Jeff take the wagon and return to his family. Dr. Parks wanted to be the one to deliver the bad news to the Bowen brothers, Joshua and Gideon, William Bowen's nephews. The young men already knew their uncle had escaped from the prison, but they didn't know that he was now dead.

After making sure that Carolyn was alright, Dr. Parks took the note from Sheriff Murphy that William had written to Jeff, and rode alone toward the Bowen's place, which was now about five miles southwest of Bruceton Mills. They and the Phelps brothers still owned the two acres in back of Dr. Parks property, but had abandoned it not long after Carolyn Parks had shot them in the behind.

It was late Thursday afternoon when Dr. Parks rode up to the hotel. Both Joshua and Gideon saw him ride in, and rushed out onto the porch to meet him, their hands extended in welcome.

"Well, Well, Joshua commented, what a pleasant surprise Dr. Parks. It ain't Sunday yet. Have you come to baptize us early, before we have a chance to backslide.?"

The expression on Dr. Parks' face told them he was not here for a social visit.

Dr. Parks asked politely, "Is there someplace private where we can talk.?"

"Sure Dr. Parks, Gideon responded, come into our private office in the back."

As Dr. Parks sat down in a plush leather chair, he took out the note, handing it to Gideon, saying, "I'm afraid I have some bad news gentlemen, and there's no easy way to say it. Your uncle William is dead."

Both Joshua and Gideon turned a bit pale as Joshua glanced at the note in Gideon's hand. They both sank into their chairs, their voices quivering.

"When Dr. Parks, and how did he die?" Joshua managed to ask. "We know he escaped from prison with uncle Wesley, but.... his voice diminished as he glanced down at the note again, reading it slowly, trying to put the picture together...a preacher, his son, the threat to kill the preacher's son, slowly things began to become clearer.

The boys had never met Jeff Townsend personally, and they only vaguely remembered him from the trial back in '66, along with a half breed, Tom Great Bear Tillotson, on the witness stand, testifying against their uncles, William and Wesley. As Dr. Parks saw the enlightenment upon their faces, he began to explain to them what had happened.

Before Dr. Parks could finish, Joshua interrupted him, as he stood up with the note in his hand. "Is this preacher by any chance Jeff Townsend? And did he kill uncle William?"

Dr. Parks could see that both the young men were now somewhat enraged, not knowing the facts of how their uncle had died. He politely asked them to sit down again, and to let him finish. The two young men had enough respect for Dr. Parks to hear him out. He began again.

"Yes, gentlemen, Reverend Townsend did kill your uncle William today, but he had no choice. Your uncle William first robbed the General Store in Bruceton Mills, then, three days later, kidnapped the Pastor's five-year-old son, Elick, and threatened to kill him if Pastor Townsend did not meet him on a ridge behind his farm before sunset. Pastor Townsend went to meet him, and beat him to the draw in a gunfight. If you need more evidence, Sheriff Clarence Murphy can collaborate what I have just told you, along with my wife Carolyn. I just wanted to be the one to bring you the news, so that you can go and claim your uncle's body, and give him a Christian burial. I have known Jeff Townsend about ten years now, and there is not a more caring and compassionate man in the world than him. In fact, it is he who is supposed to baptize the two of you this Sunday, unless you change your minds."

The two brothers looked at each other for a moment, then back to Dr. Parks.

Gideon spoke for them both, saying, "Dr. Parks, we told you at the service last Sunday that we have matured substantially during the six years since we first met you and your wife, and I guess this is God's way of giving us the opportunity to show you that we have indeed grown up since then. It's kind of hard to swallow, but we have the utmost respect for you and what you say. We'd like to meet this Reverend Townsend face to face, and hear his story ourselves, if you don't mind Sir."

Dr. Parks smiled as he stood and shook their hands, not only because of the sincere manner in which they seemed to be taking the bad news, but also because, in his entire life, this was the first time any white man had referred to him as, Sir.

"I'm certain Reverend Townsend would be glad to meet you both, and to tell you exactly what happened in his own words. If you wish, I will try to arrange for him to meet you in Bruceton Mills when you come to claim your uncle's body, if that is alright with you." It was agreed that Dr. Parks and Jeff would meet them the next day, Friday, at the Coroner's office, at about 10:00 a.m. There was just enough daylight left for Dr. Parks to make it back home before dark if he rode fast, and he rode fast, confident that there would soon be an end to this horrible, tragic nightmare.

Back at the Townsend farm, Jeff and Becky were kneeling with their children, their arms around all of them, thanking God for His tender mercies. Not many words were exchanged that evening between Jeff and Becky. Becky was at a loss for words, and Jeff didn't want to hear a lot of words. The joy and celebration of anniversaries past was somehow marred by the day's events. As they laid down in their own bed that night, Becky just laid her arm across his chest, with her head barely touching his chest, and said nothing. After a long silence, Jeff had to get up, and go outside. He walked slowly toward the little pool of water, and sat down on the grass at the water's edge, bowing his head, weeping in the darkness.

Becky couldn't sleep either. She waited for Jeff to return, but after an hour, he still hadn't come back to the house. She arose and put on a robe and her slippers, slipping silently out the front door, sitting down on the front porch, looking toward the pool of water. She could barely make out Jeff's form, sitting there in the pale moonlight, his head upon his knees. In all their years of marriage, she had never seen Jeff flinch in the face of danger, or cower to any threat. He had been her tower of strength whenever she had been weak or afraid. And now he needed her in a way that he had never needed her before. She got up and walked slowly toward him, praying that God would somehow give her something to say that would bring a bit of comfort to his aching heart.

Jeff's thoughts were rumbling through his mind like a runaway train, each thought flashed by like one of the rail cars, swiftly disappearing without his being able to see what was written on it. Every detail of his existence since he had gotten up Thursday morning flashed through his mind, none of them leaving any meaning behind. He tried desperately to slow his mind down, and make some sense of what had happened. Then he felt the gentle hand of his beloved wife touch his shoulder. She stood behind him momentarily, waiting to see what his reaction would be. He raised his head from off his knees, as she knelt down behind him, slipping her arms around his chest, holding him.

She whispered, "Jeff, there was nothing else you could have done in order to save our little boy."

No sooner had she spoken, when another hand touched Jeff's other shoulder. It was Dr. Parks, who immediately added, "She's right Jeff, your son is alive because you loved him enough to risk your own life to save his, and it is not your fault that Mr. Bowen made himself the killer that he was."

Jeff stood up, taking Dr. Parks' hand, answering, "You came all this way in the middle of the night to tell me that doc?"

"I just thought you could use a friend Pastor, and I haven't forgotten who it was that came and welcomed me and my wife to this town. And I haven't forgotten the many times you have befriended those who had no other friend. And I haven't forgotten the fact that you left your flock in the hands of a black man, something that no other white man has ever done. You trusted me with the lives of your God-given congregation without any reservation or instructions. So, for whatever it's worth to you Sir, here I am, at your service."

"I visited the Bowen brothers earlier this afternoon Pastor, and they have both agreed to meet us and the Sheriff tomorrow morning at 10:00 a.m. at the Coroner's office. I showed them this note that Mr. Bowen wrote, and explained to them exactly what happened up on that hillside, and I believe they are satisfied with what I told them. They just want to meet you face to face, and hear you say it yourself."

Jeff hugged Dr. Parks again, thanking him for caring enough to come up the valley this late at night, alone, just to offer him some comfort. Somehow, his heart felt just a bit lighter now. But he knew he would not be able to rest until he could look those two young men in the eye, and tell them how sorry he was for having to do what he did. Dr. Parks gave Becky a quick hug, mounted his horse, and rode toward home. Leaving Jeff alone, Becky waited patiently for him to return back into the house. It was midnight when she opened the front door to let him in. Tired and weary, they climbed into bed.

School was still out for summer vacation, and the two boys, Samuel and Elick wanted to spend as much time with Jeff as they could. They followed him wherever he went, and tried to imitate whatever he did. Samuel even tried his hand at sawing and splitting wood for Becky's cook stove. When they overheard Jeff and Becky talking about Jeff going into town the next morning, both of them immediately began to plead.

"Can we go Papa, please, please Papa, let us go with you.?"

Jeff wanted to spend as much time with his boys as he could also, and quickly gave in to their pleading. Becky didn't mind either, because it would get them out from under her feet for a while, so she could spend more time with the girls, she had promised she would give them a day of motherly instruction, teaching them to sew and cook.

When Jeff, Samuel, Elick and Dr. Parks arrived at the Coroner's office on Friday morning, the Bowen brothers, Joshua and Gideon, along with Sheriff Murphy were already there. Both Gideon and Joshua had spoken with Mr. Dunsen, the County Coroner. They identified the body of their uncle, and signed papers, accepting responsibility for the proper burial of the body.

The Coroner's office was right next door to the General Store. Samuel and Elick, of course, couldn't resist the opportunity to browse around in the General Store, looking at all the dime novels, the toys, the pistols and rifles, and a calendar with the picture of the newly elected President, Rutherford B. Hayes.

Samuel couldn't resist giving his little brother a history lesson, pointing to the calendar, saying, "Look Elick, that's the President of the United States, Rutherford B. Hayes."

Elick smiled momentarily, then quickly returned his attention to the small books, with pictures of western gunfighters and outlaws on the covers. He gazed at the drawing of a Sheriff, wearing a badge, beating the outlaw to the draw.

He commented to Samuel, "Our Papa is faster than any of these men."

Samuel didn't know quite how to respond to Elick's comment, but quickly took the little book from Elick's hands, putting it back on the shelf, reminding him, "Elick, you know we aren't supposed to touch anything in the store."

Mr. Martin smiled as the two Townsend boys browsed slowly up one aisle and down the other, visually examining nearly every article. He knew he could trust Samuel to keep an eye on Elick, because both Becky and Jeff had often brought Samuel into the store with them ever since he was big enough to walk, and they had taught him to keep his hands off the items in the store. After they had taken a tour of the whole place, Elick told Samuel he needed to *be excused,"* which was another way of saying that he had to use the outhouse. Samuel took him by the hand, and led him around to the back of the store, where the outhouse sat near the edge of Big Sandy Creek.

While Samuel waited for Elick to use the outhouse, he turned his attention to the gently flowing creek, watching small fish and minnows swim in the shallow water. As his eyes drifted downstream, he saw something that appeared to be a piece of clothing, a uniform of some sort! with black and white stripes!. On the opposite side of the creek was a pair of boots, lodged behind a low branch that hung out over the creek.

When Elick emerged from the outhouse, Samuel again took his little brother's hand, as the two of them walked the few steps to the front of the Coroner's office. Samuel knocked on the door. Mr. Dunsen answered the door, recognizing Samuel and Elick, and turned to Jeff, asking him if it was alright for the boys to come inside. Jeff nodded his consent. Samuel quickly informed Jeff that there was something in the creek that everyone should see. His voice was so urgent that all the men, Mr. Dunsen, Joshua and Gideon , Sheriff Murphy, Jeff, and Dr. Parks immediately followed Samuel to the spot where the prison clothes and the boots were. Jeff waded into the creek, retrieved the clothes and boots, and showed them to all the other men. On the left upper side of the shirt, just above the pocket, was a name and a number sewn into a small rectangular patch. The name was, W. Bowen, the number was 10751.

Sheriff Murphy examined the prison clothes, then handed them to Gideon, who handed them to Joshua. The two young men nodded, accepting the fact that the clothes had belonged to their uncle. Sheriff Murphy asked the two brothers if they were satisfied with what they had seen and heard since they had arrived that morning concerning the death of their uncle. They both agreed they had seen and heard enough to convince them that Jeff had done what he had to do in order to save his son's life. Sheriff Murphy asked them to wait for just another minute or two while he walked over to the General Store. He returned with Mr. Martin, who, after seeing the shirt, hat, boots, canteen, pistol, knife, and other articles that William Bowen had stolen from him, confirmed that all the articles had been taken from his store.

Everything added up, all the evidence and testimony matched, and the two Bowen brothers shook hands with Jeff, telling him they were so sorry for what their uncle had put him and his family through.

Joshua looked down at Elick, who was clinging to Jeff's leg.

"Are you alright little fella?"

Elick looked up at him, nodding his head, replying politely, "Yes Sur."

Dan Martin shook hands with the Bowen brothers also, offering, " Fellas, if you would not be offended, I would like to donate a nice suit from my store for your uncle to be buried in."

Joshua and Gideon looked at each other in total surprise, as Gideon responded.

"Mr. Martin, that is mighty kind of you, after our uncle did you so wrong. We should be the ones repaying you for the stuff our uncle stole from you."

Mr. Martin answered, "Boys, the good Lord has been mighty good to me. He forgave me of all my sins, and I must forgive all those who trespass against me. Your uncle made some bad decisions, but haven't we all at one time or another?"

The two brothers glanced at each other, then toward Dr. Parks, agreeing, "Yes Sir, we surely have."

Mr. Martin hurried into the store, coming back with an extra large, three-piece blue suit, a white shirt, and a tie to match the suit. Before leaving with their uncle's body in their wagon.

Gideon again addressed Jeff, asking him, "Reverend Townsend, if it ain't asking too much, would you do us the honor of allowing Dr. Parks to assist you in baptizing us this Sunday?"

Jeff nodded, replying, "I'd be honored to do that gentlemen."

Dr. Parks nodded, adding, "And so would I."

The Bowen family had a grave-side service for William Bowen on Saturday, June 10th, and buried him in the Bowen family cemetery, on the outskirts of Kingwood. Joshua and Gideon posted a notice in a local newspaper, which simply said:

William Bowen, one of two escapees from a penitentiary in northern West Virginia, died tragically in a hunting accident in the woods of Preston County on Thursday, June 8th. The body was discovered by the Reverend Jeffrey Townsend and Dr. Joseph Parks, who promptly notified Sheriff Clarence Murphy of Preston County. The body was taken to the Coroner's office in Bruceton Mills, and identified and claimed by Mr. Bowen's nephews, Joshua and Gideon Bowen. The Bowen family has posted this notice in the hope that everyone who reads it will be aware that the other escapee - Wesley Phelps, who escaped with Mr. Bowen, is still at large, and may be in the vicinity. The Bowen family also wishes to express their sincere gratitude to Reverend Townsend, Dr. Parks, Sheriff Murphy, Coroner Dunsen, and Mr. Daniel Martin for all the kindness and Christian charity that all of them have shown to our departed uncle and to our family in this time of tragedy. By Joshua and Gideon Bowen.

Sunday June 11th, 1876. Jenkins Memorial Baptist Church

The secret that Jeff had kept hidden for years was not a secret anymore, but only four men other than himself knew it - Dr. Parks, Joshua and Gideon Bowen, and Sheriff Clarence Murphy, and neither of them would ever tell anyone else. Neither Becky, nor Mr. Martin, nor Coroner Dunsen ever asked Jeff how it came to be that he had lived through the ordeal of facing William Bowen, and Jeff never volunteered the details. As far as the rest of the world was concerned, Jeff was still just a country preacher, a hard-working farmer, and a dedicated husband and father to his family. And as far as the people of the State of West Virginia were concerned, Sheriff Clarence Murphy was still the fastest gun alive.

Jeff put the whole sordid picture behind him, and left it alone. In the back of his mind, however, he knew there was yet one other man who might put the pieces of the story together, and come gunning for him, that man being Wesley Phelps. But he also knew there were other things that mattered far more in his life than looking over his shoulder for someone who wasn't there. He had a family to raise, a church to pastor, and a community to care for. He would simply trust his Lord to take care of those things over which he himself had no control.

The church was again overflowing on Sunday morning, with standing room only. The whole congregation waited for Jeff and his family to arrive, just to personally welcome them back home. It was a touching, heart-warming scene, with each man and woman coming to Jeff and Becky individually, shaking their hands and hugging them and their children, telling them how much they had missed them. Jeff and Becky were also thrilled to see everyone shaking hands with Dr. and Mrs. Parks, telling them how much they appreciated Dr. Parks' powerful message last Sunday.

For Becky, this homecoming was a bag of mixed emotions. But she was more concerned for Jeff than for herself. During all the years she had known and loved Jeff Townsend, she had never seen him flinch in the face of danger, nor had she seen him shrink from a task, or avoid any responsibility. He had been her pillar of strength in the most difficult times of her life. Not only was he her husband and best friend in life, he was also her pastor, her spiritual leader and teacher. In all the years she had listened to him preach and teach, she had gotten her spiritual nourishment, counseling and training from him.

But with all that had happened in the last few days, she wondered if he would be the same preacher he had always been. She wondered if he would still be as confident and as powerful from the pulpit as he had been before. She wondered if nearly losing two of their children, and killing a man, would have an adverse affect on his preaching. All her questions and fears were about to be answered. Jeff Townsend was not a man given to change. He was what he was, he knew what he believed, and why he believed it. The only change that Jeff would allow in his spiritual relationship to his God was spiritual growth. He never stopped growing in grace and in the knowledge of his Lord and Savior Jesus Christ, and neither would he allow his congregation to stop growing spiritually. He saw to it that every member of the congregation received in-depth training in the Scriptures.

After all the customary Sunday morning amenities, and all the announcements had been made, Jeff stepped into the pulpit with all the confidence and authority as he had always done. He thanked Dr. Parks for filling in for him the previous Sunday, and praised him for the fine job he had done. Then he asked the people to stand and open their Bibles to the eighth chapter of Romans, verses 33 and 34, and read - Who shall lay anything to the charge of God's elect? It is God that justifieth. Who is he that condemneth? It is Christ that died, yea rather, that is risen again, who is even at the right hand of God, who also maketh intercession for us.

He began the sermon, "This morning I will be preaching on the subject of "The mighty pillars of the Christian Faith, building upon a message once delivered by the venerable C.H. Spurgeon of England, may I describe to you four massive pillars upon which the Christian Faith and the Christian Church do rest." With only these few words, the congregation was already at full attention to Jeff's voice. The anointing of the Holy Spirit had already taken control of him, and of those who were listening. Becky smiled, breathing a sigh of relief, and almost blushing with shame because of having briefly entertained the notion that her beloved husband might not be the same man and preacher that God had called him to be.

Jeff saw the look of love and contentment in the face of his beloved wife, and continued.

"In the text we are made to observe at least four strong, nay, impervious foundations upon which our faith is built. The first impenetrable rock upon which our faith rests securely is, of course, the death of Christ."

"The regenerated child of God cannot be condemned, and neither can any charge or accusation brought against him stand, because someone who is almighty has died in his place, having taken upon Himself the full weight, guilt, and subsequent punishment that was due to the poor sinner who committed the offense. But there is something else here in this text that I greatly fear is often missed, or neglected by the casual reader. The writer, the apostle Paul, being inspired by the Holy Ghost, asks two piercing questions of his hearers, the first being, "Who shall lay anything to the charge of God's elect? That question needs to be addressed, and it needs to be answered."

"All of us who are saved, know that being a Christian, in itself, brings with it certain fundamental biases and dislikes from those who are not Christians, those who do not understand spiritual things. To make the long story short, there are many thousands, if not millions of persons who may bring charges against the child of God. But I must insist from the text that they are not justified in doing so. In fact, the unbelieving world is sternly warned against laying anything to the charge of God's elect, or attempting to condemn a child of God for any reason."

Jeff continued, "In other words, who would dare, who would be so brazen as to accuse a blood-washed child of the great King of committing sin? On the night that the children of Israel left the land of Egypt, we are told that, But against any of the children of Israel shall not a dog move his tongue, against man or beast: that ye may know how that the Lord doth put a difference between the Egyptians and Israel. "I simply must do as the Holy Spirit leads today, and say that it is a dangerous thing for anyone to employ his tongue for the purpose of accusing a child of God, and yet so many choose to do so. Why? Because they are ignorant of the Scriptures, and as equally ignorant of the divine Author of those Scriptures. When our blessed Lord was here on Earth, He once asked the question, Which of you convinceth me of sin? And if I say the truth, why do ye not believe me? (John 8:46)."

"The Son of God could not, and cannot be convicted of wrongdoing on any level. And if we are in Him, and He is in us, then neither can we be convicted of wrongdoing. Look at it another way if you will. Pontius Pilate, the man who sentenced Christ Jesus to die upon the cross was guilty of sin in sentencing the Lord to crucifixion, but as wrong and as guilty as he was, there were others who were more guilty than Pilate, the ones who accused Him, and the one who delivered Him to Pilate, namely, Judas Iscariot. And while there are those who are brazen enough to slander and accuse the Christian, as dangerous as that is, there is yet no accusation or charge that can be made to hold against him in the end. Why?

Because he has a divine Substitute who took his place, and died in his stead, clearing him, not only of his sins, but from the very guilt of having committed them. The child of God may be accused, but he cannot be condemned, because Jesus was condemned for him. And since it was Christ who was condemned for us, there is therefore now no condemnation to them which are in Christ Jesus. This, then, is the first mighty pillar upon which our faith rests, the all-sufficient, atoning death of the Son of God."

"And the second mighty pillar upon which the Christian church stands secure is the bodily resurrection of the One who is our Substitute. The Holy Spirit was pleased to move the heart and hand of Paul to write in highly expressive language the power which was employed in the resurrection of our Savior. As powerful, and as efficacious as was the dying of Christ upon the cross, Paul says of His resurrection; "yea, rather, that is risen again", as if the resurrection of Christ were an even more powerful argument for us than was His crucifixion. And indeed, if Christ had done no more than die upon the cross, without having risen from the grave, we, according to the Scriptures, would be of all men most miserable. For consider the gravity of the consequences for mankind if Christ be not risen. Paul says that if Christ be not risen, then, our preaching is vain, our faith is vain, we are found false witnesses of God, we are yet in our sins, and they also which are fallen asleep in Christ are perished. (I Corinthians 15:14-18). "I cannot be condemned because the death of Christ provided salvation for me, and because His resurrection proves it."

"And yet another powerful argument against a single one of us ever being condemned is the ascension of our Lord to Heaven from whence He came. Paul says of our Lord, "who is even at the right hand of God." But what does His bodily ascension to Heaven have to do with the fact that we cannot be condemned? It is simply this, that Christ Himself said, "Nevertheless I tell you the truth; It is expedient for you that I go away: for if I go not away, the Comforter will not come unto you; but if I depart, I will send him unto you (John 16:7)." "I ask you, how would we do without the blessed Comforter? Christ said that if He did not go away, meaning that if He did not ascend into Heaven, then the Comforter would not come. I, therefore, am glad that he ascended, for I have needed the power and presence of the Comforter in my own life on far more occasions than I care to recount to you here this morning. In fact, the great Comforter of late has been my staff and my stay, upholding me when it seemed that I would surely fall."

Jeff's mind instantly recapped the events that had taken place the last few days.

"He has been my comforter, my counselor, and my consolation in the midst of the deepest pain and suffering through which I and my dear family have ever gone. And I am certain there are many more present here today who can testify to the same fact."

Loud Amen's could be heard from every pew in the church after Jeff's last statement, with a few folks, including Becky, Sheriff Collins, Dan Martin, Mr. Dunsen, Joshua and Gideon Bowen and Dr. and Mrs. Parks rising to their feet, with their hands uplifted in praise to God. Jeff hesitated only momentarily, and began to close the sermon with his final point, adding, "And finally, the fourth mighty pillar upon which the Christian faith stands is the intercession of our Great High Priest Jesus Christ. We cannot be condemned because He died for us. We cannot be condemned because He arose from the tomb victorious over sin, death, Hell, and the grave. We cannot be condemned because He has given us His Holy Spirit to guide and to guard us against all enemies. And we cannot be condemned because He intercedes for us at any and every moment the accuser may bring a railing accusation against us."

Jeff closed his bible, asking, "And with that said, the question must be asked, upon what, or upon whom does your own hope stand? Are you able to sing with me, I need no other argument, I need no other plea, It is enough that Jesus died, and that He died for me?

As we stand together, with every head bowed and every eye closed, are there any here today who, by an uplifted hand, would acknowledge your need of a Savior."

As he stood in front of the people he had learned to love so dear, Jeff's own heart trembled as hands were raised from nearly every pew in the house. He knew the Holy Spirit had been powerfully convicting souls from the beginning of the worship service, but he didn't know there were so many there to whom the Spirit was speaking. He quickly counted thirty hands uplifted, acknowledging that they were lost. When the invitation was extended, twenty-nine of those who lifted their hands came forward, kneeling at the altar.

Twenty-nine souls were saved that Sunday morning, and along with the seven who had been saved the previous Sunday, a total of thirty-six souls were baptized in Big Sandy Creek. It was the first time in the history of the church, the county, and the State, that so many had been baptized together. It was also the first time a black Deacon waded into the creek alongside a white Pastor, and helped him do the baptizing.

Within the families who attended the Jenkins Memorial Baptist Church, there existed a certain unwritten code, a code that simply implied that every individual and every family was bound to one another, and was responsible for one another by Biblical, Christian principles, the strongest principle, of course, being their love for one another. In fact, this code was actually a written code, written upon the pages of the Holy Bible, summed up in the second commandment, Thou shalt love thy neighbor as thyself. As far as anyone in the congregation was concerned, the commandment to love one's neighbor as himself meant all of his neighbors, regardless of the color of his skin, the occupation in which he or she was employed, or the social standing of the individual or family, rich or poor, or anywhere in between. This Christian principle was demonstrated on a daily basis by the Pastor, Jeff Townsend, who led by example, and had earned the love and respect of all who knew him.

Others in the Church who demonstrated this same principle were Dr. Joseph Parks and his wife Carolyn, who on a daily basis exposed themselves to the germs and diseases of every patient who came to them, never turning anyone away, no matter how advanced the disease might be, and many times receiving no pay for their services. They did what they did because they loved people, all people, and only wanted to serve their God by serving their fellow man. And even though the pay was seldom monetary, God somehow kept blessing Dr. Parks and his practice. It seemed the more he gave of himself, the more was given to him in return. Some folks who could not afford to pay Dr. Parks with money paid him in other ways. Dr. Parks never had to buy any eggs, because his patients had now given him enough chickens and roosters to start his own chicken farm. He never had to buy meat, because one of his patients had given him a sow pig, and another had given him a boar pig, and these had produced a litter of their own (two sows and four boars). Dr. Parks raised these hogs, had, killed one for winter meat, and sold three hogs for enough money to buy a young calf, which he raised, had her bred, and thus began his own herd of cattle.

But practicing medicine was Dr. Parks' first love, and he did it well; so well, in fact, that many of his neighbors who had any extra time on their hands would often come to his farm early in the morning, and do his chores for him, so that he could spend as much time as possible doing what he did best, doctoring the sick. Many times he and Carolyn were awakened before dawn by the sound of someone out in the wood lot, chopping and stacking firewood, or feeding the horses, hogs and cows. It was their way of showing Dr. Parks their love and gratitude for his kindness to them and their families.

Being the wise and godly man that he was, Dr. Parks knew that time waits for no man, and he wasn't getting any younger. At the time, he was the only licensed black physician anyone knew within a 500 mile radius. Medical schools for blacks were non-existent in West Virginia, and the closest (and only) medical schools for blacks were the Howard Medical School in Washington, DC, and the Meharry Medical College in Nashville, TN. The chances of any black person wanting to become a physician receiving formal training were very slim. Dr. Parks was determined that if there were any young students (black or white) who showed any interest in becoming doctors or nurses, he would do everything in his power to see that they got the education and training they needed. He began by spending every possible moment he could spare sharing his own professional knowledge and skill with two very promising young students, Gloria and Greta, the twin daughters of Buford R. Williams, who drove a horse and buggy to his office every Saturday, and spent the entire day reading his medical books, observing Dr. Parks in action, and taking notes.

The good doctor was often called away to tend to the mountain folk, and today was one of those times. Carolyn lay there in the darkness. Only the shadows of the furniture could be seen by the light of the moon. She was restless, unsure of what the night had in store for her, but fearing the worst. She was trying hard to ignore the pain that was throbbing in her back. She knew it was not quite time for the baby to arrive, and she prayed that it wouldn't come tonight with Joseph away from home. It was at least two more weeks before her time to deliver. She tossed and turned from one side to the other, then onto her back, hoping to relieve the pain, but nothing seemed to work. She sat up on the bedside, slipping her feet into her soft house shoes, then wrapped herself in her house jacket. She lit the kerosene lamp sitting on the table by the bed, then walked slowly into the kitchen, pouring herself a glass of warm milk, hoping it would help her to calm down, and that sleep would soon come.

The grandfather clock showed eleven o'clock. She sat down at the kitchen table, looking around at the beautiful room. The snow-white cabinets covered the walls in the big room. The black cast iron stove sat in the corner, still warm from the evening meal she had made. So many memories flooded her mind with all the happy times that she and Joseph had shared with their family and friends they had come to know since they moved here to this small community of Bruceton Mills West Virginia. Jeff and Becky Townsend had been the best friends they had anywhere, even back in New York. The couple had been the first to welcome them into their home. Tom and Pearly Mae had been so good to her and Joseph, and then there was Rufus and Claudette, with sweet Becky Sarah.

Thinking of Becky Sarah reminded her of her precious friend Sarah Puckett. Oh how she was going to miss her, and sweet, sweet Clark Puckett, who was shot down by a crazed gunman. Sarah had later married Becky's father, and moved to Tennessee with the children, Mollie and Carter. Carolyn shuddered at the very thought of that horrible night. She remembered Sarah's screams when she was told of the terrible news of her husband's death. Her thoughts had made her forget about her pain for just a short while, but she was suddenly reminded again by a stabbing pain that didn't let up.

Joseph had been called to the Rutherford's home in the mountains. Rufus' mother, Hilda Rutherford had been struck down with a heart attack, and Joseph had gone there early last evening. Carolyn was alone, and not quite sure what to do. If these pains were signs that the baby was coming she certainly didn't want to be here in this big house by herself. She went to her bedroom and changed into a dress, packing a bag with everything she would need for the baby. She knew Joseph would head back down that mountain if he knew she was in this condition, but he didn't know, and she had no way of sending for him, so she would drive to the Townsend farm.

She knew that Becky was the only woman around that delivered babies since Sarah and Pearly Mae were gone. She trusted Becky completely, and so did her husband.

After writing a note for her husband explaining where she had gone, Carolyn carefully lit a lantern. After setting it on the porch by the front door she went back in for her small bag that she had packed. She blew out the kerosene lamp. With only the light of the moon shining brightly through the kitchen window she walked to the door, closing it behind her, and picking up the lighted lantern, she was making her way to the stable to hitch up the buggy when she saw the shadow of a man walking toward her house. She wasn't sure of what to do. "Should she run faster and get into the barn, or should she turn back and go into the house?" Before she could decide, a kind and familiar-sounding voice spoke up from the front gate.

"Are you alright Mrs. Parks? I noticed your lantern sitting on the porch and the missus told me to come check on you."

It was Harvey McAllister, Rachel's husband. Rachel was the school teacher. She and Harvey lived in a small cabin behind the school building, which was very close to the entrance of Dr. Parks' property. Carolyn was never so happy to see anyone in all her life.

"Harvey, I am so glad to see you." Carolyn said.

"What in the world are you doing out here this time of night, and in your condition.?"

Harvey asked, as he took the lantern from her hand and gently lead her back up the steps of her home.

"I was heading to the Townsend farm, I think the baby is on it's way."

Carolyn thought that she was going to have to hold Harvey up. He turned pale, stammering like a two year old.

"Th....tha baby! Oh my God! I have to get Rachel!"

Harvey turned and started running toward the gate.

"Harvey, stop!" Carolyn yelled out to him, bursting into laughter. "Just help me to get back into the house first.

"So sorry Mrs. Parks, guess I lost my head there fer a minute."

He took Carolyn by the arm, gently helping her back up the steps and into the house. He began lighting the lamps as she sat down at the kitchen table. Carolyn quickly instructed Harvey on what he needed to do. He was to bring Rachel to stay with her till he could go and bring Becky back to the Parks house. Carolyn did not want to disturb her friends at this time of night, but since Joseph wasn't here, she had no choice. But she also knew that none of them would mind, and that it was the way they would want it to be.

Harvey got Carolyn settled on the sofa and promised he would be right back with Rachel. He returned as quickly as he had left. Rachel rushed in the room and insisted that she help Carolyn into her night clothes and back into the bed. With that done Rachel hurried around in the kitchen and soon a nice pot of coffee was brewing. Rachel knew it would be a long night. Carolyn lay in her bed, feeling a bit more at peace just knowing that she was not alone, but also praying that Joseph would make it back for the birth of their first child.

At the Townsend farm Becky lay there staring up at the ceiling, unable to sleep. She had gone to bed early, knowing she had to be up at the crack of dawn to get the children off to school. The main reason she was unable to sleep was that her beloved neighbor, Hilda Rutherford, had become suddenly ill, and Becky was so afraid she would not make it. Doctor Parks had come by the house on the way up the mountain. He informed Becky and Jeff that he was going to check on her. Jeff offered to go with him, but Joseph declined, saying he would feel better knowing that Jeff was close by if Carolyn needed anything while he was gone.

"He must be home by now," Becky thought to herself. He must have came back by after she had gone to bed." Becky prayed that he was able to help Hilda. Maybe she would hear some news in the morning. No matter how hard she tried, sleep would not come. Becky slipped silently out of bed, placing a gentle kiss on her husband's cheek as he lay there sleeping peacefully. She walked to the bedrooms where her children were sleeping. After making sure that all was safe in the house she quickly poured herself a cup of coffee, which was still warm from last nights supper. She tiptoed to the door, closing it softly behind her. She sat on the swing, gazing up toward the well-lit starry sky. The moon was so big and bright it lit up the whole farm. Cricket curled up at her feet and closed his eyes.

Becky's mind recalled so many happy times on this farm, weddings, church picnics, the birth of her children, and the times that she and Jeff had romped and played like two children in the man-made pond there on the farm. Her heart felt warm at the thoughts of those romantic times. Her eyes fell on the path that led to Tom and Pearly Mae's cabin. She missed them something fierce, but she knew that Tom had to follow the Lord's plan to preach in another place. Such good times they had experienced with all their friends. It seemed so long ago now, but the memories would always be fresh in her mind. Becky only hoped and prayed that her own little family would grow up to have the same sweet memories as she had experienced.

The children were growing so quickly. Samuel was a wonderful scholar, and was very much interested in the Bible. He would sit for hours with his father, studying and discussing the scriptures. Needless to say, Jeff was one proud father. He was hoping his oldest son would follow in his footsteps, and maybe take care of the church if and when he himself became unable to do so. Ollie Marie was Miss Rachel's right hand helper. She declared that she was going to be a teacher some day.

"Just like Miss Rachel," she would say.

The twins were still like two peas in a pod, wherever you saw one, you saw the other. Elick seemed withdrawn at times, very quiet, and always very protective of the other children. Becky had noticed him always turning around and looking behind him, as if he expected to see something or someone. After the kidnapping Becky would not let any of them out of her sight for a moment. She shuddered at the very thought of that awful day. She had lived in fear that Wesley Phelps was out there in the woods, watching every move that was made on the farm. Even though it had been almost a year she still woke up in the night trembling at any little sound.

Suddenly her thoughts were interrupted by a horse and rider heading in her direction at a very fast speed. As the rider drew closer she recognized Harvey McAllister from town. He stopped at the gate and jumped from his horse. Running up to the steps he suddenly stopped at the sight of Becky sitting in the swing.

"Oh Lord Mrs. Townsend, you scared the daylights outta me," Harvey stammered, nearly falling backward, clutching his chest. Becky laughed at the expression on Harvey's face as he looked up and saw her, he looked as if he had seen a ghost.

Before Becky could say anything, Harvey blurted out in a loud shaky voice.

"Mrs. Townsend, I come to fetch you into town. Mrs. Parks needs you to come quickly, she says it's time fer the baby, and the Doc is up in the hills with some sick folks.

"My Rachel is tending to her now, they be waitin on us."

Becky jumped to her feet immediately, telling Harvey she would be ready in just a minute. She ordered him to hitch up the buggy. She rushed into the house, not noticing or caring that the screen door slammed loud behind her. She ran to the bed where Jeff lay sleeping so peacefully.

"Jeff, honey, you need to wake up!" Becky shook him gently as she continued, "Carolyn is having the baby and I must go to her. Harvey is here to drive me into town. Oh Jeff I am so excited, I will be back after the baby is born." She continued to give him instructions on getting the children to school the next morning, while she finished dressing herself. Jeff was fully awake by now and watching his wife hustle around the room, getting dressed and talking as fast as she could. To Jeff, it was quite entertaining. He loved to watch Becky when she was all excited, she was like a child at Christmas time.

"You go sweetheart, I will take care of things here, give Carolyn my blessing and I will be praying for an easy time for her and the baby." He ushered her out the door, assuring her that all would be fine here at home. Jeff walked to the porch and shook hands with Harvey, telling them to be careful as he waved goodbye. He watched as the buggy disappeared around the edge of the barn and into the night. Looking up into the starry sky Jeff whispered a prayer for Becky and Harvey to reach their destination safely, and for Carolyn and her baby to be well.

Becky and Harvey hardly spoke a word as the buggy sped along the well-worn trail into town. Each one was lost in their own thoughts. The buggy suddenly gave a jolt, as if it had a mind of it's own, a popping and cracking sound coming from the front wheel.

"Whoa," Harvey called out at the horses as he pulled back on the reins. The horses came to a sudden stop, and just in time, as the buggy sank to the ground with a sudden thud. Becky grabbed the side of the seat to keep from pitching off the buggy seat.

"What's happened Harvey?" Becky asked, leaning over to look out the side toward the ground. Harvey had jumped down from the buggy and was looking at the front wheel.

"I think we have a broken wheel Miss Becky, seems like we might just have to ride the horses on into town, don't believe I can fix it, since it has two spokes out of it."

Becky's heart sank!

She knew she had to get to Carolyn as soon as possible, and they still had a piece to go, and it would be slow traveling in the dark, on horses with no saddles. They would have to ride bareback into town. Harvey quickly unhitched the horses from the buggy and lifted the buggy as close to the edge of the trail as possible so that if other travelers came by they could get by the broken-down buggy. Becky was so afraid they would not make it to town before the baby arrived.

Mounting the horses, they headed toward town and the Parks home. The ride was rough with no saddles on the horses. Becky knew she would be sore and unable to walk tomorrow, but right now her mind was on her friend, and she didn't care what she had to go through. She was bound and determined to reach Carolyn. They had to ride slow because the lanterns had to be left on the buggy, mounted there with bolts, with which Jeff had anchored them to the front of the buggy.

The narrow road was clear and the moon was shining brightly, but they still had to travel slow because of deep ruts in the road, and the danger of the horses being spooked by a wild animal. They continued on in silence, with Harvey leading the way. He would call back to Becky once in a while, asking, "Are you ok Miss Becky?"

"I'm fine Harvey, just keep going."

In town at the Parks home the pain was growing worse for Carolyn, and Rachel was growing more nervous by the minute. She walked from the bedroom to the front porch to see if she could spot Becky and Harvey. "They should have been here an hour ago," She said to herself. Rachel had never delivered a baby by herself. She had gone up into the mountains with Becky and Carolyn before, and watched as they had delivered babies, but she was not sure she could do this all alone. She prayed that Harvey and Becky would show up any time. She heard Carolyn moaning from the bedroom, and rushed to her side.

"Are you doing alright Carolyn, can I get you something?" Rachel walked over to the bed, noticing that Carolyn was breathing very hard, and had big drops of sweat on her forehead. Rachel could see the pain on her face. She quickly wiped Carolyn's face with a cool damp clothCarolyn reached out her hand to Rachel.

"My dear, I don't think this baby is gonna wait any longer, so I need your help, and you can do this, just do as I tell you and we will have this baby here soon."

Rachel could feel the strength go out of her body, but she knew she had to get hold of herself and remain calm for Carolyn and the baby's sake. As Carolyn gave instructions, Rachel hustled around the room, preparing for the arrival of the baby. She prayed continuously as she went about her duties of delivering the baby, all the while keeping an open ear toward the front door of the house. Carolyn's pain become harder, and just as she had predicted, within a matter of moments Rachel had delivered a beautiful baby girl.

Guided by Carolyn's instructions, she soon heard the sweetest sound, the cry of a new life that had come into the world. She laid the baby in her mother's arms. What a beautiful sight! Tears rolled down the faces of both the women. Carolyn's face was beaming with joy as she planted a kiss on her daughter's beautiful face. She knew Joseph would be disappointed that he wasn't there, but he would be such a proud father. Rachel soon tided up the room, and brought Carolyn some warm chicken soup. She knew she must be tired and hungry after such a hard task. Rachel held the baby while Carolyn ate the soup.

Becky and Harvey soon saw the lights of the Parks mansion. They nudged the horses a little bit harder to urge them up the hillside. Harvey gingerly lifted Becky down from her horse. She ran upon the porch and burst into the room to find a smiling Carolyn Parks, holding a beautiful baby in her arms, and Rachel sitting by the bed with a big smile on her face. Becky approached the bed in awe as she hugged the two women and gently stroked the baby's tiny perfect hands.

"I have a daughter Becky, the Lord has given me a daughter to love and cherish."

"She is beautiful Carolyn, and I am so sorry I didn't make it here to help. The buggy lost a wheel, and we had to ride the horses on in, but I see you had a wonderful nurse with you." Becky gave Rachel another hug just as Harvey came into the room. He stopped dead in his tracks when he saw Carolyn holding the baby, beaming with joy. He hugged his wife and inquired if everyone was alright.

"See for yourself," Rachel said with a big smile, as she lead him closer to the bedside. He whispered to Rachel, telling her how proud he was that she had been here for Mrs. Parks, and apologized for not getting Miss Becky there on time.

Then turning to Carolyn and the baby, he removed his hat, saying, "she sure is a beautiful little girl, Mrs. Parks, and I'm sure Mr. Parks will be so proud."

The night was soon gone, as the bright and beautiful rays of sunlight took its place. Rachel and Harvey left to get Rachel ready for the children that would soon be arriving at school. Becky assured them she would stay with Carolyn as long as was needed.

Jeff soon arrived in the wagon with the children. After leaving them at the school he headed back to the Parks house to check on Becky, Carolyn and the new baby. Harvey and Rachel had filled him in on the details. Harvey offered to go out with Jeff to fix the buggy wheel.

Jeff pulled up at the gate just as Dr. Parks rode in from the back of the house. Jeff waved his hand at Dr. Parks.

"Hey there my friend, is everything alright? Joseph asked as he shook hands with Jeff.

"All is well sir," Jeff replied, trying hard not to show any emotion. He wanted Dr. Parks to be surprised, and he wanted Carolyn to be the one to do it, so Jeff quickly diverted his attention with a question of his own.

"How is Hilda Dr. Parks? heard she was struck ill."

Dr. Parks shook his head sadly, replying, "We lost her Jeff, she had a bad heart, and was just too weak to hold on any longer. Rufus is taking it really hard, and he has requested that you and I do the funeral at the church day after tomorrow."

"Of course I'd be honored," Jeff answered, but I am so sorry to hear the news of Hilda's death. "How is the rest of the family doing.?"

Dr. Parks' countenance saddened, as he replied, "Well, Pastor, I guess they're doing as well as can be expected under the circumstances."

He quickly added, "Come on Preacher, let's go into the house and see if we can't get Carolyn to rustle us up a good hot cup of coffee."

"Ok, sounds good to me, just lead the way," Jeff replied, trying so hard to hide the happiness on his face, knowing what was awaiting his friend just inside those doors.

As the two men walked into the big kitchen Joseph called out for his wife.

"Carolyn, honey we have company. Pastor Jeff is here and we are in dire need of some of that special coffee of yours."

"I'm in the bedroom my dear, Carolyn answered, won't you two come on in here for a moment, I have something I believe both of you will be delighted to see." Joseph looked a bit surprised, but motioned for Jeff to follow him as they headed toward the bedroom.

Jeff caught the good doctor's back to keep him from falling as he stepped into the bedroom to find his wife sitting up in their big four- poster bed holding the most beautiful child he had ever seen.

"Whoa here my friend, Jeff grunted. "Now let's get you seated before you fall."

Jeff quickly seated Dr. parks in the big chair by the bed, laughing hard, saying,

"Sorry my friend, I should have told you, but I wouldn't have missed this for the world."

After looking at the baby and making sure that Dr. Parks was not going to faint, Jeff and Becky headed out to the kitchen to make coffee, wanting Dr. and Mrs. Parks to have some private moments together. While Carolyn filled Joseph in on all the details of the birth of the baby, Becky did the same for Jeff. Jeff told Becky that Hilda had passed away, and that he and Dr. Parks were to handle the funeral. They both bowed their heads and thanked God for the new life in the next room, and for getting to know and love the precious soul that had been called home for eternal rest.

In the bedroom, Joseph and Carolyn were crying and laughing all at the same time, rejoicing over the precious child for which they had prayed so long. Now that they were together, they picked her name, Josephine Rachel Parks.

Both the joyful news of the newborn baby, and the sorrowful news of the death of sweet Hilda Rutherford traveled fast. Emotions were mixed by all who knew and loved the Parks' and the Rutherfords. Folks were happy for the good doctor and his wife, but very sad for Ralph, Rufus, Claudette and Becky Sarah. To the Parks family, God had given, and from the Rutherford family, God had taken away.

Folks from all over the county began to drop in to see the newest member of the community, then rode on up into the mountain to take food, or to assist in any way possible with the grieving family of Hilda Rutherford. All the men in the community pitched in, and soon had a grave ready for the burial. Hilda had requested that she be buried in the small cemetery by the church. The church was given an extra cleaning for the body to be brought in for the funeral on Saturday. Jeff prepared a short eulogy, as he and Dr. Parks would be doing the funeral.

On Saturday, a large crowd gathered in the church, with standing room only. The casket sat up front, with beautiful flowers covering the whole front of the room. With shoulders bent and walking very unsteadily, Ralph was escorted in by his brokenhearted son Rufus to the front row pews, followed by Claudette and Becky Sarah, their eyes streaming with tears. The neighbors flocked in, giving all the support they knew how to give. Hilda had been a great friend and neighbor to them all, and would be greatly missed.

Becky stood and lead the choir in the beautiful old hymn, "How beautiful Heaven must be." After the hymn, Dr. Parks stood and read the obituary. Before he closed with a prayer he spoke of Hilda, and all her kindness that she had shown to everyone around her. He told of her final hours, and how she had praised her Lord for the many years He had given her, and for her wonderful family. Then, just before turning the funeral over to Jeff, Dr. Parks addressed the Rutherford family on the front pew, assuring them, "Your dear mother closed her eyes, and left this world with a smile." Ralph could not contain the sobs that racked his body. Rufus, through his own grief, hugged his fathers shoulders tightly as they cried together with a mixture of both grief and joy.

Jeff approached the pulpit, clearing his throat, but still with a tremble in his voice, he began.

"Friends, family, neighbors, this is a sad day indeed for our little community. We are laying to rest today a great mother, wife, grandmother, friend and neighbor. Hilda was one of a kind, always mindful of the needs of others, but she will forever be in our hearts and minds."

He continued on, but not for long, knowing the family was tired, and that he must end this service, and the sooner the better, in accordance with Hilda's own wishes before her death. Jeff gave out encouraging words and love to the people there that day, and after all that could be said and done, Hilda Rutherford was laid to rest.

The community mourned for the family, but time has a way of healing. Ralph Rutherford was no longer the same man after the death of his beloved wife. He soon became old and frail. Three months after Hilda's death, he too was laid beside her in the little cemetery, which was no longer as small as it had been the day that Jeff and the tiny congregation had consecrated this ground, many years ago.

And yet another God-fearing, hard-working member of the congregation was Buford R. Williams, who, along with his frightened family, had wandered into the yard of the church years ago, fleeing for their lives. Buford and his family never forgot the Christian kindness that was shown to them by Jeff Townsend and the good folks of the church. The members of the church had literally prevented him and his family from starving to death. Since Buford and his family had become members of the church, they too had grown a great deal both spiritually and socially. Buford was a quiet man, never saying a great deal, but whenever he spoke, he spoke with grace, wisdom, and common sense. He never said more nor less than what he felt was necessary to say. He said what he meant, and he meant what he said.

Buford was also a very strong man, solidly built, and muscular, and necessarily so, being a blacksmith. He was also quite an intrepid engineer, constantly experimenting with different tools and methods of working with hot metals. For instance, he discovered that by using a few pulleys and chains, and a coil spring, he could rig his bellows in such a way that he could pump air into the furnace with his foot, leaving both his hands free to fashion the hot metal into whatever shape he wanted it. Keeping the metal white hot by pumping air into the fire with his foot, and using both the sharp end and blunt end of his blacksmith hammer, he could hammer the hot metal into nearly any shape he wanted. Taking strips of white-hot steel, and forging them together with his hammer, Buford would carefully and meticulously hammer the image of roses into the hot strips of steel, one rose at a time. Once Buford's skill in fashioning steel into so many different shapes was discovered, every married woman within fifty miles of his shop wanted a metal fence around their yards, with a top strip of hammered roses, or butterflies, or frogs, or any other flower or animal, or any combination of flowers and animals that Buford could hammer into the strips of steel.

Orders for Buford Williams' artful metal fences kept coming in on a daily basis, so much so that he had to work all day, and far into the night, and still couldn't keep up with all the orders that kept coming in. He knew he would either have to hire some trained help, or train someone himself in order to keep up with the demand. Mattie and the twin girls, Gloria and Greta, (who were now fifteen years young,) offered to help in any way they could, but Buford would not allow it. He wanted his girls to go to college, and to get the best education available, so he worked day and night, and saved every penny he could save to that end.

Obtaining higher education was not an easy endeavor for black students in the 1800's, but a few who had the guts and determination to obtain an education, and possessed the fortitude and character to withstand and overcome all the racial slurs, hatred and persecution of white folks (both other students and faculty) could, and did, come away with degrees, hard-earned and well-deserved degrees. Gloria and Greta Williams were two such ladies, who, with the love and guidance of their parents, and a lot of help from Dr. and Mrs. Parks, were determined to become nurses, no matter what the cost. Buford and Mattie Williams were so proud of their daughters, and no amount of self-sacrifice on their part was too much to pay to see that their girls got the best education and training available to them.

Things were changing in America in the late 1800's, some more rapidly than others. Racial equality and advancement of blacks was changing, but at a snail's pace. Every advancement in civil rights for blacks came at a very high cost. The bureaucratic wheels of *"liberty and justice for all"* turned very slowly. To put it bluntly, when all was said and done, it was still *"a white man's world"*. Freedmen who once had been the slaves of plantation owners were now the slaves of a bureaucracy almost totally dominated by whites. And while it must be said that there were many white folks who bore no innate hatred for blacks, they yet held onto an air of racial superiority. They could tolerate black folks living at a *"respectable"* distance from them, but not next door. They could tolerate black folks going to church and school, but not to *their* church or school. They could tolerate black folks becoming doctors, nurses, teachers and professors, but only as long as those doctors, nurses, teachers and professors treated, nursed, taught and lectured their own kind (their own race). The end of slavery (on paper) was by no means the end of racism and prejudice.

The Jenkins Memorial Baptist Church, then, was both a refreshing oasis and a place of refuge to the few black families who made it their home church. Pastor Jeff Townsend saw to it that every individual and family who attended the church was treated with equal respect and kindness. The time that these few black families spent at the church, worshiping their God, singing, praying, learning and teaching, was precious to them. It gave them respite from the ongoing persecution, hatred, and outright violence that some of them experienced nearly every day of their lives outside the church. It was the only predominantly white church in the area with a black Deacon (Dr. Parks,) a black pianist (Carolyn Parks,) and a black trustee (Buford R. Williams).

But Buford Williams was not simply good at his trade, he was the best blacksmith in the state, and every other blacksmith in the state knew it. While other blacksmiths were content to make a living repairing horseshoes, or forging tools and farm implements, Buford Williams was forging swords for both foreign and domestic collectors, and creating beautiful wrought iron fences for mayors, governors, senators and aristocrats, with highly decorative wrought iron gates, with handrails to match. With his business prospering and expanding at such a rapid pace, Buford knew he simply could not keep up with the demand any longer. He had to find some good help somewhere, and he knew it would not be easy, so he did what he had always done when faced with a dilemma to which he had no answer. He went down upon his knees in fervent prayer, and left the dilemma with his God, believing that God would provide him with the help he needed. Little did he know that, before he asked, God was already in the process of preparing the helper he needed, but in a way that neither Buford nor his wife Mattie would have ever suspected.

The nearest town south of Bruceton Mills was Albright West Virginia, roughly twelve miles away. Another three and one half miles southwest of Albright lay the town of Kingwood. About ten miles Southeast of Bruceton Mills was Terra Alta. Just north of Terra Alta was the hundred-acre farm once owned by Clark and Sarah Puckett. Before Clark's tragic death, he had given Buford Williams some land on which to build a house and blacksmith shop. After Clark's death, Sarah Puckett sold the whole farm to Buford, married Becky's father (Ray Davis,) and moved to Tennessee.

The Jenkins Memorial Baptist Church was situated a little less than half way between Bruceton Mills and Albright - roughly five and one half miles. Between Albright and Kingwood (just over three miles,) were the homes and businesses of Joshua and Gideon Bowen, and Jason and Travis Phelps. The Phelps brothers, of course, were blacksmiths, while Joshua and Gideon Bowen owned the Hotel. Being half way between the two towns of Bruceton Mills and Albright, the Church was easily accessible to folks from both towns. The road leading from Bruceton Mills to the Church, and the road from Albright to the Church, and the road from Terra Alta to the Church, were well-traveled. Drawing a straight line from Bruceton Mills to Kingwood, another line from Bruceton Mills to Terra Alta, and connecting the two lines at the bottom, would form a rough triangle, with each side covering approximately ten to twelve miles.

While Buford Williams' business was thriving and growing, the Phelps brothers' blacksmith shop was doing quite well also. So well, in fact, they had already employed some extra help, in the person of a first cousin on their mother's side - Sanford S. Pike, who they began to train as an apprentice blacksmith. The "S", his middle initial, stood for Sylvester. With a name like Sanford S. Pike, a nickname was inevitable. When he was younger, some folks began calling him Sandy, a nickname which he thoroughly despised. As he grew older, others called him Pike. But eventually, everyone settled for Spike instead, and the name stuck. Spike was fresh out of High School, full of energy and full of dreams. He was now eighteen, standing six feet, three inches tall, and quite handsome. He had learned to play the banjo, and loved making up his own little tunes, singing them mostly to himself.

Travis and Jason both attended the Jenkins Memorial Baptist Church, and quickly got well-acquainted with Buford Williams. Some Sundays they would actually go home with Buford and his family for Sunday dinner. After dinner, Buford took them out to his blacksmith shop, and showed them all the new equipment and tools he had accumulated over the years. The two young men were fascinated with Buford's set up, and how well-organized his shop and machinery were. Buford even shared his knowledge and skill with the two brothers, allowing them to borrow his books on metallurgy. There was even some discussion on the three of them forming a partnership. The Phelps brothers could see that Buford needed some help.

Spike Pike, was also fascinated with Buford's creations. He was also fascinated with Mattie Williams' cooking, and with Buford and Mattie's two young daughters, Gloria and Greta, but especially with Gloria, the more outgoing of the twins. Gloria, trying desperately to pretend that she was not interested, but failing miserably at it, had eyes for Spike also. Buford, Mattie and Greta pretended not to notice the two of them making eyes at one another in church, and at the dinner table. One Sunday while eating a slice of Mattie's homemade apple pie, Spike suddenly had a brainstorm, and blurted it all out at once in the form of a suggestion.

"Fellers, he began, all the folks in the State know that Mr. Williams here is the best danged blacksmith in the business."

"Now you take Jason and Travis here, they's good too, but Mr. Williams is a Master Blacksmith, and daggone it boys, he needs some help."

"There are two of you, and only one of him, and if'n nobody would be offended, why don't I just come right here and learn from Mr. Williams, and at the same time be helping him out with his backlog of orders.?"

There was a long silence at the table while everyone looked from one to the other, mulling over Spike's suggestion. Spike waited patiently for an answer. Suddenly he saw the smiles on the faces of everyone at the table, including Buford, Mattie, and Gloria.

Buford was the first to respond, replying, "Well now young man, as much as I be needing the help and all, and as much as I be liking the way this sounds, I jist don't have the heart to be taking you away from your two cousins here. It just wouldn't be Christian of me ta do that."

Travis and Jason both knew that Spike had an ulterior motive behind his suggestion, and she was sitting across the table from

Spike, glancing at their faces, searching for their reaction to Spike's suggestion. Travis cleared his throat, took a sip of his iced tea, and replied.

"Well Spike, ya shore are right. There is two of us, and I guess we could git by without ye till Mr. Williams here could git ye trained good enough to catch up on his orders. That is, bein it's alright with Mr. Williams and all."

He then turned to Jason, asking for his input. Jason smiled, knowing that both Gloria and Spike were desperately hoping for his approval also. Jason quickly agreed with Travis, replying,

"Shore Spike, Mr. Williams here is the best in the business, and ye deserve the chance to learn from the best, but now that is only if'n Mr. Williams here agrees."

Now every eye turned toward Buford, waiting for his final answer. Buford glanced quickly at Mattie, who quickly nodded her smile of approval. Buford gave his answer slowly.

"Well now, uh, Mr. Spike, shore seems that we's all in agreement that you be a comin ta work fer me. But, I must warn ye Sir, we gits up mighty early around here, an we stay up late. The work is hard, hot an dirty. An I guess ye know that some folks will be talkin, an they ain't apt to approve of ye, a white man, bein the apprentice of a colored blacksmith. Are ye ready to face the gossip that is shore ta come if'n I agree to take ye on?"

Spike didn't hesitate with his answer. He stood up immediately, taking Buford by the hand.

"Mr. Williams, I promise ta work hard, and I'll be the best apprentice I can be. And I ain't the least bit worried about what other folks may say about it. I want ta learn from the best, and all ye have ta do is tell me when I can start."

Buford smiled, answering, "Well, if'n it be alright with ye cousins here, how's bout tomorrow morning?" Jason and Travis stood, shaking hands with Buford, agreeing with the deal.

"Well, it be settled then, Buford answered. "Be here at five o'clock tomorrow morning if'n ye want breakfast."

Hiring Spike as his apprentice turned out to be a wise business decision for Buford. Spike proved himself to be a man of his word, and a hard worker, willing to listen and to learn. He showed up for work every day, early, and eager to learn everything he could about being a blacksmith. He took orders well, and followed instructions to the letter. He also proved himself to be trustworthy and honest. Buford soon discovered that, not only was Spike a hard worker, he was also highly intelligent, and had good business sense. He knew how to count money, and make change. Most of Buford's customers paid Buford with large amounts of cash. Often, when Buford was very busy with a meticulous piece of work, another customer would come to pay Buford for something he had made for him. Buford would have to stop what he was doing, and complete the monetary transaction, allowing the piece of work in the fire to cool, making it necessary for Buford to come back and re-heat the piece. Since hiring Spike, Buford could let him handle the monetary transactions, while he himself kept busy at the bellows.

Since there was no bank anywhere near Terra Alta at the time, folks in the area kept their money either in a safe, under a mattress, or in some other presumably safe place. It was during this time that the James and Younger gangs, Jesse and Frank James, and Cole Younger and his brothers were robbing, killing and pillaging all over the country, and no one knew where they would hit next. Buford kept his money in a large safe, the combination to which only he and Mattie knew. Once he learned that Spike could be trusted, he gave him the combination to the safe, and often sent him to the house with large amounts of cash to deposit inside. After more than a year of training Spike to be a blacksmith, not one penny had ever come up missing.

Spike learned a great deal from Buford Williams in a year's time, and not all of what he learned had to do with being a blacksmith. He often witnessed folks trying to cheat Buford in business deals, deals sometimes involving large amounts of cash, others involving only a few dollars. Some of those folks thought they were dealing with an un-educated backwoods colored man who didn't know how to count. They soon discovered, however, that Buford R. Williams was nobody's fool. But rather than bicker with dishonest folks over a few cents, Buford would often take the loss, and just smile and go back to work. Now that he had Spike, and knew that Spike could be trusted, he simply let Spike take care of all cash transactions. Spike grew very close to Buford and his family, and they to him.

Both Buford and Mattie knew their daughter Gloria and Spike had feelings for each other, but neither of them ever spoke of it openly. But at night, in the privacy of their bedroom, they spoke in whispers, revealing their innermost thoughts to each other. Buford was not a man to mince words, he simply spoke whatever was on his mind. After knowing Spike for over a year now, and seeing the relationship that was growing between Spike and their daughter, Buford, staring up at the ceiling, asked his wife, "Mattie, do ye think them two young'uns be in love with each other?"

Mattie didn't hesitate more than a moment, replying, "Now Buford Williams, of all the years I have known and loved you, I ain't never heard you ask such a silly question."

Buford smiled, kissing her gently on the cheek, replying, "Yeah, you be right Mattie, take a blind man not to see they's in love. Sorta minds me of us when we's their age, making eyes at each other in the church house, and trying to hide our feelings fer each other. Member them days Mattie.?"

Mattie returned his kiss on the cheek, answering with a little laugh. "There ye go again, asking a question that answers itself. Buford R. Williams, what'n the world am I to do with you, you ole handsome devil?"

Buford chuckled, taking her into his arms, looking deeply into her eyes, whispering, "I shore do love you Mattie Williams." This time she answered him with a long passionate kiss. They didn't get to sleep until after midnight.

July, 1877.

Gloria and Greta Williams made their way to Bruceton Mills every Saturday, rising long before daylight, making the twelve mile trip to Dr. Parks' clinic, where they studied, worked, and watched Dr. Parks treat the sick and wounded for as long as Dr. Parks was willing to teach them. Dr. Parks was willing to teach them from dawn till dusk. But being concerned for their safety, he always urged them to try to get back home before it got too dark. As he and Carolyn often reminded them.

"Two young beautiful black girls, riding in a fancy carriage, might be a temptation to some folks to do something less than noble."

Both the girls clearly understood the meaning of the admonition.

Being identical twins, the sisters were very close in every way that sisters can be close. They shared everything from their food and clothing to their innermost thoughts and secrets that no one except the two of them knew. Greta was not one to pry into her sister's private life, and there was no need for her to pry, because Gloria simply trusted her twin sister with every secret. By now, the fact that she and Spike had romantic feelings for each other had become pretty much common knowledge. But in spite of the fact that they had these feelings for each other, they both knew there were a lot of folks (mostly white folks) who strongly, and verbally, disapproved of, and even condemned such feelings. To most white folks (and many blacks also,) it just wasn't natural for a white man to have feelings for a black woman, and even more unnatural for a white woman to have feelings for a black man. Such was the racial prejudice and predisposition of the majority of both races in 1877. But Spike's love for Gloria, and Gloria's love for him, was stronger than their skin pigmentation, and stronger than all the prejudice of those who either could not, or would not see beyond it.

With Spike's extra hands, hard work and initiative, Buford was slowly but surely catching up on his backlog of orders for his masterful metal creations. Both he and Spike had been putting in ten to twelve hours a day, six days a week, for more than a year now, which meant that Spike and Gloria saw very little of each other. The only times they did see each other were at the table, or at church on Sunday, or on the very rare occasions when their love for each other defied all dangers and circumstances, when each of them would sneak out of bed late at night, and meet secretly behind the blacksmith shop, stealing a few precious and passionate moments in each other's arms.

With the backlog of work orders beginning to diminish with each passing week, Buford began to give Spike every other Saturday off, to do whatever he pleased, and he pleased to be with the only girl he had ever loved, Gloria Williams. On those Saturdays off, Spike rose up long before dawn, saddling his horse and riding hard and fast from Kingwood, taking every shortcut he knew, meeting Gloria and Greta about halfway between Terra Alta and Bruceton Mills. Greta would drive the carriage around a bend in the road, and wait patiently, while Gloria and Spike took advantage of every precious moment they could savor, kissing, and holding each other as if their lives depended upon it, their hearts pounding wildly with a love that was pure and deep. Neither they nor Greta knew there was another set of eyes watching them from the dense cover of the woods. Those eyes belonged to Wesley Phelps, a fugitive who had escaped from the Moundsville Prison with William Bowen more than a year ago.

Those sweet moments were precious, but they were also few, because she and Greta had to be at Dr. Park's clinic by about eight o'clock. On some occasions, Spike and Greta would change places, with Spike taking the seat in the carriage beside Gloria, and Greta riding Spike's horse for a few miles, giving Spike and Gloria a little more time to be near each other. Then, about a mile south of town, they would change places again, with Spike riding slowly and sadly back toward Kingwood, knowing he wouldn't get to be near the girl he loved for another two weeks.

Greta loved her sister dearly, and never questioned her integrity or her motives. She knew Gloria and Spike were deeply in love with each other. But she also understood the deeply rooted prejudices of people. She knew that if the relationship between her sister and a white man were to go farther than it had already gone, meaning, of course, to marriage, they would be placing their lives, and perhaps the lives of everyone they knew in jeopardy. Spike and Gloria each understood all of this also. They kept their relationship as secretive as possible for as long as possible, knowing the day would come when they would either have to make it known publicly, and get on with their lives as best they could, or end their relationship, and live in total misery for the rest of their lives.

But, as it is written in the Scriptures, love is strong as death, and theirs was such a love, stronger than prejudice, stronger than fear, and stronger than their own wills to hide or deny its existence for the sake of pacifying the prejudices and hatred of the ignorant. They decided that it was time to stop hiding. But before making their relationship known openly, they agreed they should consult their parents, their Pastor, and Dr. Parks, in that order.

When Spike broke the news to his parents, Carl and Lily Pike, his father was outraged, and backhanded his son across the mouth, screaming in his face, and cursing him, while his mother fell to her knees on the floor, sobbing, asking God where she had gone wrong in raising her son. Spike, with blood oozing from the corner of his mouth, looked his father straight in the eye, answering, "Sir, it's good to finally know how you really feel about me after all these years of pretense. I'll be leaving here now, and I'm going to ask Gloria to be my wife, and there's nothing that you or anyone else can say or do to stop me."

As He lifted his mother gently from the floor, hugging her, his father grabbed Spike by the arm, still cursing him, and telling him to leave his mother on the floor. Then, in a loud voice, with hatred in his eyes, he said to Spike.

"You never were no son of mine and never will be. I curse the day I ever laid eyes on you, nigger lover.

With one swift blow Spike hit his father for the first time, knocking him to the floor. Looking down at Carl Pike, he saw the form of a man, but the face of a low-life coward. He turned and walked quickly into what used to be his room, taking all the clothes he could carry, his rifle, and an old pocket knife his father had given him on his tenth birthday. Spike rode away from Kingwood for the last time that day, and never looked back. He rode to the home of his cousins Jason and Travis Phelps, who listened to his story with patience, understanding and respect, receiving him graciously into their home.

In the Williams household, the scene could not have been more different when Gloria came to her parents with the news that she was in love with Spike. Both Buford and Mattie, with tears of joy streaming down their cheeks, took their daughter into their arms, telling her they had known about the relationship from the first day Spike had sat down at their supper table. Buford also reminded her that he had known every time she had sneaked out of her room to meet Spike in secret, and about the meetings on the road to Bruceton Mills. Gloria, with tears in her own eyes, asked, whimpering,

"How did you know papa?"

Mattie broke in quickly, replying, "Baby, us parents know these things without being told, and you will understand when you become a mother."

Buford added, "My dear little girl, if it wuz any other man, black or white, I might have some serious reservations about it, but your mother and I both know and love Spike as if he were our own son. He is a good man Gloria, a Christian man, and honest, and faithful, and we know that he loves you with all his heart, and we give you our blessing."

Greta was listening from outside on the porch, and upon hearing the word blessing, she came running in, throwing her arms around her sister first, and then her parents, as tears of joy filled her eyes. Gloria interrupted the joyful moment with an interjection.

"But papa, he hasn't asked me to marry him yet."

Buford and Mattie laughed at the same time, replying in the same breath. "He will darlin, he will, and it won't be long in coming."

No sooner had those words come out of their mouths than Spike himself rode into the front yard, accompanied by the barking of Buford's old hound, Beauregard. Spike dismounted slowly, as Buford, Mattie, Gloria and Greta came out onto the porch to meet him. Spike had never seen them all come out to greet him this way before, and hesitated momentarily before stepping onto the porch. Buford stood still and silent, waiting for Spike to say something. Spike cleared his throat, took off his hat, and began to squeeze the rim of his hat in his hands till it was crumpled. Buford couldn't contain his laughter any longer.

"Well young man, did you come to show me how skilled you are at destroying a perfectly good hat, or are you going to ask for my daughter's hand?"

Spike's heart leaped into his throat. He dropped his hat in the dirt, as Gloria ran into his arms. He swung her around and around, and they kissed, right there in front of God and everybody.

"Now now, Buford interrupted, I think you two oughta go and see the Pastor."

"We're on our way Sir," Spike quickly shot back, as he lifted Gloria onto the back of his horse.

"Not so fast, Buford chimed in, ain't there a little something you are forgetting?"

With Gloria still sitting on the horse, Spike picked up his hat, and approached Buford slowly and respectfully, half mumbling,

"Mr. Williams, Sir, I have loved your daughter since the first day I met her, and I am convinced that she loves me. And if'n you could find it in your heart Sir, I would love nothing better than to make her my wife, that is Sir, if it's alright with you and Mrs. Williams here. You know I'm a hard worker, and I ain't afraid of getting my hands dirty, and I promise I will be the best husband to your daughter that I can possibly be, that is, if you would let me have her Sir."

Buford and Mattie both took Spike into their arms, hugging him. Buford looked Spike squarely in the eye, replying, "Spike, I've known you for a while now, and you have proven to me that you are a man of integrity. I've known from the start that you and our daughter wuz in love, and Mattie and I are proud of you both. We'd be honored to have you for a son-in-law. Now git on your horse, an go see the Pastor before I change my mind."

Spike almost fell as he half ran and half stumbled toward his horse, shouting.

"Mr. Williams, Mattie, you won't regret it, I promise you, and I thank you from the bottom of my heart."

Greta ran over to the horse just before Spike jumped onto it's back, giving him a big hug, adding, "God bless you Spike, Gloria is a lucky girl, and I also am proud of you both, and happy that I will soon have you for a brother-in-law." Spike gave Greta a big hug, thanked her, and leaped onto his horse behind Gloria, who was in the saddle, holding the reins.

The two of them decided they would stop and see Dr. Parks first, since his clinic was on the way to the Townsend farm. As they rode into the little town, they immediately noticed some folks staring at them, as if they could not believe what their eyes were seeing. A black woman and a white man, on the same horse.!

As they stopped in front of Dr. Parks' clinic, those who saw them immediately began to draw their own conclusions. Some agreed that perhaps the white man had found the black woman injured or sick on the road, and was bringing her to Dr. Parks for treatment. Others with a more vivid imagination assumed that the white man had gotten the black woman pregnant, and was bringing her to Dr. Parks to drop her off, and leave her. Still others whispered among themselves, creating the most vulgar and contemptuous scenarios their prejudiced minds could imagine against the two. But the saddest part about the whole scene was the fact that, in all of their assuming and gossiping, not one of them knew the truth of the matter, that these were two young people in love, wanting to share the rest of their lives together as man and wife.

Spike and Gloria could see and feel the contempt that was being directed toward them. It showed in the faces of some of the townspeople. They just smiled at each other, disregarding the stares and remarks, and walked hand in hand into Dr. Parks' clinic. Dr. Parks greeted them with a knowing smile, extending his hand to Gloria first, then to Spike, offering them a seat on the plush bench along the wall. There were a few moments of silence before Dr. Parks himself finally broke the ice.

"Now let me guess, you two are in love, and want to get married, and if I have the sense I think the good Lord gave me, you have already asked for this young woman's hand in marriage. Am I on the right track so far?"

He could see the look of surprise on both their faces, as Gloria spoke first.

"How did you know Dr. Parks?"

Dr. Parks chuckled slightly, replying, "There are some things that just can't be kept hidden for too long, and love is one of those things. I've known for a while that it was only a matter of time till the two of you had to do what you are doing, but why have you come to me?"

Again Gloria spoke, answering, "Dr. Parks, you and Mrs. Parks have been awfully good to me and Greta, teaching us so much, and sacrificing your time and talent, and never asking anything in return. I don't think there's another man on earth who would give of himself as freely and as graciously as you have done, that is, no man except my future husband here. You have been like a second father to me and my sister, and I just wanted you to be the first man outside of my family to know that I am engaged to the only man I have ever loved, and to ask your blessing on us."

Dr. Parks choked up instantly, tears of joy streaming down his cheeks. He dabbed his eyes with his handkerchief, and called for Carolyn to come into the clinic. She hurried in, carrying little Josephine in her arms, thinking her husband needed her assistance with a patient. As soon as she saw Gloria and Spike, without a single word being spoken, she also discerned the reason they were there. She handed the baby to Joseph, and took the young couple into her arms, hugging them tightly, telling them how proud she was of them.

Now it was Spike's turn to express his own surprise, as he asked Carolyn and Dr. Parks,

"You mean yun's both knowed all along that me and Gloria wuz in love? But how? We tried so hard ta keep it quiet."

Carolyn smiled at them, replying, "Children, Joseph and I have been married a long time, and we know love when we see it, and you two are in love, but why have you come here to us today, if I may ask?"

Spike beamed with joy, answering her, "Ma'am, we think an awful lot of you and Dr. Parks here, being in church with yuns and all, and we jist wanted to tell yuns bout our engagement, and ask fer your blessing."

Dr. Parks laid Josephine gently into her crib in the corner of his office, as the four of them joined hands. As they all bowed their heads, Dr. Parks began, "Our gracious heavenly Father, who has declared the end from the beginning, and knows all things, even to the secrets of the heart of every man, I ask you this day to smile upon this young couple, who have come to us, asking our blessing upon their upcoming marriage. But Father we would have them know that, no matter how much we love them, and no matter to what degree we are able to bless them, all true and lasting blessings must come from You alone. And so as best we can, we offer these dear ones our blessing in Your name, and ask that You bless them as only a heavenly Father can do. May you grant them courage in the face of danger, wisdom in the face of ignorance, strength in face of weakness, peace in the face of adversity, and love in the face of hatred. And Father, if it is not asking too much, would you grant them the most blessed gift of all, children to hold and cherish, as you have done for me and my beloved wife, in Jesus name, Amen."

After Carolyn, Spike and Gloria added their own Amen, Spike and Gloria hugged and thanked them for their blessing and approval. Carolyn asked them to stay for dinner, but they declined, saying they had one more stop to make before returning to Terra Alta.

Dr. Parks chuckled again, offering, "Now let me guess again, you're on your way to Pastor Townsend's house, am I correct.?"

They both nodded, smiling, and left the Parks house. As Spike lifted Gloria into the saddle, some folks were still standing around in front of other houses and businesses, watching to see if the white man came out alone, or if he would still have the black woman with him. And before Spike had climbed onto the horse behind Gloria, the rumors and whispers again began to multiply. Dr. and Mrs. Parks stood in the doorway, seeing it all, and hearing a little of it, as they waved goodbye to Gloria and Spike. The young couple looked around, expressionless, ignoring the stares and whispers, and headed north up the valley toward Jeff's farm.

As they rode through the gate into the front yard, Cricket was barking and running toward the horse, as if he were challenging him to come any farther onto his territory. Jeff was chopping firewood, while Becky was preparing supper. Samuel was stacking the firewood, Ollie was helping Becky in the kitchen, and the twins were begging for cookies. Becky told them they would have to wait until after supper for the cookies, and ordered them to go outside and ring the dinner bell, letting their brother and father know that supper was almost ready. They quickly obeyed, forgetting all about cookies, running together through the open door, jumping off the porch, each of them trying to outrun the other to the dinner bell.

The twins grabbed the rope of the dinner bell at the same time, pulling it together. Gloria and Spike had already dismounted, Becky and Ollie had come to the front door to see why Cricket was barking, and Samuel and Jeff were walking toward Gloria and Spike. Everyone stopped in their tracks, just to laugh at the twins hanging together on the rope of the big dinner bell. When the twins saw they had company, they immediately stopped ringing the bell, dusted themselves off, and stood up straight, staring at Gloria and Spike as if they had been caught doing something mischievous.

Erica spoke up. "Sorry Miss Gloria, sorry Mr. Pike."

Both Gloria and Spike came over to where the twins were standing side by side. Gloria hugged Erica, while Spike reached out his hand to Elick.

Elick responded with as tight a grip as he could manage onto Spike's hand, pumping his arm up and down, saying, "Howdy Mr. Pike."

Gloria spoke to Erica, "Well now young lady, I don't see nary reason for you to be sorry, seeing as you just let us know that we've arrived just in time for some of yer mama's good cooking."

While Gloria was talking to Erica, Spike was talking to Elick, treating him with the respect of a full-grown man, reminding him,

"My friends just call me Spike, and I consider you one of my closest friends Elick."

The twins quickly glanced at their father, as Jeff winked at them, letting them know that they were not in any trouble. Becky ushered all the children into the house, ordering them to get washed up for supper.

Samuel, being the young gentleman he was, reached for Gloria's hand first, bowing his head ever so slightly toward her, saying, "Hello Miss Williams, so nice to see you."

Gloria quickly acknowledged his welcome, curtsying to him, replying, "Likewise, Mister Townsend."

Samuel took the reins of Spike's horse, leading him to the little stream for watering. After the horse had drank, Samuel led him back to the barn, took off the saddle, and fed the horse some hay. While Samuel was tending to the horse, Jeff, Spike, Gloria and Becky walked toward the house. Becky was always excited when anyone from the church came to visit them, and both Spike and Gloria had been there before, but not together. With both of them having arrived on the same horse, Becky knew there was something extra special about this particular visit, and she was pretty sure she knew what it was. The same was true with Jeff. He had known Gloria longer than he had known Spike, but he, like so many others in the church, had seen the glances, and the way the two could hardly keep from getting as close to each other as possible, while trying hard to not draw any attention to themselves. Jeff had watched Gloria and Greta grow up before his eyes. They had grown from the frail, frightened, sad and somber little girls he had seen in the back of their father's wagon, into two happy, healthy, vibrant and beautiful young ladies.

They all gathered at the table, waiting for Samuel to come in and wash up for supper. When Samuel had sat down, Jeff asked Spike to say grace. After supper, the children were dismissed to Samuel's room, where he took his Bible from the night stand, and began to read to them from the Bible. This, of course, gave the grownups their privacy to talk. Neither Jeff nor Becky offered any presuppositions as to the purpose of this visit, but simply waited for either Spike or Gloria to tell them. After thanking Becky for the fine supper, Spike spoke first, addressing Jeff.

"Pastor Townsend, I, uh, we, uh, that is, Gloria and I, we, well, you see Sir, we are...

Jeff was about to lose his straight face, and could contain his laughter no longer, interrupting Spike slowly, helping him finish what he was trying to say, adding, "You are, deeply in love?" Spike nodded his head quickly, as Jeff continued, "And you have asked for this beautiful young lady's hand in marriage.?"

Spike glanced toward the blushing Gloria, taking her hand, nodding again, smiling at her, as Jeff added, "And her father and mother have agreed to this marriage, and now you want me to perform the wedding ceremony?"

Gloria and Spike looked at each other quickly, smiling. Becky and Gloria jumped up from their chairs at the same moment, throwing their arms around each other, as tears of joy came to their eyes, with Becky exclaiming, "Oh Gloria, I am so happy for you and Spike. We've known for a long time you two were meant for each other." Jeff and Spike stood up at the same moment, shaking hands with each other, with Jeff congratulating Spike.

"Spike, I am so proud of both of you. Gloria is a fine young woman. Have you set a date for the wedding yet?"

Spike and Gloria put their arms around each other then, as Gloria answered with a little laugh, "Well Pastor Jeff, that seems to be bout the only thing nobody knows for sure. Me and Spike have talked, and we know you to be a very busy man, with the church, the farm, and a family and all, we kinda wanted at ask you what would be a good time for you to marry us."

Jeff smiled, thanking them for their consideration, but added, "You two pick the date, and I will make myself available, no matter when it is."

Spike shook hands with Jeff again, thanking him for being so considerate, answering, "Well Pastor, Dr. Parks says that Gloria here, and her sister Greta, will both be ready to take their State Nursing exams 'bout March of next year, and Mr. Williams has already said he wants ta give us twenty five acres of land as a wedding present. So we were sorta wanting to build us a house first, and while I continue to work for Mr. Williams, Gloria can git her Nursing License, and we could be married in April."

Jeff and Becky hugged the couple again, congratulating them upon their upcoming wedding, and for their wisdom in laying some definite plans for their future. During the whole time Spike and Gloria had been in their home, neither Jeff nor Becky had said a single word about the dangers of a white man being engaged to a black woman. And neither Gloria nor Spike had mentioned it either. All of them knew the dangers all too well. Spike and Gloria had accepted the risks, and whatever consequences they might have to face by becoming man and wife. Such was their love for each other. Little did either of them know that, not far away, and in the near future, lay one of the gravest dangers of all, in the person of Wesley Phelps.

October, 1877.

The news that one of the escapees from the Moundsville Penitentiary had been killed had spread like wildfire. Until about three weeks after his death, every headline in every newspaper from the northern panhandle of West Virginia to the southernmost tip of the state noted the fact that William Bowen had been killed in a hunting accident near Bruceton Mills. Those same headlines also included the fact that the other escapee, Wesley Phelps was still at large. No one had seen or heard from Wesley Phelps since the day he and William Bowen escaped.

The news of the escape and the subsequent death of William Bowen, of course, was of local interest, and held the headlines for a little while, but only for a little while. There was more news, bigger news, of national interest, that soon eclipsed the local headlines, sending those stories to the back pages of the newspapers, captioned in small print. When compared to the news of the national events of 1877, the news of a lone escapee in the backwoods of West Virginia soon faded into oblivion. Some of the bigger stories of the day, of course, included the Compromise of 1877, making Rutherford B. Hayes the winner of the election of 1876, even though his opponent, Samuel J. Tilden, had won the majority of the popular vote.

Other major headlines included the Indian Wars, with Sitting Bull taking his band of Lakota into Canada in May of that year. In June, Henry Ossian Flipper became the first African American cadet to graduate from the U.S. Military Academy. Also in June, the U.S. Cavalry was defeated by the Nez Pierce Indians at the Battle of White Bird Canyon in Idaho Territory. In July, folks read of the Great Railroad Strike of the Baltimore and Ohio Railroad, which began in Martinsburg West Virginia on July 16th, and spread to others states, including Pennsylvania, Maryland, Illinois and Missouri, ending forty-five days later, after federal troops were called in, and 100 men had died.

In August of 1877, an Arizona blacksmith, F.P. Cahill, was fatally wounded by Billy the Kid (William Bonney), and died the next day, becoming the first victim of The Kid. And in October, the body of George Armstrong Custer, who fell at the Battle of Little Big Horn the previous year, was recovered, and buried with full military honors at West Point Military Academy.

But the one thing that preyed upon the minds and hearts of Americans perhaps more than any other during the period between 1873 and 1879 was what was called The Long Depression, during which 18,000 businesses went bankrupt, along with hundreds of banks, and ten states. By 1876, the unemployment rate had reached 14%. One can readily see, then, how that the news of one escapee being at large soon became old news. Most folks believed, and some even hoped, that Wesley Phelps would soon meet a similar fate as that of William Bowen.

And while the news of Wesley Phelps being on the loose may have paled in the light of what most folks considered more important news, his being at large still lingered in the back of the minds of a lot of folks, and especially those who lived in the vicinity of Bruceton Mills West Virginia, and particularly in the minds of the Townsend family. One other man who never let the image of those headlines fade from his mind was Sheriff Clarence Murphy. He remained ever-vigilant and cautious, never forgetting that it was the testimony of his Pastor and friend, Jeff Townsend, that sent Wesley to prison more than eleven years ago.

Wesley Phelps, in the meantime, had to live strictly by his wits. He was a fugitive from justice, with a price on his head. In the northern panhandle of West Virginia he had no relatives, no friends, and not a single acquaintance upon whom he could rely for food, shelter or clothing. He had been on the run now for more than a year. Under the conditions in which he now found himself, survival alone was the most difficult of all. He had to eat whatever he could find or kill with his bare hands. He had to risk being seen each time he drank from a stream or creek. He was on the verge of starvation, having barely survived the winter of 1876. He had managed to steal enough clothing from clotheslines to keep himself from freezing to death. And now the chilly winds of October reminded him that he was about to face yet another winter, alone, hungry, and fearing for his life with every step.

The parting words of William Bowen - *"don't follow me Wesley, or I'll kill you too,"* still rang in his conscience. But without even knowing that William was dead, his fear of William Bowen was now overshadowed by his will to survive. He had slowly made his way from the northern panhandle southward into the dense woods that formed a triangle between the towns of Bruceton Mills, Kingwood, and Terra Alta, hoping that he could somehow find his nephews, Jason and Travis Phelps, who would hopefully give him both shelter and sanctuary.

But now his eyes had seen something that had enraged his wicked soul to such a degree that he momentarily forgot all about his own condition and circumstances. He had seen a white man kissing a black woman, a beautiful black woman, to be sure, but a black woman nonetheless. It was something his demented conscience could not abide. On more than one occasion he had watched the two in each other's arms, kissing and holding each other as if they were in love with each other. But once, and only once, he had cautiously ventured close enough to hear what they were saying. They were talking about getting married!

Having spent almost ten years in prison, and more than a year as a fugitive with a price on his head had done strange things to Wesley Phelps. He was a hardened man, desperate, cautious, always looking over his shoulder, jumping at the slightest sound. For a single fleeting moment he had thought about giving himself up to the law, and facing whatever the consequences might be. But now he had arrived at the conclusion that the law would not allow him to give himself up. they would shoot him on sight, and collect whatever bounty that was sure be on his head. But now that he had seen this white man kissing a black woman, his twisted mind began to devise a plan - a plan which, to his own way of reckoning, might even exonerate him in the eyes of the law, and do the world a favor at the same time.

That white man had a horse, a saddle, a rope, a rifle, a knife, and a pistol, everything he would need to accomplish his ends. He had gotten close enough once to hear them talking without being detected, and he was certain he could do it again. Only this time he would get even closer. With the one black woman at a respectable distance from the lovers, he could sneak up on them while they were embraced, and proceed with his plan from there. In the same way that William Bowen had watched the Townsend farm for days, noting every action of every member of the family, Wesley watched Spike, Gloria and Greta, noting the distance between Greta and Spike and Gloria when they would meet. It was a distance that would allow him plenty of time to sneak in while the two were kissing, and take the rifle from its sheath. The rest would be easy - or so he thought. Like William Bowen before him, Wesley Phelps made a few mistakes, a few errors in judgment, a few miscalculations.

Spike and Gloria didn't meet in secret anymore. They sat together in church, sang together in the choir, and prayed together at the altar. Inside the Jenkins Memorial Baptist Church, every family and every individual accepted their relationship as easily as if they were both white, or both black. They did, however, use common sense and discretion when outside the church. They did nothing to deliberately attract public attention to themselves, knowing that to do so would be to invite unnecessary belligerence, hostility, or violence from those who still harbored a deep hatred for black people, and an even deeper hatred for whites who associated with black people.

Both Gloria and Greta had been honor students throughout high school, making straight A's in every subject. Upon graduation, the twins shared the high honor of being selected class valedictorian. This, added to the fact that they were both very shapely and beautiful, made for some jealousy from their fellow students, all of whom, of course, were African American. The other girls were jealous of the twins' beauty, charm and grace, coupled with the fact that every young man in the school wanted to have one of the Williams twins for a girlfriend. But wanting and having are two different things, and every young man in the school knew that Gloria was now engaged to a white man who went by the name of Spike. This, of course, enraged every young black male in the school as much, if not more, than it enraged most white folks who knew of the relationship.

The fact that Gloria, a black lady, was engaged to a white man, in itself, induced a great deal of animosity and hatred from her own race. But the thing that went un-said, and therefore unknown, was whether they hated her more for the fact that a white man had won her heart, or for the fact that they had not been able to win her heart.

But Gloria Williams and her engagement to Spike was only half of the powder keg. The other half was her twin sister Greta. While the young men who knew the Williams twins had finally and reluctantly accepted the fact that they could not have Gloria, they were yet hopeful that one of them could have her identical twin Greta. On those rare occasions when the twins were separated by more than a few feet, a few young black men were immediately in Greta's face, vying for her attention. But Greta soon let them all know that she was not interested. And that was the match that lit the fuse to the powder keg. Being rejected by one beautiful lady of their own race in favor of a white man was insulting enough, but to be rejected by her twin sister also, who was not dating anyone, that was the last straw. Add all of this to the fact that the Williams family attended a predominantly white church, where Buford Williams was now a trustee, and you have an image of the highly volatile powder keg, which could blow up at any moment.

Since the engagement of Gloria and Spike had now become common knowledge, both Gloria and Greta, and their parents, Buford and Mattie, had had to endure the whispers, the slurs, and the open insults of both races. While Buford and his family had earned the love and respect of practically everyone who knew them, there were still a few from both races who considered them traitors to their own race, and never hesitated to tell them so. But things were more difficult for the girls themselves than for anyone else. Every day brought more of the same, the taunting insinuations, alleging that both the twins had probably slept with the white boy, while others, agreeing with those insinuations, offered to show them how much better it would be with a black man. It was indeed a joyous event when the twins graduated high school with their diplomas in their hands. At least now they didn't have to hear the slanderous insults on a daily basis from upwards of seventy-five students, male and female.

The twins now concentrated fully upon their nursing studies, making the ten-mile trip to Bruceton Mills every Saturday. Dr.

Parks now offered that since they had graduated high school, they were welcome to come to his clinic any or every day of the week if they wished. But the twins respectfully declined the offer, telling Dr. Parks that they were both needed on the farm during the week. Dr. Parks fully understood, because the Long Depression, as it was named, had now made itself felt all across the country. Buford's business had suddenly declined by more than two thirds in less than three months. Thankfully, he had saved enough money during the good times to tide him over through the bad times. Buford took it all in stride, never complaining. He was still the best blacksmith in the state, and he still got enough work orders to keep his business running.

With the sharp decline in work orders, Buford now allowed Spike to come and go as he pleased, working whenever he felt he was needed. Spike spent every free hour during the week clearing his twenty-five acres, and building a house for his soon-to-be bride. On Saturdays, he would quit working early, and ride toward Bruceton Mills, taking the diagonal shortcut, to meet Gloria and Greta on their way back from Dr. Parks' clinic. Their meeting place was the same as it had been when they had met secretly, about half way between Bruceton Mills and Terra Alta. But now a few things were different. They no longer had to hide their love for each other, and instead of Greta and Spike exchanging places from horse to carriage on the way to Bruceton Mills, they now exchanged places on the return trip from Bruceton Mills. Upon arriving at the spot where they had kissed so many times, they would dismount, and re-live those stolen moments, with Greta grinning at them, insisting.

"Alright now you two lovebirds, that's enough smooching. We got to get home before dark ya know."

Saturday October 27th, 1877. Somewhere between Bruceton Mills and Terra Alta.

Gloria and Greta knew they must get in as much study and training as possible before winter set in, making the road between Bruceton Mills and Terra Alta virtually impassible. Dr. Parks and his wife Carolyn were as proud of the twins as if they were their own daughters. They studied hard, and listened attentively, paying close attention to every detail, as Dr. Parks demonstrated his skill in attending to the sick and wounded. When at church together, he and

Carolyn always made it a point to tell Buford and Mattie what a great job they had done in raising their girls. They were nearly finished with their studies and training now, and would be taking their State Nursing Exams in Charleston the following March. Dr. Parks admitted that he would surely miss their smiling faces at his clinic. As they left the clinic that afternoon, there were long hugs from both Dr. and Mrs. Parks. Carolyn insisted they take a basket of her fried chicken and some biscuits for the return trip home.

"If you don't eat it all, I'm sure Mr. Spike will finish it off for you."

Sheriff Clarence Murphy was a dedicated man, and a very methodical and meticulous investigator, never overlooking or dismissing the smallest detail in any case in which he got involved. Immediately upon being elected to the office of Sheriff of Preston County, he immediately delved into the particulars of every case that Sheriff Collins had left behind. In a locked closet in his office, he kept old newspapers from as far back as twenty years, in which were stories of old cases involving murders, attempted murders, rapes, robberies, fraudulent business deals, and countless other lesser crimes. He made a point of knowing the names of every single person mentioned in every case, and then following up on them, finding out the names of their relatives and acquaintances, their habits, and the places they were known to frequent most often. He employed every resource at his disposal in his relentless search for the truth, including the telegraph, newspapers, wills, court documents, letters, notes, and word of mouth.

Having such a virtual library of information stored in his memory, Sheriff Murphy was widely known, feared and respected for his prowess in solving cases that had been long forgotten by many others. Any criminal, or would-be-criminal who came under his jurisdiction was, by that action, placing himself in grave danger of being caught speedily. Most were caught alive, and underwent the due process of law. Some, however, were not so fortunate. There was only one man alive faster than Sheriff Murphy with a gun, and that man had now locked his pistol inside a large wooden box in his bedroom. That box was locked with a big heavy padlock, with the padlock turned toward the wall, and other heavy boxes on top of it. The key to the padlock was at the bottom of the man-made pond about a hundred yards downstream from Jeff Townsend's house.

What Jeff didn't know was that there was one other person who knew the whereabouts of that key, his youngest son, Elick, who had seen him toss the key into the pond a few days after killing William Bowen.

Sheriff Murphy had followed the case of Herb Valentine and his fellow henchmen since the day he took office. The case had been made more famous by the names by which it was called. Some had labeled it The Valentine Case, while others named it Hoods in the Woods. But to Clarence Murphy, it was yet an incomplete case, even though all of the accused had been duly prosecuted, convicted, sentenced, and incarcerated or hanged. There were still some loose ends, and Clarence Murphy would not rest until all those loose ends were tied. Two men who were either directly or indirectly involved in that case were very much alive. One of those men, Preston Jenkins, had served his full sentence, and was now a hard-working, law-abiding citizen, living with his wife in Morgantown. The other man was Wesley Phelps.

Sheriff Murphy went over the case from its beginning, reading every word over and over, trying to find something, anything, that would give him a sense of what kind of man Wesley Phelps might be, and where he might go. Perusing the back pages of some recent newspapers, he noticed the smaller stories printed there. Folks from everywhere between Wheeling and Bruceton Mills had reported things being stolen from their farms, their barns, and even their clotheslines. Upon reading these stories, his detective mind began to put two and two together. He questioned Jason and Travis Phelps, and their mother Caroline, all of whom were the only known living relatives of Wesley Phelps. Upon hearing the Phelps brothers describe the character and personality of Wesley Phelps as they had known him before he was sent to prison, Sheriff Murphy came away with an uneasy feeling in his gut. Something deep inside his well-honed sheriff's intuition told him that Wesley Phelps was either headed for Preston County, or worse yet, already there.

Just before dawn on Saturday morning, October 27th, Wesley Phelps made his way to the spot where he had first seen the white man kissing the black woman. He carefully pushed back every leaf and twig within a ten yard circle around himself, so as to make sure he wouldn't be heard when he sneaked in to grab the rifle from the scabbard on the right side of the white man's horse. He filled his belly with berries and nuts, took a long drink of water from Big Sandy Creek, and laid down for a long nap, knowing that his query would be along late in the afternoon.

At precisely ten o'clock that same morning, Sheriff Murphy, acting upon what he considered good information and a strong hunch, turned the office over to Deputy Ancel Smith, checked his pistol and rifle, making sure they were both loaded and in good working order, mounted his horse, and rode slowly toward the deep woods south of Bruceton Mills. He knew no escaped criminal in his right mind would stick to the main road, but would keep just far enough off the main road to remain concealed. He also suspected that Wesley Phelps was the man who had stolen clothing from those clotheslines. Less than a hundred yards into the woods, he found the tracks, and the prison clothes. Judging from the size of the tracks, the depth to which they had sunk into the softer areas of dirt, and the distance between them, he figured Wesley Phelps was about six feet tall, and weighed about 180 pounds. The consistent stride and direction of the tracks also told him that the man he was following knew exactly where he was going. Other tracks of the same size, depth and distance apart, going in the other direction, told him that Wesley had been to wherever he was going more than once.

The fact that not a single track pointed toward Albright or Kingwood told him that Wesley was not headed toward his nephew's home. And if he was not headed toward his relatives homes, then he was headed somewhere else, somewhere definite, and with a definite purpose in mind. Something stronger than his own family ties was drawing Wesley Phelps in another direction. Sheriff Murphy stopped and thought it all over for a few minutes, thinking, an escaped criminal, with a price on his head, with relatives well within his reach, going off in the opposite direction, toward a road that connected two towns, Terra Alta and Bruceton Mills."

Slowly he put the pieces of the puzzle together. Jeff Townsend! the man whose testimony had sent Wesley to prison, lived a mile north of Bruceton Mills. But Wesley had bypassed Jeff Townsend's farm completely. Buford Williams lived near Terra Alta, with his wife and two daughters, Gloria and Greta. Gloria was engaged to marry a white man, Sanford Pike. But Wesley Phelps couldn't possibly know Buford Williams or his family, unless...

It hit him like a bolt of lightning! Wesley Phelps was not after the man whose testimony sent him to prison, he was after someone else, someone who traveled that road on a regular basis, every Saturday.! Gloria and Greta!

His heart leaped into his throat, as he prayed that he was not too late to stop Wesley from doing what he planned to do. He knew Wesley was out there somewhere in front of him, but he didn't know how far, or exactly where. He would simply have to follow the telltale tracks and signs slowly and quietly, on foot, and pray that he spotted Wesley before Wesley spotted him. If he could find Wesley in time, he could arrest him, and all would be well, but if not; he swallowed hard, trying not to think of what the consequences might be. It was now a little past noon. Wesley Phelps was awake, and going over his plan step by step. He had no idea he was being followed by the most cunning lawman in the state. For every moment he waited and calculated, Sheriff Murphy gained another step on him.

Two more hours passed. The trail leading to where Wesley was hiding was rough and steep. Sheriff Murphy had to skirt around huge patches of blackberry briars, boulders, and dense thickets, all the while having to move slowly and cautiously so as not to be heard. He knew he could reach the road in about another hour, if he could continue at this pace without being detected. He figured Wesley was probably already at his destination, hiding, waiting for his victims to arrive. He had to assume that Wesley was armed, and therefore the more dangerous. And with Wesley being between him and Spike and the girls, he had no way of warning them of the danger into which they were riding.

Spike, Gloria and Greta arrived at their romantic spot just beyond the bend in the road at 3:30 in the afternoon. Greta was riding Spike's horse, staying as close to the carriage as possible, listening to Spike singing one of his homemade tunes. Spike and Gloria sat side by side in the buggy. Gloria was holding the reins, while Spike serenaded her, strumming his banjo, singing,

"Well, I slipped up the holler, jumpin in the rain
Goin up ta see ol Sadie Jane
She promised me a kiss on the day we met
But I still ain't kissed ol Sadie yet

But she finely gave me a smile instead
She didn't have a single tooth in her head
Now I'm runnin down the holler, dodgin the rain
Wish I hadn't seen ol Sadie Jane.

Both Gloria and Greta were holding their stomachs, doubling over with laughter. As soon as the horse stopped, Spike jumped out of the carriage from the left side, followed by Gloria. He lifted her gently from the side of the carriage. The two of them walked toward the back of the carriage, where they immediately embraced in a long passionate kiss. Greta left Spike's horse standing out in front of the carriage, and walked down the embankment to the creek for a drink of water.

The right side of Spike's horse was in full view to Wesley Phelps, while Greta was out of sight. It was the perfect moment for Wesley to advance from his cover, and ease the rifle from the scabbard. As Greta came up the embankment, Wesley stepped from the right side of the horse, poking the barrel of the rifle into her chest, putting his finger to his lips, indicating that she was not to make a sound. He then whispered for her to put her hands in the air, and walk slowly toward the back of the carriage. He pushed the barrel of the rifle into her back, pushing her toward where Spike and Gloria were standing behind the carriage.

When Greta stepped into view of Spike and Gloria with her hands up, Spike instinctively went for his pistol. Before he could draw the pistol from the holster, he saw that Wesley had his rifle in Greta's back, and started to push the pistol back into the holster. Wesley ordered him to take the pistol from the holster with his left hand, using only his fingers, and to hand it to him, slowly. Spike obeyed, handing the gun to Wesley, who stuck it under his belt.

"Now ain't this a purty picture," Wesley began, I done caught myself a dirty stinkin white nigger lover, and two trampy black whores at the same time."

Spike quickly interjected, begging Wesley, "Mister, I don't know who you are, or what you want, but if you want money, I'll give you every dollar I have, and both horses and the buggy. You can take me, and do whatever you please with me, but please let these ladies go, I beg you Sir."

Wesley didn't hesitate a moment, answering with a hateful grimace on his face.

"One more word outa you boy, an you ain't gonna live as long as I had planned to let you live. Now git your sorry ass over to this horse and cut me off three good lengths of that rope, and throw the knife into the creek."

Again Spike obeyed, cutting off three lengths of the rope, each about a foot long. Spike could see the hammer of the rifle was pulled back, so he had no chance of rushing the man without getting Greta killed instantly. Wesley saw the look in Spike's eyes, a look of helplessness. It gave him a sense of ultimate power, having the lives of three persons totally at his mercy, helpless against his superior wit. He stood there momentarily, laughing at the three of them, basking in the triumph of his easy conquest of them. And now for the most satisfying moment of his entire life, he would show them just how far superior he was. He ordered Greta to tie Spike's hands behind his back first. He then ordered Spike to stand back about ten feet away from him, and watch while Greta was forced to tie Gloria's hands also. With their hands tied, he could then safely tie Greta's hands behind her.

With a devilish grin, Wesley looked at Spike, asking, "Betcha can't guess what I'm gonna do next, can ya white bastard? Well I'm purty sure you already done it to both of 'em. But now you're gonna watch a real man do it to 'em. An your future wife here is gonna git it first. Yeah, that's right purty boy, I know all about your plans to marry the black whore. I'm just gonna break her in proper for ya. Only, when I get done with her, she ain't gonna be as purty as she is now. She's gonna have some stretch marks on her purty black neck."

Gloria somehow found the strength to speak, begging Wesley.

"Sir, if it's me you want, then do with me what you will, but please don't hurt them. Please let them go."

Wesley backhanded Gloria across her mouth, drawing the blood from her mouth. Spike's rage overcame his common sense for a moment, as he started to rush toward Wesley. Wesley allowed him to get within five feet. He quickly jerked the pistol from his belt, pointing it at Spike's head, then pointed the rifle at Gloria's head, stopping Spike in his tracks. He then ordered both Spike and Greta to stand back about fifteen feet, and watch as he looped the rest of the rope over Gloria's head, throwing the end of the rope across the limb of a hickory tree that stood in the edge of the road. He pulled on the rope slightly, putting just enough tension on it to cause Gloria to wince in pain. Tears were now streaming from the eyes of both Spike and Greta, as they both pleaded for Gloria's life. Wesley again laughed with a deep, demonic grunt, becoming more proud of himself with each passing moment.

He stood the rifle against the base of the tree, taking the pistol out of his belt, holding it in one hand, as he began to feel Gloria's body with the other, grinning, and glancing toward Spike with each stroke of his hand, relishing in the disgust on Spike's face. When Gloria began to kick at him, he grabbed the rope again, pulling it taut, almost lifting her off the ground. Spike and Greta began to pray silently. Suddenly, without any warning, something inside Wesley Phelps' reprobate mind snapped. His hatred for this black woman and the white man far surpassed his urge to rape her. He wanted her dead, swinging from this tree limb. He stuck the pistol back into his belt, grabbing the rope with both hands, to pulling downward with all his strength.

At that moment, the voice of Sheriff Clarence Murphy rang out.

"Drop the rope Wesley, do it now, or I'll cut you in half."

Without thinking, Wesley let go of the rope, and went for the pistol in his belt. The bullet from Sheriff Murphy's Winchester sank into his brain before he could pull the pistol out of his belt. Both he and Gloria sank to the ground, with Gloria falling on top of Wesley's dead body. Spike and Greta rushed forward. Sheriff Murphy quickly kicked the pistol away from Wesley's hand, then knelt beside his body, examining his neck for a pulse. Finding no pulse, he rose up from his knee, taking out his own Bowie knife, cutting the ropes from the hands of Gloria, Greta and Spike. Spike lifted Gloria into his arms, holding her tightly against his chest. She threw her arms around him, holding onto him as if she would never let him go, trembling and whispering.

"Oh my God Spike, I love you so much, you almost got yourself killed for me!"

Spike held her at arm's length, examining her neck, checking to see if the rope had done any major damage.

He smiled at her, answering, "I love you too Gloria, more than I even realized before, and you almost got yourself killed for me and your sister."

They quickly turned toward Sheriff Murphy, who was holding Greta in his arms, comforting her. All three of them began thanking him at the same time. Both Gloria and Greta hugged him tightly, each of them kissing his cheek, thanking him for saving their lives. Spike shook his hand, as Sheriff Murphy responded with a big smile of satisfaction.

"Just doin muh job."

They grinned back at him, knowing he had done far more than just his job. He had come a long distance, and had risked his own life to save the lives of his friends. Sheriff Murphy asked Spike to help him lift Wesley's body onto his own horse. They laid the body across the saddle. Sheriff Murphy climbed on behind the saddle, and was about to leave toward Bruceton Mills. But before he could leave, Spike's curiosity got the best of him. He simply had to ask Sheriff Murphy, "Sheriff, who is this man? And how did you know he would be here? And how did you know we would be here?"

Sheriff Murphy grinned, answering, "This is Wesley Phelps, one of two escapees from Moundsville. And as for me knowing he and you three would be here, I'm the Sheriff of Preston County, and it's my job to know the whereabouts of my friends, and my enemies."

Sheriff Murphy rode away slowly. He was thankful that God had allowed him to arrive in time to prevent three of his friends from being killed, but at the same time, he was sorry that one man had to die in the process. Even though he knew he had no choice, he never got used to the idea of taking another human life. This was not the first man he had been forced to kill, and he knew it probably wouldn't be the last, but each time it happened, he felt as if he had lost another little piece of his own soul. And now he was dreading facing the Phelps family tomorrow at church, and having to tell them how their uncle had died.

As Sheriff Murphy rode slowly toward Bruceton Mills, Gloria and Greta rode just as slowly toward Terra Alta. Greta was still so shaken by the incident she asked Spike if she could ride in the carriage with them. They tied Spike's horse to the back of the carriage. Spike lifted Greta into the seat beside Gloria. The twins put their arms around each other's backs for the rest of the trip. Not many words were spoken till they reached the Williams farm.

Buford had just finished putting away his tools when Ole Beauregard's low growl announced that someone was approaching. Buford immediately recognized the carriage. He stood and watched as the carriage slowly made its way along the narrow trail leading onto the farm. He suspected nothing out of the ordinary, since the three of them had arrived at about this same time many times before. Only one thing was different though, Greta was riding in the carriage with Spike and Gloria instead of being on Spike's horse. Buford just figured maybe Spike's horse had lost a shoe or something. As the carriage drew closer, however, he knew something was not quite right. Neither Spike nor either of his daughters was waving at him like they usually did upon arriving back at the farm. And Spike was not strumming his banjo and singing like he usually did. He instinctively called for Mattie to come out of the house.

As Mattie joined him, the two of them walked quickly toward the carriage, their instincts telling them that something bad had happened. Buford quickly lifted his daughters from the carriage, asking them what was wrong. They threw their arms around Buford.

"Oh Papa, it was awful, we better go to the house." Gloria said with a trembling voice.

Mattie quickly noticed the marks of the rope on her daughter's neck, but said nothing till everyone got inside the house. Spike tied the horse to the hitching post, leaving his own horse tied to the back of the carriage for now. At the table, Buford noticed the rope burn on the sides of Gloria's neck also. He glanced from Spike to Gloria, to Greta, and back to Gloria again. The expression on his face alone was enough to tell what he was thinking. He wanted answers. Gloria glanced toward Greta and Spike first. They both nodded, silently agreeing that she would be the one to tell her parents the horrible story. Mattie quickly examined the rope burns on Gloria's neck. Gloria assured her that she was alright, and nothing was broken. Mattie squinted at her momentarily, insisting.

"Just the same, I think I should put some ointment on your neck child, that don't look so good to me."

Gloria nodded, agreeing to her mama's suggestion, knowing Mattie would not sit down till she had put something on that rope burn. She waited until Mattie had returned with the ointment and a tall glass of water before beginning to speak. She took a long drink of the water, and began. As the gruesome details unfolded, Buford and Mattie grasped each other's hands, as tears filled their eyes. The only other time the girls had seen their papa cry this way was the day he had found Mattie, beaten nearly to death by The Sons of Midnight.

There was no question at all in the minds of anyone at the table that Gloria and Spike were deeply in love. There was no question in anyone's mind whether they would die for each other. Buford had gained a wholesome respect for Spike, having worked side by side with him for more than a year. He treated Spike as an equal. He and Spike understood each other perfectly. There was never any patronization nor condescension between them. Neither of them ever questioned the other's motives or intentions. Buford knew Spike loved his daughter, and would be the finest husband to her he could possibly be. But now that this near-death incident had happened, involving not just one, but both of his daughters, his father instincts took precedence over his love and respect for the man who would soon become his son-in-law.

But before Buford or Mattie could say a word, Spike had already read the questions on their faces, and knew what they were thinking. He answered their questions before they asked them, glancing from Buford to Mattie, to Greta, and to Gloria.

"Mr. Williams, I know you and Mattie have some questions to ask me, and I won't hesitate to answer them for you. You are wondering whether I or Gloria are having second thoughts about our getting married since this horrible incident."

Buford cleared his throat, glancing toward Mattie, then back to Spike.

"Well, Spike, now that you mention it, yes, I wuz thinking along them lines, and to be perfectly honest, even further beyond those lines, if you know's what I mean."

Gloria took Spike's hand, looking into his eyes, asking, "May I speak for both of us Spike?"

Spike smiled at her, almost knowing what she wanted to say, and nodded in agreement.

"Mama, Papa, Spike and I each saw a side of the other today that neither of us had seen before. We both know we would die for each other if it ever came to that, and we realize it may come to that someday. But we are willing to take that risk. But, correct me if I'm wrong Papa, but I suspect there is something else you and Mama are concerned about, other than just Spike and me, am I right?"

Buford and Mattie looked solidly into their daughter's face, nodding in agreement, knowing she could read them like a book. Gloria continued, "If the good Lord blesses us with children, your grandchildren, we understand perfectly that our children may be more white than black, or more black than white. But either way, we are also willing to take that risk, and are prepared to deal with it. We simply trust the good Lord to get us and our children through whatever we may have to face, the same way He has brought you and Mama through everything you had to face in raising me and Greta here. We know it won't be a bed of roses Papa, but neither has it been a bed of roses for you and Mama. But you survived it all, and you have instilled some good and godly teaching into us. We will make it work Papa, with God's help."

Before Gloria had finished speaking, Buford, Mattie, Greta and Spike were all wiping their eyes. Buford and Mattie both stood, inviting Gloria and Spike to come into their arms.

"Girls, I wish I could find the words to say how proud we are of both of you. I guess we have done a pretty good job with you two, if I do say so myself." Buford said.

Greta laughed, interjecting, "Now I could have sworn I smelled chicken and dumplings a cookin when we got here, and I, for one, am about to starve to death."

Mattie took the hint quickly, rushing to the stove, while Buford grabbed the plates and silverware, and set the table for supper.

The next few days were so frantic that Spike and Gloria hardly had time to see each other. Spike was busy with sheriff Murphy finalizing the report on the attempted murder of Gloria, Greta and himself. They had to go before the Judge, and give all the details, as well as to take a written report to the prison from which Mr. Phelps and Mr. Bowen had escaped.

Spike and the Sheriff got well acquainted in the few days they were together, riding side by side. One day the sheriff spoke up. "So, young man ,when are you gonna take miss Gloria to meet your parents?" Spike wasn't sure about how he was going to answer him. "Well sir, I can't wait fer my mama to met Gloria, but I don't think my step father will be too happy." He looked at Sheriff Murphy and saw the puzzled look on his face.

"Step Father!? What happened to your real father son.?" He asked Spike, stopping his horse and leaning on his saddle, waiting for Spike to answer him. Spike bowed his head a moment before answering. "It's a long story and a cruel story sir. Ya see sheriff, my Pa died when I wuz just a baby bout six months old. He was logging way back in the mountains, and a tree fell on him, crushing him to death. My mama nearly grieved herself to death, so I was told. Shortly after, this man Carl Pike, who is my step father now, well he met my mama and she had no means of taking care of me by herself, so he asked her to marry him and she did. He was good to her fer a little while, then his true colors come bustin out. He would get drunk and beat up on her something awful. Spike stopped for a moment, as tears filled his eyes.

"Take your time son, we got all day" Sheriff Murphy told him.

"Ya see, I wuz little and couldn't do nothing to protect her, all I could do was run and hide, 'cause he would slap me so hard I would just fall down, and mama would yell at him and he would only beat her that much harder. I finally got big enough to hit him with a chair or just anything I could pick up to make him stop hitting my mama. Sheriff, the day that I left home over a year ago, I left him lying on the floor like the coward that he is. I told them both about Gloria and that we wuz gonna get married, and he hit me fer the last time. I packed my things and left. Now sir, I want my mama to meet Gloria, but I am scared to take her there, I am afraid of what my step father will do or say, and I don't want Gloria to be hurt. I don't know what to do, cause you see sheriff, if he laid a hand on Gloria I would have to kill him.

"Sir, you are the only man other than my cousins that knows this story.

"I ain't told Gloria, and she wants to meet my folks, What should I do?"

Spike looked at Sheriff Murphy with sadness in his eyes, eagerly waiting for an answer.

Sheriff Murphy thought long and hard before he replied.

"Well son, when you take Gloria to meet your folks, I will ride along. I know it is out of my territory, but I want to be there as a friend. Don't you go fretting none, I will be close by, and if he harms either one of youns he will have to answer to me. So when you get ready to travel that way just let me know."

Spike had never met anyone quite like sheriff Murphy. Oh how he wished he had had a father like him! Things would have been so much better. His mama had told him so many good stories about his own father, and it grieved him so much that he had never gotten to know him. The two men rode in silence for the longest after that, each caught up in his own thoughts.

After several days all the official business was settled with the sheriff's office, the judge and the prison. Spike and sheriff Murphy had to part company and go about their daily living, each back at their jobs.

Spike was now able to see Gloria each day after work in the blacksmith shop, and Mattie and the girls always had a delicious supper waiting for Spike and Buford. They spent each evening with the family, and after the meal they had a short bible discussion. Then Spike would bring out his Banjo and they'd sing for hours before Spike headed back to his cousins home. Gloria rode her horse along with him for a short piece where they would say goodnight. Buford was not far behind, but he gave them their privacy. He did not want another attempt on his daughter's life without help close by. Gloria, Greta and Mattie were busy planning the wedding that was to take place in the church in April. Both the girls were still nervous and jumpy at any little sound. The man that had tried to destroy them was dead and gone, but they still were afraid to get out of sight of each other.

The news had reached all the neighbors, and all were very sympathetic and were very glad that Wesley Phelps had got *"what was coming to him."* Most folks all around the county had now accepted Gloria and Spike's relationship. Once in awhile they would see someone staring at them when they went into town, but their love for each other was far greater than the gossip that fell from some folks mouths.

Spike set a date to take Gloria to meet his folks. It made him sick inside to think what his step father might do or say upon meeting Gloria. He knew in his heart that he would have to kill the man if he laid one finger on her to harm her. As it grew closer to the day they were to leave, the more Spike dreaded it. And now he made up his mind that he would tell Gloria the same story he had told sheriff Murphy, the cold hard facts about his step father and the life that he had to endure growing up as a child.

That night, when they mounted their horses for their usual ride toward Spike's cousin's house, Spike knew Buford would follow them at a distance. This time, he stopped, and rode back toward Buford.

"Sir, he began, I know you are concerned for our safety, and I admire and respect that. But if I am to become Gloria's husband Sir, I must take full responsibility for her safety and comfort. I must respectfully ask you to allow us to make this trip alone. And Sir, when we return, I have something I must share with you and Mrs. Williams." Buford reluctantly agreed with Spike, shook his hand, and rode back to the farm.

Spike stopped at a beautiful spot beside the trail, where he spread a blanket on the ground. He took Gloria's hands in his own as he told her of the terrible life he had spent as a child. Gloria's eyes filled with tears as she listened to the man she loved describe a life style that she could not imagine. As he spoke, she could almost feel the pain, as he told of the beatings and the cursing, and the many times he had to hide to keep from being beat himself, while he had to listen to his mother's screams as his stepfather's big hands hit her. When all was said they held each other, both crying for Spike's mother and for the lost childhood of Spike himself.

"Now are you still wanting to go there and meet my folks?" Spike asked in a very shaky voice.

The story always shook him up every time he had to speak or even think about it.

"Yes, I want to meet your mama, she sounds like a very brave person, indeed I do want to go, and I ain't afraid as long as you are by my side."

"Then it is settled. We will go this Saturday morning bright and early." Gently taking Gloria's face in his hands, looking deep into her beautiful brown eyes he whispered, "I promise you no harm will come to you."

They talked a while longer, and true to his word, Spike rode with Gloria back to her house, where Spike told Buford and Mattie the whole sordid story of his life as a boy.

"Son, Buford spoke up, with tears in his eyes, why didn't you tell us before now, why have you lived with all this so long?"

"I was afraid yuns would not allow me to see Gloria, and Sir, I have loved her from the first time I laid eyes on her." He smiled at

Gloria as he planted a kiss on her forehead. Mattie was busy wiping the tears from her own eyes.

"Well, that settles it," Buford exclaimed, standing to his feet.

He clasped his big hands together, then raised them toward Heaven, swearing.

"Where's yuns lacks it er not, by Heaven, you young'uns is gonna have some comp'ny on yer journey."

Gloria and Spike glanced at each other quickly, not sure of how to tell Buford that they weren't alone.

Spike spoke up, "Uh Sir, that ain't necessary, 'cause sheriff Murphy is going along with us, bu-but if you insist ta go, you are welcome. I guess they might as well meet the whole family."

When Buford knew that sheriff Murphy was going with them, he relaxed, releasing a deep sigh of relief.

"Well, if the sheriff is goin along, then I guess that will be just fine, but I'm not about to let you two young'uns go by yoselves."

Having that issue settled, Spike headed home. Buford told him to come in to work late the next day since he would be arriving home late tonight.

On the ride home Spike felt as though he had a load lifted off his shoulders. He had shared his story with the people that he loved, he had told them the whole truth about himself, and they all understood, and still loved him as one of their own. He whistled the little tune he sung and played to Gloria so many times, Sadie Jane. He arrived home just before midnight, crawling into bed a happy man.

Saturday morning Spike and Gloria arrived at sheriff Murphy's office at six o'clock. Sheriff Murphy looked so different without his uniform. He was dressed in a pair of old jeans and a blue checked denim shirt, and wearing an old faded black hat. The only thing that looked the same was his gun belt, with his loaded pistol on his side.

Gloria looked him up and down, remarking, "Purdy doggone handsome."

Spike chuckled, glancing at Gloria, but intending for Clarence to hear him also.

"He reminds me of the scarecrow Pastor Townsend preached about before." They all laughed at that one, imagining sheriff Murphy hanging out in a garden on a big stick. They laughed and talked all the way to where his folks lived, but the closer they got, the less they talked, all three silently caught up in their own thoughts of what might lie ahead.

Drawing closer to the house they stopped briefly to go over the details of what they were going to do. Sheriff Murphy was going to be introduced as a friend of Spike's. If things got out of hand, then they were going to simply leave unless Carl Pike started a fight. If it came to that, then Gloria was to take Spike's mother out of the house and let the men settle this once and for all.

Sheriff Murphy assured them, "I'll tie him up if necessary, and get the sheriff of this county to come in and arrest him."

Once all that was agreed upon they approached the house.

Spike's home was on a back street of a very small settlement of maybe ten houses, mostly very poor folks living there. Despite the lifestyle they had Spike's mother kept her home clean inside and out, a small white house with an un-painted fence around it. The house had a small porch with two steps leading up to the front porch. As they grew closer, the door flew open suddenly, and out came Spike's mother with her arms open and a big beaming smile on her face. She had seen her son coming down the street with two other people she didn't know, but all that mattered was her baby boy was home. Spike jumped down from his horse, running to meet his mother. They clung to each other, both laughing and crying at the same time.

Sheriff Murphy kept his eyes on the house, expecting to see her husband come out at anytime. But then fate stepped in. It was hard for him to take his eyes off the beautiful woman who had come out that door and down those steps. He couldn't help staring, watching her holding onto her son with all her strength. She was the most beautiful creature Clarence Murphy had ever laid eyes on. Her long black curly hair, which hang to her waist over her slim figure, shimmered in the sunlight. She had dark skin, and a smile that would light up the world. In just one glance he saw all of that. "What kind of a lowlife piece of a man could hurt a gorgeous lady like that?" he asked himself.

Spike also took a moment to look toward the house, expecting his stepfather to walk out the door in a rage. His mother Lily noticed his concern, took his face in her hands, saying, "My baby you, don't have to worry about anymore beatings, anymore rages from him, he is gone and has been for nearly a year now. I am so happy. And now that you are here, my world is complete. Let's go meet my daughter-in-law. This has to be her. My, how beautiful she is! And I don't know this man, but he must be your friend. I want to hear all about your wedding. It must have been beautiful." Spike took his mother's hand as they walked toward the two still mounted on their horses. He couldn't help but smile. His mother didn't know it yet, but she would get to see their wedding. He helped Gloria down from her horse as Sheriff Murphy dismounted, immediately removing his hat.

"Mama, this is Gloria, Gloria, this is Mama." Gloria offered her hand for a handshake, but Lily took her into her arms immediately. The two embraced as if they had known each other all their lives.

"Mama, I want you to meet a good friend of mine, Clarence Murphy."

Spike felt awkward calling Sheriff Murphy by his given name. The sheriff held out his hand, stammering a little.

"It is a pleasure meeting you Mrs. Pike."

He gripped his hat tightly, hoping no one could see the trembling in his hand or the blush on his face. Lily's beauty had just taken his breath away. In her presence he felt like a school boy, falling in love for the first time.

She took his hand, and looking deep into his eyes, she thought, "Other than Spike's real father, this is the most handsome man I've ever seen." His brown eyes captivated her very soul at that moment. She let go very quickly, fearing the others would see the blush on her face. Quickly taking took Gloria by the hand, she invited them in, begging, "Please, let's go into the house and you can tell me all about the wedding. And I have a nice chocolate cake baked." Spike quickly whispered to sheriff Murphy that Carl was gone, and they had nothing to worry about.

The two men followed Lily and Gloria into the house. Spike was surprised when he walked into his mother's home. It was spotless, with no broken windows, and no broken down chairs to remind him of the ones he had once thrown at Carl Pike. Lily asked them all to sit at the table while she served them a big piece of chocolate cake with cold ice tea, all the while talking a mile a minute.

"So tell me all about the wedding son, I can't wait to hear about every little detail."

"Well Mama, we are getting married in April, and you will be there to see it for yourself." Lily's face lit up like a rising sun, as her blue eyes sparkled.

"Oh my, I am so excited, tell me everything, where is it going to be and how do I get there?"

"Mama, tell me first, where is Carl?" I see no signs of him around this place, and Mama, Mr. Murphy here is our sheriff. I told him about Carl, and he knows everything. He came along just in case we had trouble. He is one of my many friends I have back in Terra Alta, so you can talk with him freely."

Somehow, even before Spike told her, Lily knew she could trust Sheriff Murphy. His character somehow showed through his tender eyes.

"Son, she began, after he hit you that day, and you had to hit him back, then you left. He left two weeks after you did, but not before I carried another beating. Lily bowed her head briefly as though to gain enough courage to go on with her story. "I was told by some of the people around here that he was seen in different places, bad places. I was terrified for a while that he would come back and kill me, so I had a neighbor come in and change the locks on the doors and nail down the windows so he could not get in."

"So how long did you say has he been gone Mama?" Spike inquired.

"Nigh onto a year now. I suspect he is not coming back, or at least I am praying he won't."

It had turned out to be a happy evening after all. It took some doing, but Spike convinced his mother to go back home with him and Gloria. She was to stay with Gloria's family till other arrangements could be made. Spike told her he would build her a small house close by him and Gloria. Lily, without caring who saw it, quickly glanced toward Sheriff Murphy, as if asking for his approval. The beaming smile on his face said all that needed to be said. Sheriff Clarence Murphy was more than happy to help pack up the wagon for the trip back. They stayed up most of the night packing everything up. Sheriff Murphy and Lily couldn't keep their eyes off each other. Every chance they got they were talking as if they had known each other all their lives.

They were still up, sitting around the kitchen table when the morning sun lit up the small town. The wagon was loaded to the brim with everything Lily Pike owned. Lily looked all around the house to make sure she hadn't missed anything of value. There was nothing here but bad memories, so she shed no tears as they were leaving the town. The neighbors waved goodbye from their porches, and wished her well. The journey back to Terra Alta was a far more pleasant one than the trip that brought them here, and especially so for Sheriff Murphy. His heart pounded as Spike helped Lily onto the wagon seat, right beside him. Arriving at Gloria's parents home they were greeted by everyone. It was settled that Lily was to stay at Gloria's till after the wedding. Then Spike and Buford were going to build her a small cabin close to their own.

April came so quickly for Spike and Gloria. With Lily to help with all the planning the wedding was soon prepared. Gloria woke up with rays of sunlight beaming through the window. She was going to be a married woman before this day was over. She sighed with a deep breath of gratefulness as she stared at her beautiful long white wedding gown hanging on the wall at the foot of her bed. Long hours and plenty of love had been put into the making of that dress. She only hoped and prayed that she could be a good wife to Spike, and a good mother to their children. With so many thoughts running through her head she was interrupted by her sister Greta as she bounded into the room, jumping onto the bed beside her sister.

"Get up sleepy head, you gonna be married soon. We can't have no sleepin today."

She hugged her sister tightly as they lay there talking about a thousand things, from the past, present, and future.

The wedding, at the request of Spike and Gloria, was small, but Oh so beautiful. They wanted only their families, their fellow church members, and a handful of friends, including of course, Dr. Parks and Carolyn, Rufus and Claudette, all the Townsend family, and some friends of Spike's from days gone by. Dr. Parks stood as Spike's best man, and Greta, of course, was Gloria's maid of honor. To everyone's surprise, however, a few un-invited guests, young black men, who had once taunted and dis-respected both Gloria and Greta in high school, came dressed in brand new suits, and after observing the wedding, came to Gloria and Spike, extending their hands, and apologizing for the many times they had tormented them. Some of them even shook Spike's hand. One even commented to Spike, "Mister, you must be one hell of a good man, even if you is white. You got the finest lady this county has ever produced. Congratulations to you Sir."

His skill and cunning at tracing evidence and tracking men had served Clarence Murphy quite well as a Sheriff. Not one criminal who had ever come under his jurisdiction had been able to elude him for very long. But not only was he a student of investigative science, he was also a student of human nature, another tool that had served him well. Reflecting upon his long and distinguished career as a lawman, he sometimes wondered which had contributed more to his success - his knowledge and skill as a detective, or his careful study of human nature. But the one truth that stood out perhaps more than any other to him was the fact that there were only two kinds of criminals, those who were very dumb, and those who were very smart. The dumb ones were usually very easy to catch, and not very dangerous, except to themselves. The smart ones were not as easy to catch, and were usually very dangerous to anyone and anything that got in their way. But another valuable lesson that Sheriff Murphy had learned about all criminals, the one thing they all have in common, was that they all make mistakes. The crafty lawman had only to uncover those mistakes, then use them to his own advantage.

Some other criminal attributes that Sheriff Murphy had observed were that some criminals were very bold, brave, or even fearless, while others were outright cowards, yellow to the core. But sometimes the coward, when cornered, could suddenly become more dangerous than the bravest man alive. A coward was far more likely to shoot you in the back than a man with the courage to face you. It was therefore the duty of the lawman, if at all possible, to know what kind of man he was after, before going after him. But with all of this, he also had to remind himself that his job was to arrest the criminal, if he could do so without killing him or being killed, and bring him to the proper authorities, and hope that justice would be served. He was not the jury, and he was not the judge, he was only a Sheriff, and nothing more.

But now he was faced with a slightly different kind of case. The man he was after had not been formally charged with a crime, and was most likely somewhere beyond his own jurisdiction. In Sheriff Murphy's mind, Carl Pike was indeed a criminal, and one of the worst kinds of criminal, and a coward to boot. As far as he was concerned, any man who would beat his stepson and his wife with his fist was the lowest of the low. But with no formal charges laid against him, he could not be arrested. Lily Pike loved her son too much to put him through the embarrassment of having to see his stepfather tried as a wife beater, and so she had endured his abuse for all those years. Sometimes she had stepped between Spike and his stepfather, taking the beating herself, in order to stop him from beating Spike.

Sheriff Murphy had a personal stake in finding Carl Pike. All he wanted was the man's signature on the divorce papers, and he and Lily could be married legally. The woman he loved, and the fine young man whose life he had saved were waiting anxiously for him to return with that signature. Lily and Spike, more than anyone else on earth, knew how dangerous Carl Pike could be when confronted. But they also knew the courage and wisdom of Clarence Murphy, and were praying that his quest would be over quickly and successfully, with no one being hurt.

Armed with only what he had learned from Lily and Spike about the character and personality of Carl Pike, he headed toward Morgantown, stopping briefly at every saloon and house of ill repute along the way, just to ask if anyone had seen a man fitting Carl's description. He was not surprised to learn that Carl had visited nearly every one of those establishments, some more often than others. Just before he crossed the county line, he removed his Sheriff's badge. So far, so good. He was headed in the right direction. If Carl hadn't suddenly changed his mind, and gone off in another direction, he would most likely find him in Morgantown.

But Sheriff Murphy had learned the hard way not to take the habits of criminals for granted. Men like Carl Pike could be unpredictable, and Carl Pike was certainly no fool. By asking the right questions of the right people, Sheriff Murphy quickly learned that this was not the first time Carl Pike had left his wife at home, and made the journey to Morgantown. It turned out he had come this way often, stopping at several saloons, hotels, and brothels, spending large sums of money on liquor, prostitutes, and a few willing wives of other men. In the process, Mr. Pike had made some enemies, and some friends - enemies who would like to see him dead, and friends who would like for him to stay alive, so they could enjoy his money.

This was the mistake Sheriff Murphy had been hoping Carl would make, and he took full advantage of it. At the Lakeview Saloon, a certain Abe Doddery, one of Carl's better friends, upon hearing Sheriff Murphy asking questions about Carl, slipped out the back door, mounted his horse, and galloped off in a hurry toward Morgantown to warn Carl that someone was looking for him. Abe grossly underestimated the wisdom of Clarence Murphy. Sheriff Murphy let him get about a hundred yards in front of him, and simply followed. He would not even have to search for Carl Pike, because Abe Doddery would lead him straight to him.

It was Saturday night, and the Larkspur Ladies Emporium, as it was called, was bristling with patrons, including a few city councilmen, local businessmen, and anyone else who could afford the price of a fine suit, a bottle of champagne, and an hour or two of company with a lady consort. A huge candelabra hung from the ornamented ceiling, shedding brilliant light upon the whole ballroom. A chamber orchestra played Mozart and Beethoven, while well-dressed ladies entertained well-dressed gentlemen at the finely-polished imported mahogany tables. Upstairs were twenty stately rooms, each one elegantly furnished with large paintings, a private bath, a complementary bottle of champagne, and a canopied bed with satin sheets and pillowcases.

Abe Doddery was stopped at the front doors by a matron dressed in a floor-length black silk gown. One look at him, and she quickly assured him he was at the wrong place. She was about to close the door when Abe quickly informed her that he had an important message for one of her patrons, a man who went by the name of Carlos Pickering, which, of course, was the alias which Carl Pike used whenever he visited the Larkspur Ladies Emporium. The matron told him to wait outside while she located Mr. Pickering. Carl was just about to take the arm of his lady consort to go upstairs when the matron whispered in his ear, telling him there was a man outside with an important message for him.

When Carl opened one of the big double doors, he saw Abe Doddery handcuffed to the hitching rail. Sheriff Murphy stuck the barrel of his revolver into Carl's ribs, and nodded silently for him to step outside. Carl obeyed instantly. The two men walked around to the side of the building, with Carl in front of Sheriff Murphy. When

Sheriff Murphy ordered him to stop, he immediately holstered his pistol, and stated his business.

"Mr. Pike, I'll make this short and sweet. I am Clarence Murphy, Sheriff of Preston County. I'm not here to arrest you Carl. All I want is your signature on this divorce paper, and I'll leave you alone, and with any luck at all, you and I will never see each other again."

Carl's face grew blood-red instantly. Clarence could see the rage and hatred in his eyes.

"I know who you are, Murphy. Carl answered.

"Everybody knows the great Clarence Murphy, the Sheriff who always gets his man. I just got one question Murphy, who's the sorry bastard the sorry bitch is sleepin with?"

Before he could blink, Sheriff Murphy's fist sank deep into Carl's gut, doubling him up, knocking the breath out of his lungs. He sank to his knees, gasping for air. Sheriff Murphy grasped his necktie, lifting him to his feet, shoving him up against the wall.

"I'm the sorry bastard Mr. Pike, and we're not sleeping together. And if I ever hear you call her that again, I'll kill you where you stand, do you understand me Carl?"

Holding Carl up against the wall with one hand, Sheriff Murphy handed the divorce paper to him with the other hand. When he was sure that Carl could now stand on his own, he reached into his vest pocket, pulled out a fountain pen he had brought for the occasion, spun Carl around facing the wall, and demanded, "Now sign at the bottom Mr. Pike, and our business will be done here."

In the moment it took for him to sign the divorce paper, Carl Pike realized how Sheriff Murphy had acquired his reputation, he had earned it! Carl knew he was dealing with a man far superior to himself, in character, courage, intelligence and integrity. Carl had pulled his bluff on a lot of men. He had convinced some men, men like Abe Doddery, that he was their superior. But in his entire life, he had never faced an adversary one on one, in a fair fight. In only the last few minutes, he had learned what it meant to be a man. And in spite of the fact that he hated Clarence Murphy, every fiber in his being respected him.

Clarence took the paper from Carl's trembling fingers, looked at the signature, and walked around the corner to where Abe Doddery was handcuffed. He motioned for Carl to come over and join them. Before removing the handcuffs from Abe' hands, he asked Abe, "Mr. Doddery, I have a question for you, and I want you to think about it seriously before you answer."

Abe nodded, answering, "S--ure mister Murphy, I certainly will."

"Take a good look at me Abe, and take a good look at Mr. Pike here, and tell me, for which one of us do you have the most respect?"

Without a moment's hesitation, Abe replied, "Oh, Mr. Murphy, it's you Sir, no doubt at all, I have the most respect for you."

Sheriff Murphy grinned, slowly turning the man around, unlocking the handcuffs.

"Then you won't mind signing this piece of paper for me will you, as a witness?"

Abe didn't even look at the writing on the paper. Sheriff Murphy handed him the fountain pen. Ole Abe signed his name below Carl's signature. Sheriff Murphy looked at the signature, waved the paper up and down a few times, to make sure the ink was dry, folded it, and put it back in his vest pocket. He mounted his horse, tipped his hat to the two men, and just before turning his horse toward the road, he made one final remark to the men.

"It's been a pleasure gentlemen, ya'll have a good night."

Neither of the men spoke until they knew Sheriff Murphy was out of earshot. When it was safe to speak, Abe now looked at Carl with a look of disdain, commenting, "And to think I came all this way to warn you. You ain't nuthin but a yellow-bellied coward Pike. Or is it Pickering? I heard the Sheriff call you Pike. So you've been lying to everybody all along, even about your real name, ain't yuh Pike?"

Carl shot back, "Go to hell Doddery, I got a hot dame waitin on me inside."

Abe managed to find the courage somewhere within himself, and backhanded Carl across his mouth, drawing blood from the corner of his mouth. Carl took out his handkerchief, wiped the blood from his mouth, and turned toward the door, saying nothing, and not looking back. Abe mounted his horse and rode toward home.

When Carl knocked on the big door, the matron answered, took one look at the dirt on his knees, and his crumpled suit, and told him he was no longer welcome there.

Carl Pike straightened his crumpled suit as best he could, dusting the dirt from his knees, answering, "Well that's just fine madam, 'cause this ain't nuthin but a glorified whore house anyway. I can take my business elsewhere, where I can get a little respect."

The matron closed the door in his face, and left him standing there, cursing till he ran out of curse words. He pulled his flask of brandy out of his suit pocket, drank the contents straight down, and stomped away angrily, mumbling to himself, stumbling into the nearest saloon, where he drank himself into a stupor, and was thrown into the street at 2:00 a.m. He was awakened by the pouring rain on Sunday morning. His flask and his wallet were gone. He had no money, no friends, and no place to go.

Carl Pike wandered through the streets and alleys of Morgantown for three weeks, begging for food to eat, living off nothing but the kindness of strangers. He slept in barns and livery stables, stealing whatever he could steal in order to survive. One generous bartender gave him a bottle of whiskey. It would be the last bottle he would ever drink. On the fourth Sunday after he had arrived at the Emporium wearing a $100.00 suit, he was found hanging from a crossbeam inside a barn. He was buried by the County, in the paupers field outside of town. A wooden cross was placed at the head of his grave, with the name Carlos Pickering carved across it. On the vertical part of the cross was carved the date of his death - Sunday, May 26th, 1878.

With Judge Elias W. Bracken having retired, and his son, Elias W. Bracken II being a Law Professor at a local University, Elias W. Bracken II became a good candidate to fill his father's shoes. The day the old Judge retired, the Governor sent a telegram to Elias' son, asking him if he would be interested in the position. And as much as he loved his position at the University, he simply could not refuse the honor of stepping into his father's shoes as Circuit Judge, presiding over three counties.

With the divorce paper in her hand, signed by Carl Pike and Abe Doddery, Lily and Clarence went together to see the new Judge. Looking at the paper and the two signatures, Judge Bracken granted the divorce by signing the document himself. He had known Sheriff Murphy a long time, and asked no questions as to how he had obtained the signatures. He stood, shaking hands with Clarence and Lily, first congratulating Clarence upon his good taste in women, and asking them if they had set a date for their wedding. They had not yet set an official date, but Lily quickly spoke up.

"Yes, your Honor, we have. It's set for Saturday afternoon, June 29th at the Jenkins Memorial Baptist Church, and you and your wife are invited to come."

Clarence beamed with approval. He wanted Lily to become his wife as soon as possible, and June 29th was only two weeks away! Announcements were sent out quickly, some by mail, other's by word of mouth. Everyone who heard of the glorious occasion said there was not a couple more deserving of happiness than these two wonderful people. Once again, another beautiful wedding took place at the Jenkins Memorial Baptist Church. Sheriff Clarence Murphy stood in front of the church beside his best man, Joseph Parks, and the pastor Jeff Townsend. The house was overflowing with folks from all around. Their beaming smiles showed their approval of this event. As Carolyn played softly on the piano the wedding party marched in. Becky had taken her place by Carolyn at the piano ready to sing a beautiful song when the time came. Gloria was the maid of honor, and the first to march down the isle, her beautiful smile like a ray of sunshine. She was followed by her twin sister Greta, sprinkling rose pedals on the floor, as she gracefully marched to the front to stand by her sister. Carolyn Parks began playing the wedding march as Lily appeared in the doorway, walking proudly, being escorted by her handsome son Spike. Sheriff Murphy gasped at the sight of her beauty. The long white gown only slightly enhanced the beauty of the lady wearing it. Her long black hair draped over her shoulders and down her back to her slender waist.

They stopped in front of Jeff as he asked, "Who gives this woman to be married to this man?"

"I do" Spike answered, as he planted a kiss on his mother's rosy cheek.

They joined hands, and stood beaming with joy before Jeff and the congregation as they exchanged sacred vows, and each placed a golden wedding band on the finger of the other. The celebration carried on far into the night. When the last person said good night the happy couple retired to their home which Clarence Murphy had made sure was a perfect place for his beautiful bride.

Becky was determined to find her son Elick, who had left home months ago, and she knew he had made friends with two new boys from town whose last names was Collins. He had also made friends with two others from up on the mountain, Charlie Miller, who was at least eight years older than Elick, and Curt Flemmins, Claudette's younger brother who had a twin named Burt. Had not Burt volunteered for the Army he would most likely have been with the other boys. Elick, Charlie and Curt had met the Collins boys, Jimmy and Gilbert, two days after they had moved into town. The Collins family moved into Bruceton Mills very quietly, hoping no one would notice them. They moved into a run down shack on the outer edge of town, a place not fit for a family to live in. They arrived in an old broken down wagon with a few pieces of furniture and a big brown dog tied to the back with a rusty chain around it's neck. The Collins family was a black family. Their mother had moved them here hoping to have a better life. No one knew where they came from, and no one asked.

Bruceton Mills, in spite of the economic downturn, was booming at this time. Several families, black and white, had moved into the small community for the same purpose, to try to find a better life for themselves. Walter Collins was a lazy, no- good- for- nothing, ne'er-do-well type of man, constantly dodging the law. The only occupation he had ever known was making moonshine. When Becky learned from the stories she had been told that Elick was hanging around with the two Collins boys, she could only imagine the worst. She figured if he was running around with the Collins boys, then maybe she could find out where they were staying.

Early one morning she hitched up the buggy and drove into town and headed toward the Collins place. As she approached the house, both the sight and the stench of the place sickened her. The hole in the roof was as large as a small cave, and was covered with a piece of vinyl table cloth. The windows in front were boarded up with pieces of thin planks covering the broken glass. Becky walked across a small plank through the muddy yard to the steps. The giant brown dog stood at the edge of the porch growling at her, it's long white sharp teeth reminded her of an angry wolf. Only the large rusty chain around it's neck prevented it from coming any further. The door opened when the dog began barking and growling.

"Git back from thar you sorry varmint," a loud angry voice yelled, as a man opened the screen door and approached the dog. With one hard kick in the face he sent the poor animal whimpering against the wall of the porch. Becky wasn't sure if she should speak or run. The man was very dark-skinned, with a half frown and half smirk on his face, as he eyed Becky from head to toe, making her feel very uncomfortable.

Now he glared menacingly at Becky, and in that same loud angry voice growled.

"State yur business woman, ain't got no need fer folks comin 'round here."

"Well s--sir, Becky stammered, I...I was just dropping by to invite you and your family to church." her heart was pounding.

"Huh? church?" the man grunted, still glaring at her, he spit a mouthful of tobacco onto the ground at her feet.

"My name is Becky Townsend, I am the pastors wife." Becky continued, not giving up.

Becky had made her way as far as the rickety steps leading up onto the porch, extending her hand. She was no longer afraid of the wounded dog that glared at her from the back of the porch. She was sure the man would kick it's face in again if it moved. The man stopped her in her tracks!

"I ain't got nary bit uf bizniss in comin to yer meetin house, ain't nary thang thar that I be wantin, now git off'n my place, fore I untie this crazy dog on ye."

"Now shoo! Get back to yo big fancy house an meetin place, 'cause I ain't comin, and you need to git goin." The man waved his hands wildly at Becky.

Becky never moved an inch, even though she was terrified of the man. He took a step toward her. She braced herself for a possible blow from his big dirty hand. About that time a woman walked out the door drying her hands on a pretty white-and-blue apron. In a voice even more authoritative than the man, with both hands on her hips, she reprimanded him,

"Walter Collins! Ya shore ort ta be plum ashamed o yo self, can't ya see ye be talkin at a lady?" She gestured her hand toward Becky. Then, to Becky's great surprise, and great relief, the woman spoke to her in a very sad, apologetic, and soft voice.

"Misses, I be so sorry fur tha way Walter here spoke to ya. Sumtimes he jist ain't right in tha head. Now bring yourself in child."

She held out her hand to Becky to help her up the steps. Glaring at Walter she scolded him.

"Mind yer manners old man, and don't let me be hearin another word from that thar foul mouth o your'n."

Becky grinned as she stepped past Walter. In an instant, the mean old monster had become a shrinking violet. He cowered against the wall like the dog he had kicked, as Becky and her new friend, with a triumphant stride, walked into the house.

The woman who introduced herself as Lucy Collins. Despite the outside condition, the house was clean. It smelled old and musky, but clean nevertheless. Becky could tell that someone (Lucy, no doubt,) had gone to great lengths to make the place livable. The furniture was worn, and showed signs of being moved around, scratched and faded from years of use. In a matter of a few minutes, Becky determined that she had never met a nicer woman in her life. It turned out that Walter was a brother to her late husband Frank, who had died in a logging accident. Lucy had two sons, Jimmy and Gilbert. Lucy was a very beautiful woman, her slim figure giving her the appearance of a young girl. She wore her hair up in braids wrapped around the base of her neck. Becky noticed her dress was faded, and her brown shoes worn till the color had skinned off the toes and heels.

She served up the best cold glass of tea Becky had tasted in a long time. They sat at the little round table, on the only two straight back chairs Lucy owned. The two of them talked as if they had known each other all their lives, sharing stories of their families. Tears filled Lucy's eyes as she told of her husbands accident, and how Walter was sorry and no good, and had led her two sons down the same path that he had gone all his life, stealing, making moonshine, and just anything other than making an honest living with his own two hands. Walter had moved in on them after her husbands death and had, to a great degree, taken over their household. For years now they had to been moving nearly every month, being evicted from every house, all because of the no good, stealing, and bad attitudes of Walter and the boys. White folks had run them out of the last town, warning them not to return. Lucy wiped her eyes again, confiding in Becky how she missed the good clean life they had enjoyed when her husband was alive. Everything had fallen apart since he had died, and Walter had taken over their lives. The boys, Jimmy and Gilbert, were completely out of control, so when she had heard that Bruceton Mills was a fast growing town, with a wonderful church, she prayed that she could get her sons here, and just maybe they could get a job somewhere, and things would be better for them.

Becky described Elick to Lucy, asking her if he had been there to visit. Lucy said she did remember a young man "fittin" that description, along with two other young men coming by the house several times, the last time about a month ago, to pick up Jimmy and Gilbert. She said that Walter had let it slip that they were all headed to the mountains.

"Miss Becky, she whispered softly, as she reached over and touched Becky's hand, I have spent many nights on my knees praying for the boys, and for Walter."

Becky quickly answered, "Well Lucy, now you have one more heart and mouth that will join you in those prayers." Becky liked Lucy right off the bat, they agreed to join together and pray for their sons to return home safely.

"Miss Becky, I am so much obliged for you coming to visit, and I promise you I'll be to church Sunday. Our whole family went to church faithfully when my husband Frank was alive. "But old Walter, well, he just gets plumb ornery and mean with me an the boys if'n I mention God or church."

On the way home Becky's mind drifted back to the last time she had seen Elick. In her memory she could see him the day He marched into the house to collect some clothing, informing her that he was going into Morgantown to look for a job. She remembered pleading with her son to stay home, but he would not hear of it, almost shouting at her.

"Momma I don't want to be here, can't you understand that? I hate this farm and all this religious stuff is more than I can take. Samuel is always with Papa, Ollie is at the school and Erica tries to follow me everywhere I go. I need something different momma, please don't try and stop me, my mind is made up."

Her heart broke all over again, remembering watching her son, a son she loved more than life itself, walk away without a backward glance. She again felt that sickening, sinking feeling that her son was slipping away from the family forever. Ever since that horrible day long ago, when he and Erica had been kidnapped, and he had been forced to watch his father kill a man, he had never been the same. He had succumbed to bitterness, and at least for a while, tried to push all his love for family, and all his godly teaching to the back of his mind. He told himself there was something more, something better, somewhere out there for him, and he was determined to find it, wherever and whatever it was.

Like his father Jeff, Elick was not afraid of anyone or anything, he was no coward. He held no fear of the unknown, and felt he was now ready to venture beyond the confines of home, family, and religion. His young heart was simply pounding with youthful wanderlust, his spirit was restless, and he felt he had to go out there and challenge himself, to conquer his inner curiosity about what lay beyond the fences of the farm. He had often asked his older brother Samuel why God had allowed him and his sister to be kidnapped, why his father had been forced to kill that bad man, even though he knew the man deserved to be punished. He couldn't understand why a good man like his Papa had to shoot someone.

Samuel had tried valiantly to answer all his little brother's questions, but to no avail. With each answer, Elick had invented another question. Now Becky feared for her son's life. She and Jeff spent hours on their knees on his behalf, praying to God. As yet Elick had never accepted Jesus into his heart, and during family devotion time at home he would head for the door, letting it slam behind him. He was angry, but held all his thoughts and emotions inside. Becky prayed and cried for her son every day. She and Jeff searched for him everywhere they went, asking folks if they had seen him, or any of the other boys.

True to her word, Lucy came to church on Sunday. Everyone of both races accepted her as if they had known her all their lives. She had such a sweet spirit about her, and before long, she was singing in church, both in the choir, and as a soloist. Whenever she finished a song, there was not a dry eye in the building. During prayer time, Becky and Lucy would join hands and kneel at the altar, praying together for God to bring their boys home safely. Word began to spread around the county that they were looking for the boys. As the news spread farther, some folks would ride by the farm just to tell Becky and Jeff the boys had been seen in a nearby town. Some began to report that they had items stolen from their barns, smokehouses and chicken houses.

Then one Saturday, word came that five boys fitting their description had been spotted up in the mountains, in the area where the biggest moonshine still in the county had been busted years before. A lone hunter, riding through that area, saw five young men camping there, three white and two black, with an older black man. Jeff was certain it was Walter Collins, Lucy's brother-in-law, and the five young boys.

Jeff, fearing the worst, rode into town to speak with sheriff Murphy. Arriving in town at the sheriff's office Jeff told sheriff Murphy all he knew about the boys and all the rumors he had heard from different ones who passed by the farm.

"Well Bro. Jeff, the sheriff responded, meet me here in the morning around 3:00 a.m., and we'll head up the mountain and take a look see around. If them boys are up there, we will get a chance to sneak up on'em before they get up."

"Sheriff, I've been told there's been a lot of stealing, breaking into people's homes, and even some folks have been hurt. What if my son Elick has been one of those who has been doing these things, what will happen to him.?"

Jeff's eyes were sad, and that tired and weary look was beginning to show on his face.

"Won't be easy on him preacher, will depend on the Judge, but since he is young, and if they prove it is his first offence, then they might go easy on him."

Clarence placed a big calloused hand on Jeff's shoulder, assuring him he would do all in his power to help his son. Jeff thanked him, and headed toward home to tell Becky the plans that he and the sheriff had made.

Meanwhile, high up in the mountains at a camp site, five young men were busy as beavers, making moonshine under the watchful eye and iron fist of Walter Collins. The light from the fire brightened up the area around the still. Elick Townsend looked over his shoulder every few minutes, imagining he heard footsteps in the woods behind them. Elick, Charlie, Curt, Jimmy and Gilbert had been making and running moonshine for Walter Collins for nigh unto six months. They would drive a wagon as far as Morgantown to deliver a load. Walter did the dealing, pocketing the money, while the boys unloaded the goods. On the way back to the mountain camp site to make more moonshine they would steal clothes off clothes lines, chickens and eggs, and meat from smoke houses. Once they stole a nice fat pig and slaughtered it at the camp site.

Elick knew what he was doing was wrong. He also knew that his Mama and Papa would not approve of the way he was living. He also knew they were most likely sick with worry. With each passing day, and each sorrowful night, his heart wrenched with agony, as he missed his twin sister Erica, his big brother Samuel, and his loving Mom and Dad. He knew he was in too deep with this gang, but at the same time, didn't know quite how to free himself from their tight circle. He kept telling himself he was now a man, earning his on way, and could leave any time he set his mind to, but, as he was to learn the hard way, it wasn't quite that simple.

Walter kept promising them he would pay them their wages at the end of the year. With each sale of a load of moonshine, he grudgingly gave them just enough money to keep them working for more. With each small payday, Elick and the others congratulated themselves upon having earned hard money, never considering the unlawful manner in which they had earned it. With a few dollars in his pocket, Elick often lay awake, counting the money in his head, secretly congratulating himself that he had rebelled against everything he had been taught, and was determined to do all in his power against the law, because the way he had it figured, the law had not done anything to stop William Bowen from taking him out of his yard that day, and his Papa had to take the law into his own hands to get him back, even to the point of killing the man.

He asked himself, "Where was the law then, when his family had needed it?"

He had also asked his brother Samuel that question so many times. Samuel had tried to reason with him, but Elick only grew angrier, and more rebellious each time. He told himself, "It didn't happen to Samuel, so what would he know?"

Elick worked hard to finish sealing up the jars of moonshine while Jimmy and Gilbert Collins loaded it into the wagon. Curt Flemmins and Charlie Miller were gathering up firewood for the next batch. They knew Walter would be here at the crack of dawn, and if they were not loaded and ready to go, he would cuss and rave like a madman. His body tired and aching, Elick climbed into his makeshift bed. He lay there, staring up at the dirty canvas above his head, wondering what his family was doing at home, wishing he could be more like them. But some kind of inner force kept pushing him at breakneck speed toward what he knew would, sooner or later, be utter destruction. He wished he could pray like he had heard Samuel and his father do so many times, but his heart somehow felt so empty.

He had met these so-called friends months ago, and it seemed the more they did to hurt others the more they wanted to. That, in itself, was the one thing, more than any other, that tore at his insides. He never meant any harm to anyone else, and it grieved him knowing he and these other young men had brought a lot of pain and suffering to those who did not deserve it. Tears flooded his eyes as he wondered how many little children had gone to bed hungry as a result of his having stolen their chickens, their eggs, or their supply of meat. Elick knew it was wrong, Curt knew it was wrong, and the others just didn't seem to care. Lying there looking at the stars, he suddenly realized he was tired, tired of running and tired of the filthy life into which he had been caught up.

He could see his family gathered around the table with the Bible open, discussing the great and many wonderful things Jesus had done while walking here on earth so long ago. He closed his eyes, with tears flowing freely. Lying there, lost and lonely, Elick began to pray.

"Lord, if you are real, save me from all this mess I am in, forgive me for my sins, for stealing, and for hurting my family. God give me the courage to go back home like the Prodigal Son that I have heard Papa preach about."

Now his tears were no longer the tears of young rebel trying to be a man, but the tears of a broken-hearted child, reaching for the forgiving hand of a loving Heavenly Father. With those tears still streaming down his face, and not caring who saw or heard him, he felt an inner peace he had never felt before. He knew in that moment that Jesus Christ had come into his heart, and had made him a new creature.

Slipping out of his blanket, he gently shook Curt awake, telling Curt he was going home, and that he wanted him to go home too, and to get out of this mess before they were caught and sent to prison. Curt was more than happy to get off that mountain and go home. The boys mounted their horses, and as quietly as possible turned toward the East, heading toward Curt's home, where they would spend the night. Curt's father and mother both had died some years before. Curt was staying in their house, taking care of the place till Burt returned from the army. Elick's plan was to go on down the mountain at daylight. He knew it would do no good to talk to the others, because they had their minds made up to continue this life of crime. He paused for a brief moment, as he whispered a prayer for the friends he was leaving behind.

Jeff met sheriff Murphy at exactly 3:00 a.m. Without a word they turned their horses up the rough trail toward the site where long ago General Horton and his uncle Burley Crawford had set up and run the biggest moonshine still in the State. Jeff's mind again went through the whole ordeal of the time when General Horton and his uncle had ambushed him and some of the men from church while they were on a hunting trip. He remembered his best friend Clark Puckett being gunned down in cold blood, and Rufus Rutherford being shot in the back. He recalled the lightning quick response of Tom Tillotson, who had shot the two assassins in the chest, with three well-placed bullets in each man. Jeff shuddered at the very thought that his son might be mixed up with the wrong people, and something like that was likely to happen to him. He whispered a prayer for his son.

The trail was narrow and rough. The horses hooves slipped on the rocks as they groped in the darkness. The sudden howl of a wolf spooked the horses, nearly throwing the two men off. "Whoa! Here feller, easy now, nothing is gonna hurt you."

Gaining control of the animals they continued up the rough path, only the light of the moon made the trail visible. The men rode in silence so as to not be heard by anyone. After what seemed like hours they spotted the dim light of an open fire, only a small flicker could be seen. They dismounted so they could go in on foot. As they neared the fire they spotted three bodies lying on blankets close by. Sheriff Murphy stepped quickly up to within two feet of the sleeping men, while Jeff quietly skirted around them to the opposite side, glancing at every one of them, trying to spot Elick. Clarence drew his gun from it's holster.

"You! by the fire, get up with your hands in the air and don't anyone move." he commanded. The figures jumped to their feet. One started to run, but stopped at the sound of the sheriff's gun, as he fired it at his feet. Jeff prayed it wasn't Elick.

Jeff recognized Charlie Miller, who lived there on the mountain. He was much older than Elick, and Jeff, knowing that Charlie was trouble just waiting to happen, had tried to keep them apart. Standing there with their hands in the air, the three started pleading for their lives. Sheriff Murphy found the wagon of moonshine loaded and ready to go. He told the boys that things would go much easier on them if they talked now, and told who was at the head of this ring. The boys looked at each other wildly. Jeff noticed two more blankets nearby that appeared to have been slept in. The boys were more than glad to talk. They quickly informed Clarence that Walter Collins was the mastermind of all this, and that they only delivered the shine for him to different places. When asked who the other two blankets belonged to, no one would say a word

"Gonna go hard on you boys if ya don't tell everything ya know. Ya shore ya don't know who slept here last night?"

Sheriff Murphy questioned, giving them an opportunity to confess all. Charlie Miller looked straight at Jeff.

"It was your boy preacher, and one other, Curt Flemming, don't know where they be, musta tuck off when they's hurd yun's riding in."

Charlie was happy to be telling on the other two boys.

Jeff's heart sunk!

The sheriff kicked the fire up with his foot. Then placing more wood on with his left hand, he instructed the young men to sit down on the ground by the fire. Neither of them was eager to try to run again.

"Now who wants to tell me about this Walter Collins, who he is, where he lives, and where I can find him?" sheriff Murphy commanded in a very stern voice.

Jimmy Collins spoke up, "Sir he be my uncle, and we's expecting him by morning light, he be coming to help us with the load of shine here." Jimmy pointed toward the loaded wagon.

"Shut up Jimmy!" Charlie Miller reached over and shoved Jimmy, almost knocking him in the fire. At the same time, Gilbert

Collins leaped up, and with one swift kick to Charlie's mouth caused the blood to spurt out like a stuck hog. Jeff and the sheriff quickly subdued Jimmy and Gilbert before they killed poor Charlie.

"Now, now, we'll have none of that," sheriff Murphy warned, as he gave the bleeding Charlie his handkerchief, then sat down between the two brothers and Charlie. The plan was that Jeff and the sheriff would take the two empty blankets, and pretend to be asleep. When Walter got there, they would surprise him. The boys promised they would not warn Walter, because the sheriff promised he would talk to the judge for them if they would help him capture Walter. Jeff knew these young men had a chance at life if only they would get away from people like Walter Collins.

That morning at the edge of first light Walter came riding in on his freshly stolen horse, cussing and yelling for them to get up.

Sheriff Murphy slowly rolled over in the blanket, pointing his gun at Walter's head.

"Now real easy like Mr. Collins, drop yer rifle and gunbelt, and git down real slow, and put yer hands behind yer head." he ordered.

Walter obeyed the first order, dropping the rifle and pistol. Upon touching the ground, however, he made the most stupid mistake of his life, he took a wild swing at Sheriff Murphy. From that point, Clarence was not gentle with Walter at all. One quick, powerful left uppercut put the big black man on the ground, moaning. The seasoned lawman rolled him around in the dirt a few times with his boot, before telling him that he was under arrest for bootlegging moonshine, stealing, and hurting innocent folks. The boys, watching the sheriff roughing up 'ole Walter, were more than glad to spill their guts. They told Jeff that Elick and Curt must have slipped away in the night, and they really did not know where the two had gone.

"But preacher, Curt lives in a house on the east side of Old Crimson Creek, I bet him and your boy are holed up there." Charlie informed Jeff.

After busting up the still and pouring out the moonshine, keeping only one jug as evidence, they loaded the three boys and Walter onto the back of the wagon, with Walter's hands tied behind his back. Jeff rode down the mountain with the sheriff to the jail house. Walter was placed in one cell, and Charlie Miller in the other.

Charlie was twenty two years old, and the sheriff had no choice but to treat him as an adult.

The Collins brothers were still minors, and were escorted home by Jeff and the sheriff. Lily saw them coming, and came running, nearly missing the plank that lead across the muddy yard. She didn't mind a little mud on her shoes, her son's had come home! They fell into her arms crying like the fourteen and fifteen year olds they were. The sheriff explained to her that the boys would have to testify against their uncle and Charlie Miller, and that they would have to own up to all the meanness they had done in the last six months. They promised their mother they would gladly take their punishment if they could only come home. Lily smiled from ear to ear. This was the answer to her prayers, and her new chance to become the mother she had longed to be ever since Frank had died. She told the boys they would have to get jobs, get back to their book learning, and that uncle Walter was not welcome there anymore.

Sheriff Murphy assured her that Walter would be gone for a long time after the judge got finished with him. The boys shook hands with Jeff, saying they hoped he found Elick soon.

"Mr. Townsend, Jimmy offered, in spite o all we done, we knowed all the while your boy was a fine young man at heart. He jest wound up in the wrong place at the wrong time, and got in deeper than he really wanted to. We really came to like Elick, an not fer him stoppin us Mr. Townsend, we'd most likely done more harm than we did."

Jeff thanked them for their kind words, then, as he and the sheriff parted company, Jeff headed toward Old Crimson Creek with a heavy but hopeful heart.

Jeff had learned a lot from Sheriff Murphy by just observing the way the sheriff paid close attention to every detail of every situation. Things which most folks would lightly pass over, or miss altogether, Clarence Murphy noticed, and took notes on. He never forgot a single word a suspected criminal said to him, and he could describe every criminal he had ever arrested, including what they had been wearing at the time. This trait, of course, had earned him quite a reputation as a lawman. Most criminals, or would-be criminals who heard his name feared him, knowing there was only one sure way to get by sheriff Murphy, and that was to kill him. But, as so many had learned the hard way, killing sheriff Murphy was not an easy thing to do.

As Jeff rode toward Old Crimson Creek, he remembered that one of the boys had told him that Elick and Curt may have gone to Curt's house. He stopped at the foot of the mountain, pondering slowly the whole scene he had just left behind. He began to recount every detail of what he had seen and heard while at the campsite. If Elick and Curt had ridden their horses down the mountain that night, their tracks should still be fairly fresh, fresh enough for him to find and follow. He smiled as he thought of how easily and forcefully Sheriff Murphy had taken command of the whole situation. In a few short minutes, he had earned the trust and respect of the three boys, simply by being the man he was, and doing what knew was right. But in the same way Sheriff Murphy had disciplined himself to follow his instincts, while upholding the law, he, Jeff Townsend, had learned to follow the leadership of the Holy Spirit, and to obey that spiritual voice that often spoke to his heart. Bowing his head, he asked God for guidance in finding his son Elick. When he said Amen, he looked out in front of his horse, and there in the short grass, just a few feet off the trail, were hoof prints! Two horses, headed in different directions, one toward Old Crimson Creek, the other toward Bruceton Mills. In a single moment, he knew without any doubt that God had heard and answered his prayer. The two boys had split up right here, with Curt going to his home, and Elick headed toward his home. His heart leaped with pure joy, as he spurred his horse into full speed, his coat tail flapping in the wind.

Becky had a hard time falling asleep after Jeff left to meet sheriff Murphy. She lay there praying to God to let Jeff find Elick and bring him home. She had worried herself sick over her son for month's now. She could not imagine where he might be, but she had nightmares of him getting killed by some drunken man. Her mind wandered back to the day Elick had been kidnapped, and the look on his little face when his father had carried him back to the house. She wished she could somehow wipe that part of his, and her life away. Still praying, she drifted off to and uneasy sleep.

Becky was suddenly awakened by the barking of the dog Cricket. He sounded excited, like he knew the person or persons he was seeing. Becky hurriedly sat up on the side of the bed, slipping her feet into her shoes, throwing her robe around her shoulders. She walked quickly through the dark house, with only the moon light shining through the windows guiding her way. She didn't want to draw attention to herself by using a lamp. Cricket had stopped barking now, as Becky heard the voice of a young man talking softly to the dog. She was unable to recognize the voice at first, but when she looked out the window from the front room there was no doubt in her mind who the young man was frolicking in the yard with the little dog. Becky fumbled at the door latch, as her heart leaped into her throat. It was Elick. Her son was home!

"Elick!" She screamed with tears of joy in her voice.

She ran down the steps with her arms open. Elick fell on her shoulder with tears streaming down his face. They were both laughing and crying, with Elick stammering to Becky how sorry he was for leaving home and begging her to forgive him. Becky held him tighter than she had that day years ago, when Jeff had handed him to her after the kidnapping. She held him at arm's length, looking into his eyes.

"Oh, my sweet, sweet boy, there is nothing to forgive. You were forgiven the day you left us son, and no matter what you may have done, you are our son, and we love you just as much as we ever have. I just thank God you are home, and unharmed."

They sat at the table for hours, talking. Elick told his mother all that he had been doing, and that he had asked God to forgive him. He told her of the peace he had found that night. Becky shouted out loud when he told her he had asked Jesus into his heart.

"And that's not all Mama, I prayed with Curt, and he too has given his life to the Lord. I couldn't stay away another minute Mama, I left Curt at his folks home, and headed on down the mountain."

Becky told Elick about Jeff and sheriff Murphy going up to the campsite, and that they were probably there now. She and Elick bowed their heads, praying that no harm would come to Jeff, Sheriff Murphy, or any of the other boys. They even included Walter Collins in the prayer, asking God to change his heart. After prayer, Elick took Becky's hand again.

"Mama, I know there will be consequences for the bad things I've done, and I'm ready to face whatever those consequences may be. I'm going to see Sheriff Murphy in the morning, and tell him everything." Elick confessed.

For right now, Becky and Elick were just enjoying each other's company. Then the other children came into the kitchen, half-asleep. Upon seeing Elick, Erica screamed with delight, throwing her arms around him, kissing his cheeks, then swatting him on his behind.

"Brother, I oughta wear you out, but since you're home, and alright, I guess I'll spare ya this time."

Elick smiled, hugged her tightly, and thanked everyone for praying for him." Now they were all gathered around the big table, laughing and talking. Such was the scene that greeted Jeff as he walked into the room. As the eyes of a father and son met, no words were needed, their tears of joy said everything, as Elick ran toward Jeff, who stood with his arms outstretched. All was forgiven, the lost son was home.

December 25th, 1888. The Townsend farm.

New inventions and new technology were sweeping the nation by the year 1888. The use of electricity in major cities had now become widespread, with turbine engines powering electric grids. Cameras now contained roll film. Many carriages and buggy's now used pneumatic tires, replacing the old steel-rimmed wheels. The Michelin Tire Company was incorporated in May of 1888. It was also a leap year, and an election year, with Benjamin Harrison (Republican,) winning the election by receiving the majority of the electoral college vote, over the incumbent Grover Cleveland (Democrat,) who won the majority of the popular vote. It was also the year of the midnight massacre, which took place on New Year's night, involving the famous Hatfield vs. McCoy feud. But modern technology had not yet made its way into the deep hollows, valleys and mountaintops of West Virginia. Most folks still used coal oil lamps, candles and lanterns for lighting, hardly anyone had indoor plumbing, and no one except the affluent had pneumatic tires on their wagons or buggies.

Sitting at the table with all the family around them, celebrating another Christmas dinner together, Jeff and Becky were both lost in their own thoughts and emotions. This year was made extra special since Rufus and Claudette Rutherford, who were now considered family also, had joined them for Christmas dinner. As they glanced around the table from one child to the other, remembering each one's birthday, and the most memorable events in their lives, they glanced at each other, each trying to decipher the other's thoughts. They had grown to know and understand each other so well over the years, they could almost repeat what the other was thinking, just from the expression on his or her face.

Becky's mind was immersed in memories of the beautiful wedding of her son, two years earlier. She glanced from Samuel to Becky Sarah sitting beside him, holding his hand, as she recalled the grueling ordeal of Becky Sarah's birth, twenty years ago. Jeff was smiling, remembering Samuel announcing his calling to the ministry, and his ordination four years ago, at age seventeen. Becky Sarah was beaming with pure joy, waiting for the right moment to make the announcement that she was pregnant with their first child. Samuel's heart was pounding with anticipation, waiting to see the reaction on the faces of his parents, his in-laws and siblings when the announcement was made.

Ollie Marie and Erica were up and about the kitchen, bringing in large platters of sliced ham, turkey, biscuits, and mashed potatoes. They insisted that Becky sit still, while they did all the serving this year. Elick put more wood into the fireplace, glancing back into the big kitchen, watching and listening to his family laugh and swap precious memories. His heart was so touched by the scene he had to remain by the fireplace for a while to keep the tears from accumulating in his eyes. He realized he had such a loving and gracious family, a family who loved him unconditionally, in spite of the fact that he had gone astray for a while, and had done some foolish things. Not one of his family ever brought up his past to him. It was as if none of it had ever happened.

When all the food was finally on the table, and everyone had been seated, Elick was a little bit surprised when Jeff asked him to give thanks, something that Jeff usually reserved for himself at Christmas time.

Becky Sarah figured this was the most opportune moment to make the announcement. Just before Elick bowed his head, she cleared her throat, glanced around the table, and inserted.

"If I may, I'd like to make an announcement just before we pray."

Everyone smiled, nodding their approval, as Becky Sarah looked into Samuel's eyes.

"Papa, Momma, Jeff, Becky, family, I am proud to announce that I am with child, Sam and I are going to have a baby. You four are going to be grandparents.!"

Everyone suddenly forgot about all the food in front of them. Jeff, Becky, Rufus and Claudette were so excited they all jumped up at the same time, throwing their arms around Samuel and Becky Sarah, as tears of joy appeared instantly. Then it was time for everyone else to take their turn at hugging the two. The excitement and joy of the moment far surpassed the fact that the food was getting cold by the moment. After everyone had hugged the two, and congratulated them, Becky wiped her eyes with her apron, nodding to Elick to go ahead with the prayer of thanksgiving.

His voice trembled slightly as he bowed his head and began to thank the good Lord for the many blessings He had bestowed upon the Townsend household. As Elick prayed, Erica's mind drifted back to that awful day when she and Elick had been kidnapped by William Bowen. She subconsciously reached up and touched her own cheek, where that mean man Bowen had slapped her so hard. She remembered the look of rage on her father's face when he had seen the mark of William Bowen's hand on her cheek, and how he had taken her into his arms, and held her so tenderly. She, like everyone else at the table, had so much for which to be thankful. Dr. Parks had taken her under his tutelage as a nursing student on her sixteenth birthday, and in one more year, she would be ready to take her State Nursing Exams.

Becky, with her head bowed, holding Jeff's hand, recalled Jeff's words that day long ago, as he strapped on that gun belt, promising, **"I'll be back, with our son."** She re-lived the sheer terror of hearing the three gun shots, and then the pure joy and relief of seeing Jeff coming back with Elick in his arms. She had never once questioned Jeff about the horrific details of that encounter with William Bowen, and Jeff was glad she hadn't.

Ollie Marie Townsend, now nineteen, was a quiet, somewhat shy and reserved young lady. She inherited her mother's good looks, and her father's personality. She listened intently to every word that was spoken, and always gave everyone the benefit of a doubt. But she also had a keen sense of discernment. Like her father Jeff, she always looked people straight in the eye when they were talking to her, and seemed to know when someone was trying to deceive her to any degree. This sense of discernment, of course, was a great asset to Ollie Marie, who had now become the new school teacher at Bruceton Mills Elementary School. Sitting here with her beloved family, her own heart throbbed with thanksgiving for so many precious gifts and sweet memories.

As Elick continued to pray, Jeff's thoughts flashed back to two separate occasions in which he had stood by the Flemmins family, as Dr. Parks had amputated the legs of Foster Flemmins, who later died from the effects of diabetes. And thinking of Foster's death, he was reminded of Foster's beloved wife Cleo, who, upon the death of her husband of fifty-eight years, simply grieved herself to death only one month after his passing. He thought of Homer Rutherford, Becky Sarah's great uncle, who had sailed to Africa, where he spent the rest of his life as a missionary to the Zulu tribes.

Samuel and Becky Sarah, of course, were busy with their own sweet memories, remembering how they had chased each other all over the playground in elementary school, and Samuel standing up to any and every other boy who tried to steal his girlfriend. Samuel was re-living their first kiss, underneath the old silver maple tree that stood just to the south of the pond-the same tree to which Tom Tillotson had tied his horse the day he had sneaked up the valley with plans to rape Becky.

Rufus and Claudette were holding hands, silently giving thanks for a beautiful daughter, a handsome son-in-law, a soon-coming grandchild, and for the love and self-sacrifice of Clark Puckett, who had died with his arm around Rufus' neck. They thanked God for Tom Tillotson, who ran eight miles to get Dr. Parks. They thanked God for Dr. Parks, who, along with Tom, had run the eight miles back into the woods to cut the bullet from Rufus' back. They thanked God for Pastor Jeff, who had helped Dr. Parks carry Rufus the eight miles to the clinic, where he and his wife Carolyn had cared for Rufus for several weeks. They thanked God for each other, for life itself, and for every blessing they had enjoyed as husband and wife for twenty-one years.

Samuel Jeffery Townsend was now twenty-one, and what a fine young man he had grown up to be! Ollie Marie was nineteen, and the twins, Erica and Elick, were seventeen. Jeff and Becky were now forty-five. And if it is true that the apple never falls too far from the tree, that saying found its fulfillment in Samuel. His parents, Jeff and Becky, still called him Samuel, as they had done since the day he was born. Most of his friends just called him Sam. And if ever there was a son who wanted to be like his father, it was Samuel. He admired and respected his father more than any other man on earth. By his fifteenth birthday he, like his father before him, had memorized four books of the Bible - Romans, Hebrews, Galatians and Ephesians, and was working on several others. He had determined that he would someday memorize at least twelve books of the Bible, one for each of the twelve Apostles, and on his 21st birthday, he had accomplished it. He could now quote Romans, Hebrews, Galatians, Ephesians, Philippians, Colossians, First and Second Thessalonians, James, The Gospel of John, Jude, and Philemon, word for word.

This, in itself, was an amazing feat, considering the fact that Samuel had also worked side by side with Jeff on the farm since he was big enough to pull a crosscut saw, and had finished high school at age seventeen. He was the same height as Jeff - six feet four inches tall, and had the same dark hair and blue eyes. He walked like his father, and he talked like his father. In other words, he was the spittin image of his father, Jeff Townsend, both in appearance, character and personality. Often, when they rode in the wagon or buggy together, dressed alike, sitting side by side, from a distance it was difficult to tell the two apart. Jeff and Becky, of course, were both mighty proud of Samuel. If no one else listened to every word Jeff preached, Samuel did. From the day he had accepted Christ as his Savior at the age of nine, down in Cleveland Tennessee, he had never missed a single sermon Jeff had preached. His soul was stirred each time the invitation was given, and folks came forward, as he had done long ago. He went out with his father on many trips, to revivals and camp meetings. But there was one place in particular Samuel loved to visit more than any other - the mountains, where Rufus, Claudette and their daughter, Becky Sarah lived.

Jeff made it a point to visit every member of his congregation whenever any one of them was sick, hurt, or had a death in the family. And every time Jeff mentioned going to the mountain, Samuel immediately volunteered to go with him. Samuel and Becky Sarah had been childhood sweethearts ever since elementary school, and Samuel had never had eyes for any other girl except Becky Sarah.

In high school and college, Becky Sarah often had to tell all the other young ladies to back off, because all of them had eyes for the tall-dark-and-handsome Sam Townsend, and they all let him know it, in their own way. And the same was true for Sam Townsend with regard to Becky Sarah. Every red-blooded young man with normal vision couldn't help but notice the beautiful face and lovely figure of the gorgeous, blonde-haired, blue-eyed Becky Sarah Rutherford. But once they all witnessed big Sam Townsend picking a fellow much bigger than himself off the ground by his shirt collar for flirting with Becky Sarah, everyone knew she was Sam's girl, and they left her alone.

It seemed everyone at the table could sense somewhat of the thoughts of all the others. Each person, while reminiscing over his or her own fond memories, could also relate to some, if not all, of the past experiences of the others seated around that table. It was a gathering of individuals, united by so many common threads, love being the strongest of them all, which made them into a unit - a unit called family. The bonds that held the Townsend family together were forged by love, time, experience, and an unshakeable faith in God and His Holy Word. Each person at the table could recall one or more crisis or tragedy through which he or she had come, and, looking back on it, could see the hand of God in his or her survival in and through that crisis or tragedy. They had all learned that God does not keep us from trouble, but He keeps us in the trouble, and goes through it with us, helping us to bear it.

And yet another common thread that ran through the Townsend family was their willingness to listen to what the others had to say. Each family member could remember something each of the other family members had said to them over the years, some precious, unforgettable statement that endeared that family member to them in a special way. As Elick was about to close his prayer of thanksgiving, Erica suddenly remembered his last words to her that day William Bowen had kidnapped Elick, and carried him into the woods. Just as William had clasped his hand over Elick's mouth, she had heard his muffled cry, **"I love you Sissy."** She recalled seeing the tears in Elick's eyes, and the expression on his face that day, an expression that said far more than words could have said. It was a look of both desperation and fear, and yet with a glimmer of hope. And even though the situation at the time seemed hopeless, both she and Elick had somehow known they would, someday, somehow, be re-united. And now, looking back on it, they were both thankful to God that He had arranged that reunion, even though it had cost William Bowen his life.

It seemed as if each word Elick said in his prayer of thanksgiving sparked another memory in the mind of someone at the table. Then, as Elick began to close his prayer, each heart throbbed with gratitude, a tear trickling from every eye, as Elick finished with his prayer.

"And Father, in addition to being so grateful for all the material blessings You have given us, I think I can speak for everyone at this table in saying, we thank you most of all for saving our souls, and for each other. Thank you Lord, for the best Christmas I have ever had, and for the greatest family any man could wish for. In Jesus name, Amen."

The winters in the mountains of West Virginia were often very harsh, and the winter of 1888 was no exception. On several Sundays during the winter months, no one could make it to the church, simply because the roads were impassable by any means. It was not uncommon to wake up with two or three feet of snow upon the ground. But life did not stand still for anyone in the area. The cattle and chickens still had to be fed, the cows had to be milked, the firewood had to be carried in, and paths had to be shoveled to each out-building, the barn, the outhouse, the smokehouse, and the woodshed.

Most of this work was now done by Jeff and Elick, since Samuel and Becky Sarah had moved into the cabin that used to belong to Tom and Pearly Mae Tillotson. Both Jeff and Samuel had now accumulated large herds of cattle, including cows, bulls, horses, and hogs. Samuel's own herds kept him and Becky Sarah pretty busy just keeping all the animals fed. Whenever possible, Jeff and Elick made the ride across the open field to Samuel's place, and helped him out with the more difficult work of sawing and splitting firewood, birthing a calf, or butchering a hog, while Becky Sarah did the lighter chores, like milking the cows and feeding the chickens.

So much like his Dad, Samuel took as much of the work as he possibly could off his beloved Becky Sarah, not wanting her to over-exert herself in her delicate condition. But Becky Sarah, like the lady after whom she was named, insisted that she not be coddled, and was determined to do her share of the work, in spite of her delicate condition. The two of them finally reached a compromise, with Becky Sarah doing the milking, and Samuel carrying the heavy pails of milk to the house.

As they lay in bed each night, after a hard day's work, and counting their blessings, each of them fell silent for a while, lost in their own hopes and dreams for their family, before drifting off to sleep. Little did they know their thoughts were virtually identical. Each of them wondered if their first child would be a boy or a girl. Each of them secretly hoped for a son, but would be just as happy if it were a daughter. Becky Sarah, like her mother-in-law Becky, longed for a son to mold into the image of her husband. Samuel wanted a son, but smiled as he contemplated the possibility of a little girl with the same good looks, character, and personality of Becky Sarah.

Samuel never fell asleep without talking to God about his family, his ministry, and his life, asking for wisdom, courage and strength, and thanking God for every blessing. His thoughts often drifted back to his boyhood days, watching his Mother and father work hard every day on the big farm, and then preparing hot meals for the children. He thought about how tired and weary they often looked at the end of a hard week, and yet going to church twice every Sunday, singing and smiling as if they weren't tired at all. He remembered his father Jeff preaching many a sermon so fervently his clothes would be wringing wet with sweat, and then ride for miles to kneel by the bedside of a sick friend, and pray for them, and even sit the whole night with them if he felt he was needed. Before falling asleep, Samuel always reminded himself of the commandment, Honor thy father and thy mother, that thy days may be long upon the earth. He determined that he would always honor his parents, not only in words, but in deeds, and in character. He silently vowed that if God did grant him a son, he would do his best to raise that son as he had been raised, in the fear of God, and in the light of the Holy Scriptures.

July 1st, 1889. The Townsend farm.

Samuel rode hard and fast toward Jeff's house, slapping his horse's flanks with his hat.

"Papa, Mama, it's time, it's time, the baby is coming! I'm gonna be a father today!"

He yelled as he reined his horse in quickly, stopping just long enough to grab Becky's arm and swing her up onto the horse behind him. The trip that usually took about thirty minutes now only took about ten minutes.

Jeff ran to the corral, opened the gate, leaped astride his new horse Razor, and headed toward Dr. Parks' house in Bruceton Mills. Dr. Parks heard Jeff yelling before he rode into the yard. He grabbed his medical bag from Carolyn's hand, knowing it was time for Becky Sarah's baby, without Jeff saying a word. He leaped up behind Jeff, waved quickly to Carolyn, and they were off toward Samuel's house, full speed.

Dr. Parks jumped off the horse before he stopped, outrunning Jeff into the house, with Jeff one step behind him. Becky had already examined Becky Sarah, and informed Dr. Parks the baby would be here any minute now. She was holding Becky Sarah's hand, telling her to push and breathe, push and breathe. Dr. Parks put his stethoscope to her chest, then to her stomach, smiling, telling everyone that all seemed to be alright so far. Jeff and Samuel quickly stepped out of the room, bowing their heads in prayer in the living room. As they looked into each other's faces, no words needed to be spoken. Their hearts pounded wildly, anticipating another new life about to come into the world, another Townsend baby, a child for Samuel and Becky Sarah, a grandchild for Jeff and Becky.

The minutes seemed like hours to Jeff and Samuel, as they both paced in front of the fireplace, their hands in their pockets, their faces turned upward, then downward, as Becky Sarah screamed in pain. Then there was silence, a silence that seemed like an eternity. And then they heard a cry - the cry of a newborn baby. Father and son embraced each other tightly, with tears of joy streaming down their faces. They each lifted their right hands toward Heaven at the same time, thanking God for another miracle, and another blessing upon the Townsend household.

Dr. Parks cut the umbilical cord, gently handing the eight-pound boy to Becky, who immediately began to wash him in warm water, kissing his cheeks, while Dr. Parks tended to Becky Sarah. Samuel and Jeff stood in front of the fireplace, every muscle taut, waiting for someone to tell them to come into the bedroom. Dr. Parks walked into the living room with a big smile on his face, motioning for them to come in. Jeff reached out his hand, motioning for Samuel to go in first. Becky had now handed the baby boy to his mother, who held him in her arms as only a mother can, staring at his cherub face, counting his fingers and toes, and kissing him ever so tenderly. In the same breath, Becky Sarah and Becky announced softly to Samuel and Jeff.

"It's a boy!"

The two of them stood in awe for a moment, unable to say a word because of the big lump in their throats. Samuel sat down on the bed beside Becky Sarah, stroking her hair and kissing her forehead, then staring into the face of their firstborn son. His heart swelled with both pride and thanksgiving. Jeff and Becky stood speechless for a few moments, holding each other, and staring at the wonder of a new life, a life that was an extension of their own lives. Samuel took the baby gently from Becky Sarah's arms, held him in his own arms for a few moments, and stood up, walking slowly and carefully around the bed to where Jeff and Becky were standing. Knowing that Becky had already held the Baby, he held him out to Jeff's open arms.

"Papa, meet your new grandson."

As Jeff took the little boy into his arms, his heart pounded with purest joy. He held him as if he were a doll made of china, afraid he would break. Dr. Parks stood at the foot of the bed, silently thanking God for a healthy child and mother. He glanced from one beaming face to another, taking in the pure joy of the moment. It was another one of those precious and happy moments that would go into his memoirs years later.

Becky Sarah was the first to break the joyful silence.

"Samuel dear, have you thought about a name for our big beautiful boy?"

As Jeff handed the baby back to Becky Sarah, Samuel smiled, glancing around the room, as if to ask.

"Are you asking me to name him?"

Becky Sarah smiled back, answering his un-asked question.

"Yes Samuel, I want you to name him."

Samuel looked around the room again, from Jeff to Dr. Parks, and back to Jeff again.

"How does Jeffrey Joseph Townsend sound?"

Without a moments hesitation, everyone in the room responded with a loud, "Amen." Then, with the baby in his mother's arms, all the others joined hands in a circle of prayer, giving thanks to the good Lord for this precious gift.

After examining the baby and mother one more time, Dr. Parks assured everyone they were both fine. Just before he and Jeff left for Bruceton Mills, Dr. Parks remarked to Samuel and Becky Sarah.

"I am deeply honored that you would add my name to the name of you firstborn son. It is an honor I have never known before in my entire career, and I will cherish it all the days of my life."

Before he got all choked up, he quickly added, "But you all know now that everybody is gonna call your son J. J. don't you?"

Everyone in the room laughed as Becky Sarah added, "We don't mind at all Dr. Parks, because all of us know the two good and godly men after whom our son is named."

Dr. Parks was now so choked up he couldn't respond, but just nodded his head as he and Jeff left the house. As they rode toward Bruceton Mills, Dr. Parks silently thanked God that he, a black country doctor, had been honored in having the son of a white Baptist preacher, and the grandson of a white Baptist preacher named after himself. It made him proud to be called the friend of men like Jeff and Samuel Townsend. Jeff and Dr. Parks stopped at Jeff's house just long enough to tell Elick and the others about the new baby, and to have Elick ride up to the mountain to inform Rufus and Claudette that they had a big healthy grandson.

Like his father before him, Samuel Townsend was, first and foremost, a God-fearing man. His father and Mother, Jeff and Becky, led by example, and instilled in all their children a set of Christian principles by which they hoped and prayed their children would always abide. But being a Christian, and practicing those Scriptural principles as best a parent can, is not an ironclad guarantee that the children will always abide by those same principles. But both Jeff and Becky simply claimed the promise of the Lord, as written in the Scriptures, Train up a child in the way he should go: and when he is old, he will not depart from it (Proverbs 22:6).

The Townsend children were by no means perfect. They were sometimes disobedient, sometimes rebellious, sometimes stubborn, and got into trouble from time to time just like every other child. But the older they grew, the more mature they became. They had all been exposed to an environment in which certain priorities were established, and wherein love for, and loyalty to God, family and friends were strictly observed on a daily basis. When they were very young, Jeff and Becky made their decisions for them. But as they slowly matured, and began to develop their own personalities and character, they then began to make decisions and choices on their own. But one thing that always made Jeff and Becky so proud of their children was the fact that, even after they were grown, they would often still come to their parents for advice and counsel when confronted with decisions and choices of which they were not certain. And no matter what situation or challenge they ever faced, there was always one thing of which the Townsend children could be certain, and that was the fact that they were loved by both father and mother, and would always receive the very best advice their parents were capable of giving.

Sam Townsend was now a father, and an ordained Baptist minister. He made the decision to establish a certain order of principles in his own life. God came first, his family second, and his ministry third. Everything else would be relegated to its proper place in accordance with the teaching of the Holy Bible, and with the guidance of the Holy Spirit. His God, his family, and his ministry, in that order, were things for which he was willing to die at any moment.

Sam and Becky Sarah enjoyed a relationship that was just as close, and as intimate as a marriage could possibly be. They were always totally honest with each other, keeping back no secrets from each other. Both of them had seen in their own parents a tenderness and caring for each other that transcended most other marriages. Like their parents before them, they loved each other with a love that forbade any outside influence from affecting their relationship.

They had eyes for one another, and for no one else. Their hearts throbbed each time they looked into each other's eyes, each time they touched the other's hand, and each time their lips met. Becky Sarah was never far from Samuel's thoughts, and Samuel was never far from Becky Sarah's. They were both physically and emotionally drawn to each other, and they never let an opportunity to say "I love you," pass them by.

Life expectancy in the 1800's in America was about 40-45 for women, and about 50 for men. By 1889, those numbers had only increased by about 2 years. Jeff and Becky were now 46 years old. Some factors, of course, that contributed to those numbers were the geographical location in which folks lived, and the conditions under which they lived. Living conditions in the mountains of West Virginia in the 1800's, to be conservative, were harsh at best. In many families, every single day was a fight for survival, a struggle against nature, disease, and the economic conditions under which they lived and worked.

For many, the economic conditions under which they lived and worked were created by folks other than themselves. The vast resources of coal, oil, natural gas and timber in West Virginia sparked the interest of wealthy and powerful magnates outside West Virginia, resulting in the sale of millions of acres of land for a fraction of it's real worth. These resources, all of them, of course, had to be extracted from the earth, and shipped to their final destination, which created the necessity for better roads, and especially railroads. The expansion of railroads and the merging of railroad companies, alongside the demand for the high-quality coal from West Virginia and other states also sparked a colossal boom in immigration - workers looking for a better life for their families.

This expansion also sparked an unprecedented population surge. In the late 1800's, in McDowell County alone, the population increased by 600 percent.

With huge tracts of land being sold off to the railroad companies and mining entrepreneurs, much farming land suddenly vanished. Many farms now became industrially oriented rather that subsistence oriented. But those smaller farms located off the beaten path, out of range, or out of reach, of the profit-minded industrialists, remained what they had always been - a means of day to day existence for the folks who owned them. Both Jeff and Samuel were offered $50,000 each for their farms by an agent for the booming railroad industry. Both Jeff and Samuel turned down the offers. They were determined to leave the land to their children and grandchildren, unspoiled by modern machines.

Keeping the farms running on a daily basis took its toll on both body and spirit from every family member, and no one worked harder than Jeff and Samuel Townsend. And no one within a fifty-mile radius of Bruceton Mills had a more beautiful and well-managed farm than the Townsend farms. At age forty-six, Jeff still put in twelve to fourteen hours a day, every day except Sunday, working, keeping his land looking pristine and lovely. This, along with tending to 150 head of cattle, and being the Pastor of a thriving church, began to take its toll on his body. Samuel began to notice the subtle, but visible changes in Jeff's physical appearance.

July 3rd, 1889. Barbourville, Kentucky.

Mary McAllister-Tillotson had now lived twice as long as the average life expectancy for women, she was 82 years old. Her husband Avery, was now 83. Tom and Pearly Mae were now 61, and their son, Thomas Clark, would be 19 in four more months, on Thanksgiving Day. Avery Tillotson was not only a retired Army Officer, he was also a very astute businessman and entrepreneur. He had anticipated the rapid expansion of the railroad, coal, gas and timber industries, and had invested heavily in each of them. As a result of his wise investments, he and Mary had lived quite comfortably ever since his retirement from the Army. They had now moved into one of the finest homes in the county. The little two bedroom house Avery had bought when he first retired was now a rental property, and the one-acre farm had now expanded into a five-hundred acre spread. But now they were very old, and both were looking their ages. Avery had long since put all his affairs in order, making sure that if Mary outlived him, she would be well taken care of financially.

Mary had been a loving and faithful wife to Avery, and they had lived happily for nearly sixty-two years. And since they had been re-united with their son Tom, and now had a beautiful daughter-in-law and handsome grandson, they looked back upon their lives as having been blessed beyond measure. Ever since the day they had recognized Tom at the church, they had attended the church on a regular basis. There was only one thing more that Mary wanted in life, but she had never mentioned it to Avery until a few days ago. She wanted to go to Barbourville Kentucky, and find the graves of her parents. She remembered Captain Daniel Smith telling her that her parents were buried in Barbourville. Avery immediately ordered a farm hand to ride to the train station, and buy them a round trip ticket. They left Cleveland Tennessee at 8:00 a.m., and arrived at the Barbourville depot at 10:45 a.m. on the morning of July 3rd.

Harvey and Rachel Fowler-McAllister had now been happily married for fifteen years. Rachel had retired from teaching, Harvey had retired from the Postal Service. They had both also invested their money wisely, and had lived quite comfortably. Having been born in Barbourville Kentucky, Harvey also had a longstanding desire to return, not only for the big Fourth of July celebration, but also to visit the graves of his parents and grandparents. Rachel was ready and willing to do some traveling, and to see as much of the country as she could see from the window of a passenger train. They left the Albright train depot at midnight, arriving at the Barbourville depot at 11:00 a.m., fifteen minutes behind Avery and Mary Tillotson.

The Barbourville Cemetery was approximately a half mile from the train depot. By the time Avery and Mary had hired a carriage to drive them to the cemetery, Harvey and Rachel were only minutes behind them. Mary had no idea where in the cemetery her parents might be buried, so she and Avery simply walked up and down the rows of graves until they spotted a tombstone engraved with the names Elizabeth M. McAllister, born May 10th, 1780, died April 6th, 1810. The name beside Elizabeth's name was, Whitley McAllister, born April 26th, 1780, died April 6th, 1810. Right beside the tombstone of Elizabeth and Whitley McAllister was another tombstone, engraved with the names Susan McAllister, born October 8th, 1807, died November 10th, 1887. Beside her name was the name of her husband, Michael McAllister, born April 3rd, 1805, died June 6th, 1885.

As Mary and Avery slowly drew closer, Harvey was telling Rachel the story about how his grandparents had died back in 1810. Mary listened intently as the story unfolded.

"My father here, Michael McAllister, was only five years old at the time. "He had gotten up before everyone else that morning, and had gone out to the outhouse about fifty yards from the cabin. When he returned to the cabin, the front door was open, and there on the floor lay the dead bodies of my grandparents, Whitley and Elizabeth, who are buried right here next to Mom and Dad. "When I was ten, my father told me the story about how the Indians came and murdered my grandparents, and kidnapped my Aunt Mary. I haven't heard of her since that day.

Harvey continued, "A neighbor found my father sitting between Grandpa and Grandma, crying his heart out. That neighbor took my father, and he and his wife raised him as their own son, but never adopted him. Their last name was Jones, but they let my father keep his last name, McAllister."

Mary nearly fainted. She trembled and wept upon hearing Harvey's words. Avery quickly tired to catch her before she sank to the ground, but wasn't strong enough to hold her up. Harvey responded quickly, catching her just before her head would have hit the tombstone. Rachel began to fan Mary with her paper fan. As Mary slowly recovered from the shock, Harvey and Rachel asked Avery if she was going to be alright, and were about to leave when Mary reached out her hand, begging Harvey to wait.

"Sir, she stammered, I am Mary, Mary McAllister-Tillotson, your Aunt. You are my nephew. These are my parents, and your father, Michael, was my brother."

Now it was Harvey's turn to almost faint. He turned pale, gasping, stammering, "No, it can't be true!"

Mary quickly assured him, "Yes, Mr. McAllister, it is true, I am Mary, your Aunt. I was kidnapped by the Cherokee, who killed my Mother and Father when I was three years old."

The sincerity and passion in Mary's words were convincing enough for Harvey to listen to what she had to say. He remembered his father telling him that his little sister Mary was only three when she was kidnapped.

When he and Mary had regained enough composure to speak without stammering, they embraced, weeping and kissing each other's cheeks. Harvey introduced Rachel to Mary and Avery, then Mary introduced Avery to them. They both knew they had a lifetime of catching up to do, so they agreed to meet at the D&W Cafe for supper that evening. Mary and Avery were simply too tired to go anywhere else at the moment without getting some rest first.

Their hired carriage took them to the Blackstone Hotel, directly across the street from the Courthouse Square. Exhausted from the trip itself, and now also from the emotional experience of learning that Mary had a living nephew, both she and Avery fell asleep almost as soon as their heads touched the pillows. As Mary drifted off, her eyes filled with tears again. She was thinking about how the trauma of seeing her parents lying on that floor eighty years ago, and hearing the sound of her mother's voice calling out her name, then being abducted by the Indians, had almost totally erased her already vague memory of a brother. But now that she had met Harvey McAllister, and had seen the tombstones of her parents and her brother, suddenly the whole scene flashed into her mind again. But she refused to dwell upon the past now. God had spared her life, and had given her a loving husband and a son, and now a nephew.

She thought, "Dear Lord, I cannot thank you enough for the tender mercies you have shown me, and the long and happy life you have granted me. And Lord, if I should not live to see another day, I can die knowing that I am so richly blessed."

Avery kissed her forehead softly, and he also drifted off to sleep, but not before praying.

"Dear Lord, sometimes it seems our lives are being guided in a strange direction, and we don't quite understand why, and neither do we know the outcome of a single day's journey, but you certainly have been good to Mary and me Lord, and I just want to thank you for all the happiness you have granted me in more than eighty years of life. And Lord, I think Mary and I can both agree that if this were our last day on earth, we are satisfied with all you have allowed us to experience."

They were awakened at 6:30 that evening by Harvey and Rachel. The four of them hired a carriage to take them to the D&W Cafe. The atmosphere was charged with excitement, with Harvey and Rachel wanting to know everything that had happened to Mary from the day she was kidnapped by the Cherokee. Mary was just as excited to know about her brother Michael, his wife, and all the stories he may have told Harvey about his own life. Mary took her time, slowly and calmly telling them the whole story about her abduction, being taken to the Indian village, being raised as Ahyoka,

The Townsend Legacy: Heavenly Places II

and being married to Small Deer, the son of Great Elk. Harvey and Rachel listened intently to her every word, as she described her life among the Indians, her escape from them, and how she had been abandoned by Small Deer, and rescued by a handsome Lieutenant by the name of Avery Thomas Tillotson. Avery smiled, pointing to himself. Mary continued, telling them about finally having a son, and naming him Thomas Avery Tillotson. Her countenance saddened a bit when she recounted how Tom had suddenly vanished, and had gone missing for thirty years. When she mentioned the name Tillotson again, something rang a bell in Harvey's memory. He turned pale, gasping.

"Aunt Mary, surely you're not talking about the Reverend Tom Tillotson, the Pastor of the Copper Springs Baptist Church in Cleveland Tennessee, are you?"

"Yes, Harvey, that's the one. Have you heard of him?"

"Heard of him? Aunt Mary, our Pastor, Jeff Townsend, was there back in '76, he and his wife Becky, and his son Samuel. He told us about a Pastor Tom Tillotson, who was half Indian and half white, and about his son Samuel being saved that day. But never in my wildest dreams did I imagine Tom Tillotson being related to me.!"

"That's the man, Harvey, and Avery and I were there that very day. In fact, that was the day we saw Tom for the first time in thirty years. And yes, we met the Reverend Townsend and his wife Becky, and their son Samuel."

Rachel had been relatively silent during the whole conversation, hanging onto Mary's every word. But now she chimed in.

"My, what a blessed set of coincidences this trip has turned out to be! Harvey, since we have nothing else to do but travel, why don't we take the train back to Tennessee with Mary and Avery, and you can meet your long lost cousin Tom?" Harvey's face beamed in agreement.

"Oh my, that would be such a blessing. Avery, Mary, would you mind if we join you on your trip back to Tennessee?"

Both Mary and Avery smiled their own approval, with Mary answering, "We'd be pleased and honored to have you go with us. And I know Tom and Pearly Mae would be absolutely thrilled to learn that Tom has a cousin. And, by the way, Tom and Pearl also have a son, Thomas Clark."

"Well, it's settled then, when were you planning on returning?"

"Actually, we were planning on leaving on the evening train today, if that's not too soon for you and Rachel. The train leaves at 10:00 p.m. tonight, and is scheduled to arrive in Cleveland around 12:30 tomorrow morning. We really wanted to be home on the 4th, for the big celebration."

"Then we will celebrate the 4th with you and your...excuse me, *our* family." Harvey said.

The four of them quickly finished their meal, as Harvey and Rachel hurried to the train station to buy their tickets, while Avery and Mary returned to the Blackstone Hotel to rest again. The Hotel clerk woke them up at 9:30. They met Harvey and Rachel at the train depot at 9:50, and the train departed on schedule, at 10:00 p.m. on the evening of July 3rd. Avery and Harvey sat together, facing Mary and Rachel. A fine mahogany table separated them.

At precisely midnight, the train suddenly started slowing down. Avery pulled out his gold-plated pocket watch, noticing the time. He knew the train shouldn't be slowing down this early. They were still about thirty miles from Cleveland. The train suddenly lurched, as the grinding, screeching sound of steel on steel pierced the night. The windows of the luxury car in which they were riding were suddenly shattered by a hail of bullets, followed by flaming arrows. Avery's first impulse was to protect Mary. Harvey's first impulse was to protect Rachel. As each man rose to throw his own body in front of his wife, a flaming arrow sank into Avery's back.

He sank to the floor, moaning, "Mary", "Mary".

Mary's mind flashed back to that day, eighty years ago. She was hearing the voice of her dying mother calling, "Mary", "Mary". The train had now stopped. As the last breath left Avery's body, a stray bullet pierced Mary's throat before she could get Avery's name out of her mouth. Harvey was unarmed, but saw the pistol hanging at Avery's side. He grabbed it quickly out of the holster, firing five quick blind shots out the shattered window. He used the last bullet to shoot out the opposite window, and almost threw Rachel out the window. Rachel screamed as her body landed in the loose gravel. In a split second, Harvey was out the window, and had Rachel in his arms, running toward the woods as quickly as his legs would allow, expecting either a bullet or an arrow to kill them both any second.

What Harvey didn't know was that his five blind shots had killed three of the five attackers. The two remaining men were more interested in looting the dead bodies on the train than in catching and killing the two who had escaped.

Harvey ran with Rachel in his arms for as long as his lungs gave him enough air to take another step. He ran up the slope of a low hill, and down the other side. Totally exhausted, he fell with Rachel in his arms, in the middle of a narrow stream of water. They looked into each other's eyes, wrapped their arms around each other, and waited for what they believed to be certain death. After what seemed like an eternity, they realized they were not being followed. They looked up and saw the glow of the fire from the burning train cars. One of the horses of one of the men Harvey had shot galloped over the top of the hill. Harvey figured the robbers had gotten what they wanted, and had set the train cars on fire, with the dead bodies still inside, and had hightailed it away from the scene.

He whistled for the horse, talking gently to him, walking ever so slowly toward him. The horse stood still, as if waiting for his new master to come and take command of him. Harvey gently took the reins of the bridle in his hands, stroking the horse softly, and led him down the slope to where Rachel had now crawled out of the stream. She started to get up and walk toward Harvey, but fell immediately. Harvey quickly tied the bridle rein around a bush, and ran to her. Her ankle was slightly swollen. He soaked his handkerchief in the cold stream, wrapping it loosely around her ankle. They waited another thirty minutes. Not a sound came from the direction of the train. There were no more flames from the train, only smoke. Satisfied that the killers had left the scene, Harvey lifted Rachel into the saddle, and climbed up behind her. They rode slowly and cautiously toward what was left of the train. As they approached, the stench of burnt flesh almost made them vomit.

Harvey dismounted and took the handkerchiefs from the three men lying dead a few yards from the train. He couldn't help but notice they were white men, dressed and painted like Indians. The rifles, pistols, and bayonets lying by their bodies were U.S. Army Issue. He quickly tied a handkerchief over his own nose and mouth, and handed the other two to Rachel, who did the same with hers.

Harvey picked up two of the pistols, handing one to Rachel, and shoving the other underneath his belt. He also picked up one of the rifles, and one of the bayonets. Another one of the dead men's horses was standing about twenty yards away. Harvey whistled for the horse. The horse responded immediately, walking slowly toward Harvey as if he were its owner. Harvey suspected these were military horses, trained to obey immediately upon hearing a man whistle to them. He checked the brands, and sure enough, there was the U.S. Army brand, with the additional identifying brand, Seventh Cavalry, directly beneath it.

These men had either been soldiers themselves, or had killed the soldiers to whom these horses had belonged. But right now, Harvey didn't have time to speculate about the identities of these dead men. He had some other dead bodies to attend to. Rachel waited in total silence. When she and Harvey slowly approached what was left of the luxury car from which they had escaped, there lay the charred bodies of Avery and Mary Tillotson. Harvey walked quickly to the front of the train, where he found the dead bodies of the engineer and fireman. Running back to the caboose, he found the dead body of the brakeman. All the other train cars were filled with dead bodies also, eight men, eight women, and four children. Harvey counted twenty two dead bodies besides the bodies of Mary and Avery. There were eight Derringers in the hands of the eight dead men.

With two fresh horses, Harvey and Rachel rode into Cleveland at 8:00 a.m on the morning of July 4th. They went immediately to the Sheriff's office. Rachel put her arm around Harvey's shoulder, limping into the Sheriff's office. Sheriff Todd Jackson took her other arm around his own shoulder, as he and Harvey helped her to a padded bench along the wall. Before either Harvey or Rachel could introduce themselves, Sheriff Jackson ran out the door, headed toward the office of Dr. Arville Jones. He returned in less than three minutes with a white rag full of chipped ice from Dr. Jones' ice box. He gently removed the handkerchief from Rachel's ankle, filled it with the ice, wrapped it around Rachel's ankle, and elevated her foot onto a chair. Rachel smiled gratefully, feeling some relief almost immediately.

Harvey showed Sheriff Todd Jackson the rifles, pistols, and the bayonet, along with the Army handkerchiefs. After Harvey explained to the Sheriff what had happened last night, Sheriff Jackson immediately dispatched several wagons to the scene to bring back the bodies. When Harvey told him that two of the victims were his Aunt Mary Tillotson and her husband Avery, Sheriff Jackson turned pale, and sank into his chair.

"Why, that's Pastor Tillotson's Mother and father."

"I know Sheriff, Tom Tillotson is my cousin."

Tears filled Sheriff Jackson's eyes, as he asked, "Oh my God, how am I gonna break this to Pastor Tom?"

"Sir, I'd like to go with you, if you don't mind, and if you like, I'll break the news to Tom myself."

"No, Mr. McAllister, it's my job, and I'll break it to him as best I can. But you're welcome to come along if you want. It might help a little to have a living relative near when I tell him and his family. But we need to go to the telegraph office first, and get a telegraph message on the wires to every Sheriff's office in the tri-state area, and warn them, there are still two killers on the loose."

Sheriff Jackson was only twenty-one years old, the youngest Sheriff ever elected to that office in the county. But what he lacked in age, he more than made up for in courage, wisdom, and his knowledge of the law. More than a few men had learned the hard way that he was no amateur with a pistol. He was also a man of compassion, never mistreating a prisoner, or jumping to conclusions about the guilt or innocence of anyone accused of a crime. He was also single, very handsome, and an eligible bachelor. Whenever he was not actively enforcing the law, he was studying the law, hoping someday to become an attorney. He was a member of the Copper Springs Baptist Church, meaning, of course, that Tom Tillotson was his Pastor and friend. He knew it wasn't going to be easy breaking the news of the deaths of Tom's parents to him.

The swelling in Rachel's foot was now almost totally gone. Sheriff Jackson took another look at it, wrapped it tightly with the white rag, handed her a walking cane left behind by a former prisoner, and asked her if she could walk with the cane. Rachel rose slowly, putting just a little weight on the foot, took a few steps, and smiled.

"Well, Sheriff, or should I add - doctor Jackson? That feels so much better. I can walk just fine with this cane."

"You stay here Mrs. McAllister, while Harvey and I take your horses to the livery stable and get them fed and watered. I'll see if I can borrow a carriage from cousin Fred, and the three of us can go and tell Tom and Pearl the bad news."

Tom, Pearl, and Thomas Clark were just about to leave home, headed uptown for the big Fourth-of-July celebration, when the carriage arrived. They all immediately recognized Sheriff Jackson. Of course none of them recognized the other man and woman in the carriage. Sheriff Jackson stepped out first, motioning for Harvey and Rachel to remain in the carriage for just a moment while he spoke to Tom alone. Pearly Mae and Thomas Clark stood silently, as Sheriff Jackson and Tom walked a few yards away. As Sheriff Jackson slowly broke the news to Tom, Pearl saw Tom's face turn white. She knew something was wrong. Sheriff Jackson put his arm around Tom's shoulder, as the two of them came back toward the others. Sheriff Jackson motioned for Harvey and Rachel to join them. Tom took Pearl and Thomas Clark by their hands, quietly saying, "Let's all go inside."

Telling the gruesome story to Tom and his family was harder than Sheriff Jackson had anticipated. Sheriff Jackson and his family had become close friends with the Tillotsons ever since Tom had baptized Sheriff Jackson, ten years ago. He finally got so choked up he asked Harvey to finish the story. Harvey began with his gaining, and losing, an Aunt and Uncle in a single day. Upon hearing that Harvey was his first cousin, Tom managed a weak smile, as he and Harvey, and Pearly Mae and Rachel, embraced in a long hug.

By the time they got back to town, the wagons were arriving at the morgue across the street from the Sheriff's office. Tom went straight to the telegraph office, sending a telegraph message to Jeff. It read:

(Mother and father dead. Come quickly - Tom).

As the bodies were removed from the wagons, Sheriff Jackson counted thirty-two bodies. Harvey asked him to count them again, because he was certain there should be only twenty-seven, that was, of course, assuming that three of them were the three killers who had been killed during the robbery. Re-counting the bodies together, Sheriff Jackson, Harvey, and the Coroner all counted thirty-two bodies. The men who drove the wagons explained the additional five bodies. About half way between the burnt train and town they had discovered the five dead bodies of five soldiers, all from the Seventh Cavalry. Two still had arrows in their backs, and three had been shot in the back. They had been ambushed by the five murderers. One of them was Master Sergeant Cleotis Raines, who had served with Tom's dad Avery - the Sergeant Raines who had painted the portrait of Mary many years ago.

Two hours after the telegraph was sent, Sheriff Clarence Murphy delivered it to Jeff. Two hours later, Jeff, Becky, Ollie, Erica, and Elick boarded the train, headed for Cleveland Tennessee. Samuel and Becky Sarah stayed behind to tend to the two farms while the rest of the family was gone. The train arrived in Cleveland Tennessee at 3:00 a.m., on July 5th. Tom didn't know how many of Jeff's family would be coming, so he asked Sheriff Jackson to hire three carriages to bring the family back to his home.

Tom, Thomas Clark, and Sheriff Jackson met Jeff and his family at the train depot. Jeff got off the train first, lifting Becky gently off the steps to the ground. They were followed by Ollie. When Ollie Marie Townsend appeared in the doorway of the train car, Sheriff Jackson's heart skipped a beat. The light from the lanterns on either side of the door illuminated her face and figure. Never in his life had Todd Jackson been so smitten by a young woman's beauty. His heart raced. For the few moments she hesitated in the doorway, his reason for being there completely escaped his mind. As Tom was embracing Jeff and Becky, it seemed to Sheriff Jackson as if time had frozen. Even all the noises around him, including the loud hum of the train's engine, were eclipsed by the sheer beauty of this angelic creature in front of him. Jeff, Becky, and Tom all turned around to see Sheriff Jackson and Ollie staring at each other. Tom was about to help Ollie down from the train when Sheriff Jackson was suddenly jarred back to reality. He quickly stepped in front of Tom, lifting his hands toward Ollie, offering,

"Please Reverend, allow me."

Jeff, Becky and Tom all grinned knowingly as Sheriff Jackson took Ollie's hand in his. He removed his hat with his other hand, held it to his breast, and spoke as softly as his stammering voice would allow.

"May I help you, Miss....?"

"Townsend, Sir, Ollie Marie Townsend."

Jeff stepped forward, offering Sheriff Jackson his hand, as Tom introduced them.

"This here is Reverend Jeff Townsend, Ollie's father, and this is Becky, her mother."

Sheriff Jackson looked up at Jeff's tall form, and felt the strong grip of his hand, glancing from Becky to Jeff, to Ollie, responding, "Well, I can see why Miss Townsend is so beautiful."

Jeff and Becky grinned, accepting his compliment as both a compliment, and an apology for staring at their daughter. And now that Sheriff Jackson had met three of the Townsend family, another one stepped into the doorway of the train. It was Erica, now seventeen, and every bit as stunning and lovely as her older sister. Before anyone else could offer to help her down from the train, Thomas Clark Tillotson rushed forward, smiling from ear to ear, with his left hand extended toward her right hand, and his right hand toward her left. As Erica started to step forward to allow him to escort her down the steps, she stumbled slightly over the threshold, literally falling into Thomas' arms. He caught her in his powerful arms, holding her as if she were as light as a feather. The shock and awkwardness of the moment was immediately overcome by Erica's sweet smile. She quickly dismissed her own embarrassment by asking.

"Is this the way you introduce yourself to all the ladies, Sir, or just me?"

"Uh, well, no ma'am, uh, I was just, afraid you would get hurt, uh, so..."

"So you caught me. And I thank you for that. You're a real gentleman. Now you can put me down, if you don't mind, Sir."

Everyone including Jeff had to chuckle, in spite of the sad circumstances that brought them there. Elick was standing in the door of the passenger car, holding several suitcases, watching the whole scene. He quickly asked, "Would any of you big strong gentlemen care to help me with some of this luggage?"

Both Thomas and Sheriff Jackson responded immediately, taking two suitcases apiece from Elick, hoisting them into the back of their carriages. Jeff helped Becky into the back seat of Tom's carriage, Elick rode up front with Tom. Ollie offered her hand to

Sheriff Jackson, who was more than happy to lift her into the front seat of his carriage, as Thomas gently lifted Erica onto the seat of his carriage, as if it were a foregone conclusion that this was the way it was supposed to be. The two girls glanced at Jeff and Becky momentarily, as if asking for their approval. Jeff simply nodded at them, and the three carriages headed toward Tom's home.

Between the train station and Tom's house, Tom explained to Jeff and Becky how his Mom and Dad had died. At the same time, Sheriff Jackson and Thomas were telling Ollie and Erica the sad story. Jeff and his whole family were all shocked, but pleased, to learn that Harvey McAllister was Tom's first cousin. In the midst of all the horrible circumstances that once again brought the Tillotson and Townsend families together, there was that single ray of sunshine, in losing both his parents, Tom had gained a relative he never knew he had.

One thing that was a foregone conclusion was that Jeff was to deliver the eulogies in the funerals of Mary and Avery Tillotson. Upon hearing about their tragic deaths, Tom knew there was only one man he wanted in the pulpit, his lifelong friend, Jeff Townsend.

The bodies of Mary and Avery had been burnt beyond recognition. In fact, if not for the fact that Harvey and Rachel had been in the same train car with them at the time, no one would have been able to identify them. Their caskets would not be opened during the funeral. Sheriff Jackson said a quick goodbye to all of them, and hurried back to town.

The mortician in Cleveland had thirty-two bodies on his hands, and twenty-six of them were severely burned. The Coroner could only give the families one small ray of comfort, telling them their relatives had died from either their gunshot wounds, or possibly from smoke inhalation, or both. He simply didn't have the heart to tell them their loved ones had burned to death. The grief of their loss, and the shock of the cruel and inhuman manner in which these folks had perished, left the entire town with a mixture of emotions. In the midst of their grief and sorrow, many also felt a sense of rage toward the murderers. Many vented their emotions, saying they were glad that three of the murderers had been killed. But with all the grief and sorrow, there was also that lingering sense of fear that the two killers who had escaped might be somewhere near. But in the back of everyone's mind, there was also the unshakeable confidence that it would only be a matter of time until Sheriff Todd Jackson would find those men, and bring them to justice.

The only bodies among the dead which were not completely burned by the fire were the bodies of the engineer, the fireman, the brakeman, and the three killers. Sheriff Jackson ordered that every stitch of clothing, and every article found on the bodies of the three killers be preserved, pending his own investigation of them. Among the articles found were the pocket watches of three of the five dead soldiers, and fifteen dollars in money. Each killer had five dollars in his pocket.

Sheriff Jackson shook his head, murmuring, "They each died for a watch they would never use, and five dollars they would never live to spend."

But in the hip pocket of one of the killers, Sheriff Jackson found one particular piece of evidence that intrigued him. It was a short poem, printed in ink, on a scrap of paper. The poem read -

I don't know why the rest of you are making such a fuss,
'Cause I don't mind at all if Clubfoot Jim should ride with us;
Can he be of any help to us, I ask, who really knows,
What difference does it make if on one foot he has no toes?
As for me I must admit I'd rather ride with Jim,
Than with that dirty nasty stinking Sligo Slim.

Sheriff Jackson immediately ordered all the boots be removed from the feet of the three men. All three of them had all ten toes. That meant, of course, that one of the two who had gotten away from the robbery scene was probably the Clubfoot Jim to whom this man had referred. Sheriff Jackson ran out the door of the morgue, straight to his office. He opened all his desk drawers, sifting through all the old Wanted posters. At the bottom of one stack of posters was the picture of James Lockard, a.k.a. Clubfoot Jim, wanted for murder and armed robbery in three states!. Right next to that poster was another, with the picture of Clifton Slade, a.k.a. Sligo Slim, also wanted for murder and armed robbery. The posters were dated 1879. Clubfoot Jim and Sligo Slim had been able to dodge the law for ten years. Sheriff Jackson smiled to himself, chuckling softly.

"Now talk about poetic justice, I'm coming for both of you boys."

He tucked the poem and the posters into his vest pocket, and rode out to Tom's home. He asked Tom if he had decided when to have the funeral for his parents. Tom had been advised by the mortician not to keep the bodies above ground one minute longer than necessary. The funeral was set for Sunday, July 7th. Sheriff Jackson showed the Wanted posters and the poem to Tom, Jeff, Harvey, Thomas and Elick. Without his even asking, all of them volunteered to serve on a posse, and go after Clubfoot Jim and Sligo Slim. It was agreed they would all meet at his office Monday morning, and be deputized.

James Lockard got the nickname Clubfoot Jim by being greedy and stupid. Before he became an outlaw and a fugitive, he killed bear and buffalo for a living, selling buffalo hides and bear skins to whoever would buy them from him. In 1879, he murdered another hunter who had trapped a huge grizzly in a bear trap. The other hunter was about to shoot the trapped grizzly when Jim happened upon the scene. In a single moment of greed, he shot the other hunter in the back, then killed the raging grizzly. He murdered a man for a bear skin. He wasn't strong enough to open the steel bear trap with his hands, so he took hold of one side of the trap with his hands, and placed his left foot against the other side, trying to force the trap open enough to get the bear's foot out. The spring of the trap was too strong for him. His foot slipped. The razor-sharp teeth of the steel trap seared through his leather boot, and almost cut off a third of his left foot.

Clifton Slade had now been on the run for more than eleven years, dodging the law and bounty hunters. He left Sligo Louisiana in 1876, having robbed the bank and the freight office in the same day. He literally shot his way out of town, killing a Sheriff and three deputies in the process. He was a slender whip of a man, measuring six feet, eight inches tall, and skinny as a rail, thus the nickname, Sligo Slim. He had the reputation of being the second fastest gun alive, second only to a Sheriff in West Virginia by the name of Clarence Murphy. Sligo Slim vowed that he would someday find Sheriff Murphy, and prove to the world that he, and not Sheriff Murphy, was the fastest gun alive. He was on his way to do just that, and had made it as far as Tennessee, when he heard the screams of a man who sounded like he was caught in a bear trap.

Had not Sligo Slim come along that day, James Lockard would have bled to death beside the bear whose skin he had so coveted. Sligo glanced at the other dead hunter, then at James and the dead bear. His proposal was short and to the point.

"Your life for that bearskin mister."

It was an offer James Lockard was in no position to refuse. He quickly wrapped Jim's foot and leg in a blanket, and got him to Dr. Jones' office. He held Dr. Jones and his nurse, Miss Smith at gunpoint, forcing them to treat James Lockard. Dr. Jones managed to save what was left of Jim's foot. Thus Sligo Slim and Clubfoot Jim met, and became partners in crime.

Sunday July 7th, 1889. Copper Springs Baptist Church.

Bad news travels quickly, and the news of the murders and robbery of the train had spread like wildfire. The news that four children, and the Mother and Father of a local Pastor were among the victims only added fuel to the journalistic flame. Pictures of the burnt train appeared on the front page of every newspaper within a hundred mile radius of Cleveland. Thankfully, all the bodies had been removed from the train before pictures could be taken.

The church was overflowing. Tom and Pearly Mae, and their son Thomas Clark, were well known, and well loved by all who knew them. And no one in the congregation had forgotten Jeff and Becky Townsend from more than a decade ago. But Tom knew if there was one person in the world who understood his grief and sorrow at this moment, it was Jeff Townsend. Although they had not seen each other in years, their friendship was just as strong as it had ever been. Tom somehow knew there was no one except Jeff who could say what needed to be said in a time like this, and he was right. When Jeff stepped behind the pulpit, he said absolutely nothing about the murderers, or the manner in which Mary and Avery had died. He was certain everyone already knew the gruesome details. He simply looked down at the two caskets in front of the pulpit, then toward Tom, Pearly Mae, Thomas Clark (who now had Erica by his side,) Harvey and Rachel, and Sheriff Jackson, who now had Ollie Marie sitting by his side. He also noticed that Mollie Puckett was now sitting beside a handsome young gentleman, who, as it turned out, was Michael Stewart, Tom's associate Pastor. Mollie and

Michael had now been married two years. He turned to the fourteenth chapter of the Gospel of John, and read.

Let not your heart be troubled: ye believe in God, believe also in me. In my Father's house are many mansions: If it were not so, I would have told you. I go to prepare a place for you. And if I go and prepare a place for you, I will come again, and receive you unto myself; that where I am, there ye may be also. And whither I go ye know, and the way ye know. Thomas saith unto him, Lord, we know not whither thou goest; and how can we know the way? Jesus saith unto him, I am the way, the truth, and the life: no man cometh unto the Father, but by me.

"Dear friends and family, when our blessed Lord spoke these words, He was nearing the time of His departure out of this unfriendly world, and there were certain things He wanted his beloved disciples to know. Our dear friends, Mary and Avery Tillotson, have departed this unfriendly world, and if they could speak to all of you now, I'm sure they would want all of you to know these same things. And although they left without having had the opportunity to tell each of you face to face individually, I am certain that each of you will agree with the four things I am about to mention to you, concerning Mary and Avery Tillotson."

"Back in the thirteenth chapter of John's Gospel, we read,

Now before the feast of the Passover, when Jesus knew that his hour was come that he should depart out of this world unto the Father, having loved his own which were in the world, he loved them unto the end.

"That's the first thing He wanted them to know, the fact that He loved them. And is there anyone in this assembly today who has any doubt that they are loved by the Lord Jesus? And is there anyone here who has any doubt that you were loved by Mary and Avery Tillotson? I am sure there isn't one, because they showed their love for you by being here in church with you every Sunday, having fellowship with you, and worshiping our Lord with you. And in the same way that our Lord has done countless things for you that endear Him to you, I am also sure that each of you can think of many other things that Mary and Avery said or did that endeared them to you as friends and family, and as a brother and sister in Christ."

"The second thing our Lord wanted His disciples to know, and the second thing Mary and Avery would want all of you to know is where they went. Our Savior told the disciples He was going to His Father's house. That's where Mary and Avery have gone also, to the Father's house, which we all know is just another way of saying Heaven, for Heaven is our Father's house. It is there, in our Father's house, that folks like Mary and Avery feel most at home, and the most comfortable, safe and supremely blessed and loved. It is a place that is indescribable in human terms for its beauty and comfort, being occupied by saints and angels, and by the Lord Himself. But even if I, or anyone else could use our words to paint a vague portrait of that place, what good would it do any of you, if we couldn't, or didn't, tell you how to get there. And that is the third thing Christ wanted His disciples to know, and the third thing that Mary and Avery would want all of you to know - how to get there to the Father's house."

"Jesus was asked by Thomas, who, for all intents and purposes, was speaking in behalf of all the rest of the disciples, for I believe they all wanted to ask the same question - how can we know the way. And the answer, of course, was sitting right there in front of them. But to satisfy their longing, unanswered question, He plainly told them that He is the way, the only way, to Heaven. The departed souls of our friends Mary and Avery Tillotson are in Heaven today because of Jesus Christ, and His finished work. And if any of us hope to see them again, it is through Jesus Christ that we must go, for there is no other way, and finally, our Lord wanted them to know that He would see them again, saying that He would come, and receive them unto Himself. I am certain that Mary and Avery Tillotson would want all of you to know that, if you, like them, know the Way, then they will see you again. When we leave this place today, we will all carry with us our own sweet and precious memories of these two beloved friends, and many, of not all of us, will weep, not for them, but for ourselves, having to say farewell to two dear and precious loved ones. But in the midst of our sorrow, we have a blessed assurance, we will see them again. I know that I shall see them, and I am going to leave this place today with the hope that everyone under the sound of my voice can safely say the same."

The entire congregation followed the funeral procession across town, to a lovely spot that Avery and Mary had chosen years before, beneath the shade of a grove of pine trees. The bodies of Mary and Avery Thomas Tillotson were buried on the Tillotson estate, about three hundred yards from their home, thus beginning the Tillotson family cemetery.

That night, Jeff told Becky about he and Elick volunteering to join the posse, and go after the two killers. Becky started to object, but quickly let it go, knowing Jeff's mind was made up. Her mind quickly flashed back to that day long ago, seeing Jeff strap on that gun belt, promising, "I'll be back, with our son."

Monday morning, July 8th, Sheriff Jackson's office 8:00 a.m.

Sheriff Jackson wasted no time in filling all the men in on the character and deeds of Clubfoot Jim and Sligo Slim.

"These men are armed, and extremely dangerous. They will not hesitate to kill the first man who poses a threat to them, and I seriously doubt that either of them will be taken alive. In fact, rumor has it that Sligo Slim has vowed that he will never be taken alive. Gentlemen, if any of you have any reservations about serving on this posse, I totally understand if you wish to re-consider. Sligo Slim is feared as the second fastest gun alive, second only to Sheriff Clarence Murphy of West Virginia. He has sworn an oath that he will kill any man who tries to stop him from proving he is faster than Sheriff Murphy. Any questions?"

Jeff and Elick shot a quick glance toward one another, saying nothing. All the men raised their right hands, repeating the oath after Sheriff Jackson, who pinned a badge on each of them. Everyone except Jeff was already wearing a gun belt. Sheriff Jackson took one down from a peg on the wall, slowly handing it to Jeff.

"That's a Colt .45 brother Townsend, you might want to familiarize yourself with it before we leave. Would you like to take a few practice shots out back first?"

Jeff removed the Colt from the holster, twirled it around his trigger finger a few times, and shoved it back into the holster.

"I'm praying I won't have to use it Sheriff, but if I do, God help the man on the other end."

Sheriff Jackson squinted slightly at Jeff's remark, adding, "These two men have a big head start on us gentlemen, and they may have already crossed the Tennessee line. If they have, it will be up to someone between here and West Virginia to arrest or kill them. I'm guessing they're headed northeast, toward West Virginia. So if we're gonna catch them before they cross the line, we'll have to ride hard and fast. Harvey, you and Elick take point, and take these binoculars. Us three will be right behind you. We will start at the site of the train robbery, and pick up their trail from there. If they haven't crossed the state line, I intend to find them, and bring them back, dead or alive. Harvey, if you or Elick spot them, don't shoot, or confront them alone, is that clear?"

Harvey and Elick nodded in agreement. Sheriff Jackson looked at Tom and Jeff, waiting for some kind of response from them. Tom and Jeff only stared at each other, as if they hadn't heard him. There was a silent conversation going on between Tom and Jeff that only the two of them could understand. They both remembered that situation long ago when the two of them had brought a little band of murderers to justice without firing a shot. Sheriff Jackson simply gave the two of them the respect that comes with age and wisdom, and dropped the conversation.

Five men, a young Sheriff, an even younger farm boy, a retired Postal worker, and two Baptist preachers set out to find, and hopefully arrest, two desperate killers.

At the site of the train robbery and multiple murders, two sets of tracks led off from the others, headed northeast, just like Sheriff Jackson suspected. Harvey and Elick took the lead riding side by side, with the other three men riding three abreast a few yards behind them. They all knew the two men they were following were four days ahead of them, so they rode hard and fast for almost the whole day, stopping only to feed and water their horses, and grab a bite to eat themselves.

Sligo Slim had no intentions of keeping Clubfoot Jim around for a minute longer than he was needed. At the moment, he was nothing more than an extra gun in case of trouble. And if he was unable to follow orders, he would either kill him, or leave him behind to survive by his own wits, and Jim had already shown that he did not possess a lot of those. He was quickly becoming extra baggage to Sligo Slim, and Jim sensed that fact. The only things that kept him from trying to kill Sligo was his fear of him, and the slight twinge of gratitude he still felt for Sligo having gotten him out of that bear trap, and taking him to doctor Jones' office that day long ago. There was not an ounce of friendship between them. Sligo Slim was totally obsessed and consumed with the idea of finding and killing Sheriff Clarence Murphy. He didn't care how long it took to do it, and he would kill any man who stood in his way.

Clubfoot Jim couldn't understand why Sligo wasn't in any hurry to get out of Tennessee. They had ridden slowly and had made camp every evening for four days long before sunset. It almost seemed as if Sligo Slim was hoping he was being followed. He was so confident and arrogant about his own prowess with a gun, he simply believed he could shoot his way out of any situation. He was in no hurry. That arrogance and carelessness allowed Sheriff Jackson and his posse to close the gap between them rather quickly. The distance covered by Sligo and Jim in four days was almost covered in one day by the posse. One hour before sunset, they were within five miles of the campsite of the two outlaws.

Sligo and Jim had made it to within fifty miles of Jellico Tennessee, just south of the Kentucky border, where they made camp. Jim insisted they keep going until they crossed the state line, which would eliminate at least one lawman being able to pursue them any further. Sligo hurriedly reminded Jim that he was in charge, barking,

"I ain't scared of no Tennessee lawman, nor any other lawman for that matter. That little Jackson feller back there is still wet behind the ears, and he ain't gonna follow us this far. An even if he does, he won't live to tell about it. You understand me Jim? Now shut yer trap and see if yuh can catch us a mess o fish fer supper."

Clubfoot Jim quickly obeyed, fashioning a homemade fishing pole from a thick grove of bamboo. Before Sligo Slim got the fire going, Jim had already caught five good-sized catfish. Sligo Slim gave him the only compliment he had heard in his life, telling him,

"Now, see there old man, what ya can do with a little effort? You might not be totally useless after all."

Clubfoot Jim took the insult for what it was, an insult. But he also heard something else in Sligo Slim's remark. It was more than an insult, it was also a reminder, and a warning that he could be disposed of at any time Sligo pleased. He took the warning seriously, cowering to Sligo's every demand, fearing that if he didn't, Sligo would show him just how useless he was, by murdering him.

With less than an hour of daylight left, Harvey and Elick rode about another mile or so ahead, making sure the tracks they had been following still led in the same direction. Elick lifted the binoculars, scanning the valleys and hills below them.

Suddenly he gasped, "Oh my God Harvey, I think we've found them."

He quickly handed the binoculars to Harvey, pointing straight ahead and downward. Harvey saw the thin plume of smoke rising from the campfire.

"I think you're right Elick. I'd say they're about three miles ahead."

They rode back to their own campsite, dismounting hurriedly, anxious to tell the others what they had seen. Sheriff Jackson leaped astride his horse immediately.

"Show me." he ordered.

After seeing the smoke from the campfire himself, Sheriff Jackson and Elick rode back to the others.

"He's right fellas, they're camped about three miles upstream. That means they've settled in for the night, and it also means they ain't in no hurry. It's getting too late to go in after them tonight, and our horses need rest, food and water. We'll camp here tonight, and close in on them first thing in the morning, if that's alright with all of you."

Everyone agreed they should wait till dawn to descend the mountain, and close in on the two killers. About an hour before dawn, Jeff eased the binoculars out of Elick's hat, slipped quietly to his horse, led his horse to a safe distance away from the camp, and mounted up, riding cautiously toward the deep valley ahead. He wanted to get to the killers before everyone else, and try to talk them into surrendering without a fight. His motive was to keep Elick and the others out of danger, at the risk of his own life.

About an hour later, Tom was the first to wake up, quickly noticing that Jeff and his horse were gone. He woke the others immediately. Sheriff Jackson didn't know what to think or say. He finally managed to say what he was thinking,

"You mean to tell me he skipped out on us, even his own son? What kind of coward is he anyway?"

Tom quickly put his hand against Sheriff Jackson's chest, scowling,

"Now you hold on just a damn minute Sheriff, Jeff Townsend ain't no coward. If I know Jeff like I think I do, he's probably gone out after those two murderers alone."

"Well if he has, he's gonna get his-self killed. He don't stand a chance against those two madmen." And Tom, you know yourself, he has no business out there alone."

Elick quickly cut into the argument, facing Sheriff Jackson,.

"You don't know my father very well Sheriff. He can take care of himself."

"I'm sure he can son, but we are not gonna let him even try that."

Sheriff Jackson quickly dismissed the argument, seeing the admiration and determination in the young man's eyes.

"Let's mount up and get after him, maybe we can over take 'em before he gets too far."

He yelled out an order for them,

Three hundred yards from the outlaws campsite, Jeff looked through the binoculars. Just to the north of the outlaws campsite stood a huge beech tree. He saw the tall lanky figure of Sligo Slim step from behind the tree, pulling up his pants. Clubfoot Jim was dousing the campfire with water from the stream. They were getting ready to pull out. He quickly pulled out his white handkerchief, tied it around the end of a long stick, and fired a single shot high above the campsite. The two killers and the posse all heard the shot. Sheriff Jackson was sure that Jeff was dead. They rode faster, toward the campsite. When they finally saw Jeff, he was riding slowly toward the big beech tree, holding the white handkerchief high above his head, waving it from side to side.

Sligo Slim ordered Jim to climb up into the beech tree, where he couldn't be seen. When Jim was two limbs above the ground, Sligo threw his rifle up to him. He waited for whoever had fired the shot to come into view. When he saw Jeff riding toward him with the white handkerchief waving, he didn't know quite how to react at first. Should he order Jim to kill him now, or wait and see who this fool was? His lust for blood overcame his judgment. Whether this stranger was a friend or foe didn't really matter. He and Jim had the advantage. He let Jeff come within fifty feet, then yelled at him. "That's far enough mister. State yer business, or die young."

Jeff had been a student of human nature long enough to notice the slightest movement of a man's eyes when he was hiding something. He knew there were two killers here, and the other had to be somewhere near, watching his every move, waiting to put a bullet in him at any moment. He figured the other was either behind that tree, or up in it somewhere. He shot a quick glance upward, and saw the tip of a boot sticking out of the leaves. He knew he had no time to waste making small talk.

Sheriff Jackson and the others had now come close enough to hear the conversation.

They heard Jeff saying,

"I'm Jeff Townsend, a friend of the Tillotsons, the people you and your friend up there in that tree murdered. I've come to offer you a deal Sligo. You can either give yourselves up, and face a rope, or you can try to kill me. If you can kill me in a fair gunfight Sligo, me and the Sheriff back there will let you and Clubfoot Jim both go free, ain't that right Sheriff.?"

Sheriff Jackson was dumbfounded, glancing from Tom, to Harvey, to Elick.

"Has that preacher lost his mind? He doesn't stand a Chinaman's chance against those outlaws." Todd stated.

Elick cut in again, "Don't shortchange him Sheriff, I've seen him use a gun before. Let him follow through, and see if Sligo will take the bait."

Sligo Slim grinned from ear to ear, squinting his eyes in pure hatred at Jeff.

"You're either very fast, or very foolish stranger, and I'm bettin foolish. He muttered.

"You just signed your own death warrant mister. How 'bout it Sheriff? You gonna let us ride outta here after I kill this damn fool?"

Sheriff Jackson looked at Tom and Harvey momentarily, as if asking for their advice. Tom grinned at him,

"It's your call Sheriff, but my money's on the preacher."

Sheriff Jackson reluctantly agreed to the deal, yelling back to Sligo Slim.

"Alright Sligo, you got a deal, but I must advise you to re-consider."

Sligo Slim took two steps forward, covering about ten feet of ground. Jeff threw the stick and handkerchief to the ground, pulling back his coat, revealing the Colt at his side. Sligo Slim's confidence in his own skill and swiftness was based upon how many men he had gunned down in his lifetime. He had never lost a gunfight, and he had faced some pretty fast gunslingers. But there was something about this man in front of him he had never seen or felt before. This man had ridden in as bold as a lion, and challenged him to a fair fight.

Slim thought, "He may be as good as he thinks he is, or maybe he's got a death wish. Either way, there's no turning back now. He's my last obstacle to Murphy. I'll make an example of him. I'll fill him full of holes before he clears leather."

Clubfoot Jim was frozen stiff with fear. He couldn't move a muscle. He could barely breathe. His eyes were fixed upon the stranger in the black suit and white shirt. He looked like such a nice and decent fellow, certainly not like a gunfighter. What a shame, such a good looking fellow had to die this way, at the hand of a wanted murderer like Sligo Slim. He half wished the stranger would somehow get off a lucky shot before dying, and maybe at least wound Sligo real bad.

Elick's mind flashed back to that steep hillside, where he had been held helpless by a big man named William Bowen. He remembered Jeff demanding that the big man let him go. He remembered the fear that had chilled his heart the moment Mr. Bowen swung that pistol toward his father. He also remembered seeing the man sink to the ground, dead. Now his heart pounded in his chest. Jeff was older now, and as far as Elick knew, he hadn't fired a gun at a man since that day. He remembered Jeff throwing the key to that big wooden box into the pond. So many thoughts and memories rushed through his mind at once. Was his father about to be killed right there in front of him? He began to pray.

Tom was praying also, remembering leaving his whip and gun belt hanging inside Jeff's barn many years ago. He had never seen Jeff with a gun at his side. And now here he stood, facing a man who was feared across the country. In a single moment, his very best friend would either be dead or alive.

He thought, "Dear God, if ever we needed a miracle, now would be a good time."

Sheriff Jackson was tempted to draw on Sligo himself, but he had given his word, and now it was too late to back down.

He thought, "How will I ever face Ollie Marie again if Jeff dies here? She's the only woman I've ever cared for, and now I've put her father's life in jeopardy by making a foolish deal with a murderer."

Harvey was praying, "Dear Lord, I love my Pastor, and he has been the best friend Rachel and I have ever known. Please don't let him die this way."

Sligo Slim was so confident he offered to let Jeff go for his gun first, growling, "Make your play mister, since you only got a few more seconds to live anyway."

Jeff stood expressionless, watching Sligo's eyes, replying, "I have all of eternity to live Sligo, and in a much better place than this. I really wish you'd drop your gun belt, and let me tell you about my Lord and Savior Jesus Christ."

Sligo Slim's heart jumped in his chest. So that's what was so strange about this man, he's a preacher!. His gun hand quivered slightly. Jeff noticed the quivering. Sligo swallowed hard.

"It's too damn late to preach to me padre. They've got a special place waitin fer me in Hell already. But you ain't gonna be the one who sends me there."

Sligo knew Jeff was not going to draw first, and that would be the narrow advantage he needed to kill him. Jeff saw the hatred in his eyes, silently counting the seconds before he knew Sligo was going for his gun. The men watching couldn't tell which man went for his gun first, but a split second after the barrel of Sligo's pistol had cleared the holster, a single bullet from Jeff's Colt had ripped his chest open. The force of the .45 caliber bullet knocked his lanky frame five feet backward. He crumpled in a pool of his own blood. Clubfoot Jim instantly dropped his pistol and rifle to the ground, and came shinnying down the tree trunk like a spider monkey, throwing both hands in the air, screaming.

"I give up mister, please don't kill me, I give up right now."

His face was white, and his entire body trembled, as he continued to stammer, "I ain't never seen a draw that fast mister, you just beat Sligo Slim, the fastest gun west of the Mississippi!"

Sheriff Jackson's jaw dropped. He shook his head, murmuring, "Well, he tried to tell me, there's always someone just a little bit faster."

Harvey sat astride his horse, stunned. He couldn't say anything except, "Thank you sweet Jesus."

Elick ran to Jeff, throwing his arms around him, saying nothing. Jeff glanced toward Tom, who grinned, nodding his head, saying not a word. Sheriff Jackson handcuffed Clubfoot Jim, shook hands with Jeff, and started to offer an apology, when Jeff stopped him.

"Sheriff, I know you've got eyes for my daughter, and if you want to court her, I'd appreciate it if you kept this little incident between us." Sheriff Jackson nodded in agreement.

"I'll take care of it Mr. Townsend, no one but us will ever know you're the fastest gun alive."

"Now if you're planning on being my son-in-law, you can drop the mister, and call me Jeff."

"Yes Sir, I'll do that Sir, er Jeff."

They buried Clifton Slade right there beneath the beech tree. Jeff fashioned a cross from two sticks, sharpened one end of the upright stick, and pushed it into the ground at the head of the grave. Tom prayed a short prayer, and the group headed back to Cleveland Tennessee. One thought lingered upon Jeff's mind. Not only had he just killed a crazed gunman, he had also saved the life of Sheriff Clarence Murphy, because, as he had noticed, Sligo Slim was indeed just a split second faster on the draw than Sheriff Murphy.

Becky, Pearly Mae, Mollie and Michael, Rachel, Ollie Marie, Erica, Tracy Michelle, Thomas Clark, Sarah and Daniel Ray were all having their own prayer meeting in the living room of Tom's home when they heard the men's voices out in the yard. The women all nearly ran over each other getting to the man they loved. Sarah and Daniel Ray were a bit slower getting out the door. Jeff's heart swelled with gratitude as he watched Ollie Marie throw her arms around Sheriff Jackson, kissing him, and holding onto him as if her life depended upon him. Then Becky was in his own arms, squeezing him with all her strength, tears of joy running down her cheeks. Harvey and Rachel were also embraced, and kissing each other's cheeks, while Erica was being swung around and around by Thomas Clark. Elick had Tracy Michelle in his arms, holding her tenderly, looking into her eyes,

    Clubfoot Jim had never seen an outbreak of love and tenderness like this in his life. His heart pounded, and tears filled his eyes, as he thought to himself, "I wonder how it feels to be loved that way by another person."

    Jeff walked over to where Jim sat astride his horse. He could almost hear Jim's thoughts, and feel his emotions. He looked up at Jim, offering, "Jim, it's never too late to make things right with God, if you haven't turned Him away for the last time."

    Jim knew he was soon to be tried and hanged, and he knew he was headed for a lost eternity. Jeff's kind words came with a tenderness and sincerity he had never heard before.

    "You mean there's hope even for a no account varmint like me preacher.?" he asked.

    "Yes there is Jim, and that hope is in Jesus Christ, the Son of God. If you feel the need of salvation in your heart, and ask Him, He will forgive you this very moment Jim, and save your soul, and cleanse your heart as if you had never sinned at all."

    Everyone else in the yard had now gathered around Jim and Jeff, listening, and praying silently. Jim bowed his head for the first time in his life, asking the Lord Jesus to forgive him of all his sins, and to come into his heart. He raised his head a changed man, forgiven, cleansed, and a new creature. With tears of joy streaming down his face, he asked Jeff if he could be baptized before he was taken to the jail in town.

    Sheriff Jackson nodded, replying, "I'm sure that can be arranged Jim. The creek is on the way to the jail."

    "Then let's go right now Sheriff."

    The whole crowd followed Sheriff Jackson and Jim to the creek, where Sheriff Jackson removed his handcuffs. Tom and Jeff both led him into the deep water, and baptized him.

    Jim came up out of the water with his hands raised, praising God. "No matter what happens to me now Sheriff, I'm ready to meet God in peace, even if it is at the end of a rope."

James Lockard, a.k.a. Clubfoot Jim was tried, convicted, and sentenced on Wednesday, July 31st, 1889. Due to his age and poor health, the jury recommended clemency. The judge, The Honorable Vance Wickersham, sentenced Jim to life in prison. He lived four years, dying at the age of fifty-four, and was buried on Boot Hill, the cemetery specially reserved for gunfighters and other convicted criminals who died with their boots on.

Although their trip to Tennessee had been for a sad occasion, Becky wanted to surprise Jeff with a second honeymoon to celebrate their wedding Anniversary. Dismissing all the events that had taken place the last few days, she quickly made all the arrangements for a nice romantic evening of dinner and dancing in the arms of her wonderful husband, followed by a peaceful quiet night in the best hotel the town had to offer. She broke the news to Jeff when he asked her if she was ready for the ride back home. Becky smiled that smile of hers, the one that told Jeff she had something up her sleeve, something more than what the present situation or conversation called for.

"You just get dressed up in your suit handsome, 'cause I have a surprise for you. Meet me at the carriage. It will be waiting to take us to a secret place."

Jeff did as she said, and was waiting at the carriage when she came out of Pearly Mae's house. After all these years, her beauty still took his breath away. Becky was dressed in a long red gown with a white silk wrap around her shoulders. Jeff smiled, extending his hand to help her into the carriage.

Climbing up beside his lovely wife, he asked, "Where to madam?"

"To the Garden Palace kind sir."

"Oh my, why such a fancy place dear lady?"

"I am spending an evening with my true love sir." she replied.

"Well, I must say he is one lucky man." Jeff gently shook the reins.

The horse took off, stepping high and proud. Jeff smiled, so thankful to know he was that lucky man. He knew Becky had made some plans, and her heart was set on this special time, before they had to go back home, back to every day living on the farm. He was excited to see what she had in store for them.

The drive to the Garden Palace was short, less than a mile. Upon arriving they stopped the buggy in front of the big, fancy, well-lit building, where they were met by a tall man in a white uniform, who, after helping Becky down from the carriage, took the horse's reins from Jeff. Jeff slipped the man two dollars. The gentleman smiled, tipped his hat, glanced toward Becky, and winked at Jeff as he drove away.

Inside the hotel, Becky asked for the key to their room, which was on the second floor. She had come over earlier that day, bringing their bags, and reserving the room. The room was beautiful, with a balcony overlooking a small pond with a garden of flowers spread out around it. Two white swans were swimming in the beautiful blue water. Becky freshened up in the big powder room. Coming out onto the balcony, she informed Jeff they had reservations in the dining hall.

They were seated at a small table in a quiet corner of the room. Yellow roses decorated the table, with a white candle burning in the middle. Yellow roses were Becky's favorite flower, but she knew Jeff liked them also. When the waiter had taken their order, four men with violins suddenly appeared at their table and began playing the Tennessee Waltz. All eyes turned toward the couple as they rose to their feet. As Jeff took Becky into his big strong arms, they floated ever so gracefully across the dance floor.

Suddenly, they were in a world all their own. They seemed temporarily transformed into a King and Queen, dancing in front of their subjects, being admired by all who saw them. Becky's black hair shimmered in the light of the chandelier hanging from the high ceiling. Jeff's handsome face beamed with purest delight, gazing into the eyes of his beautiful wife. He gently pulled Becky closer, as they both felt the same feeling they had felt so many years ago, as two young people in love. That same love was still as powerful as it had ever been. The song was over much too quickly. Amidst the thunderous applause of a standing ovation, the two sat down at their table while the men kept playing, song after song, very softly behind them.

The meal of Duck a'lorange was exquisitely prepared, and graciously enjoyed. And once again, Jeff and Becky Townsend were lost in each others company. It seemed like forever since they had gotten away from the farm by themselves. This night was even more special since they were celebrating their wedding anniversary. Becky had been secretly planning for a long time to make this the best celebration they had ever shared. She loved Jeff so much, and prayed silently that they would have many more. After hours of dancing and the great food, the couple walked hand in hand around the beautiful gardens. Finally retiring to their room, they lay in each other's arms, their minds reflecting upon the wonderful day they had shared, and the romantic night that was yet to come. It was an anniversary neither of them would ever forget.

Both Jeff and Becky were unusually quiet for the first few miles of their trip home, each of them silently reflecting upon the recent events in their lives. As Becky leaned her head against his shoulder, he gently took her hand in his, holding it ever so tenderly. He tuned his face toward hers, smiling warmly. She saw something in Jeff's eyes she had never seen before, something she couldn't quite read. They had always been able to read each others eyes and facial expressions so easily. But now there was something different, something in the way he looked at her. Jeff saw the questioning look on her face. He lifted her hand to his lips, kissing her hand

"I love you Becky, everything's gonna be alright." he whispered.

She smiled back at him, looking up into his blue eyes, replying, "I love you too Jeff, more than life itself. And I know everything will be alright, just as long as I have you next to me."

Jeff put his arm around her, pulled her close to him, and kissed her hair.

"Let's try to get a little sleep sweetheart. It's a long way home."

Becky tried to dismiss the uneasy feeling in her heart, guessing that maybe Jeff was just missing the children so badly he couldn't talk about it, or perhaps he was silently thinking about his sermon for Sunday. She leaned on his shoulder again, holding his hand till he fell asleep.

Sunday April 23rd, 1893.

It was unusually cold for late April, as Jeff rose early to build a fire in the fireplace, just to take the chill out of the house. Every joint in his body ached with pain. After getting the fire going, he decided since he was already up, he might as well build Becky a fire in the cook stove. He knew she would be up soon, so the stove would be good and hot for her to prepare breakfast. Soon the whole house was warm and comfortable.

Jeff also decided to go ahead and milk the cow for Becky, just to give her a little more rest on Sunday morning before church. He crept silently into the kitchen, took the big milk pail off the shelf, and crept quietly back into the living room, where he pulled on his jeans and a plaid wool shirt. He took his hat off the peg, slipping silently through the house to the back door. Stepping outside, he heard the sweet sound of birds singing, announcing the coming dawn. The dim light from the window and the breaking dawn revealed the sparkling dew drops on the grass. He smelled the sweet fragrance of honeysuckle just beginning to blossom. The air was crisp and clear. He turned the corner of the house, glancing southward toward the little pond. There was just enough light to show a soft shimmer on the surface of the water. He stood perfectly still, taking it all in, his heart pounding with thanksgiving for the life his God had given him.

He lifted his eyes toward Heaven, whispering, "Thank you dear Lord, for the many blessings you have given me. I suppose I am the most richly blessed man on Earth. You gave me the most beautiful and honorable woman any man could hope for. You gave me a home and a farm, and four wonderful children. And you gave me a great church to serve for these many years. You have blessed me with so many good and faithful friends. I just want to say thank you Lord, and tell you I love you with all my heart."

As if an angel had been standing by his side, listening to his prayer, Jeff felt a deep settled peace sweeping over his soul. He smiled toward Heaven, and started to walk toward the barn, when he felt the sharp pain in his chest. He hesitated momentarily, taking in deep breaths, exhaling slowly. The pain lasted for about five minutes, then eased a little. He walked slowly to the barn, and milked the cow. Carrying the big pail of milk back to the house, he noticed he was very short of breath, something he had never experienced before.

Just as he reached for the door handle, Becky opened the door. There she stood in her woolen robe, smiling as always, thanking him for the fire and for milking the cow for her. He set the pail of milk down and took her into his arms, kissing her passionately. She held him close to her, whispering.

"Well, if that's how you're gonna greet me, I'll stay in bed every morning, and let you milk the cow every day big man."

Jeff grinned, sniffing the air. He couldn't decide what smelled best, the bacon and coffee, or Becky's perfume.

The heavy pain in his chest returned. Becky saw his face wince with pain, something she had never seen since she had known Jeff.

"What's wrong Jeff. Are you alright?"

"Yeah, I'm fine honey, just a little indigestion from last night I think. I probably had too much of your good cookin."

"Well, breakfast is ready now, so you hurry and wash up."

After breakfast, they waited for Samuel and Becky Sarah to get there so they could all ride to church together in the big double carriage Dr. Parks had given Jeff and Becky as an anniversary gift. Jeff and Becky sat in back, with Jeff bouncing little Jeffrey Joseph on his knee. Feeling the pain in his chest again, he handed him to Becky.

"Son, would you like to do the preaching today?" He inquired of Samuel.

"Haven't heard you preach since last Sunday."

Samuel chuckled, answering, "Oh no papa, you ain't gettin off that easy. We're all looking forward to hearing you today. Ain't that right Mama.?"

"I'm not getting in the middle of that argument with you two again. You'll have to settle it yourselves. Ain't that right Becky Sarah.?"

"Exactly right Becky, me neither."

Samuel laughed, elbowing Becky Sarah in the ribs, "A lot o help you women are. Can't get a straight answer outta neither of ye." they all laughed, continuing on toward the church.

The church yard was overflowing, with horses, buggy's, wagons and carriages lined up all the way around the church, with others hitched to the little fence surrounding the cemetery.

Jeff didn't know it, but the deacons and their wives had a surprise birthday celebration planned for him. His birthday wasn't until Wednesday, but the church always managed to surprise Jeff by having him a birthday celebration a few days before his birthday. As they pulled up to the entrance of the church yard, Dr. and Mrs. Parks met them. As Jeff was about to lift Becky down from the carriage, the pain hit him hard in his chest. He grabbed his chest, wincing in pain.

Dr. Parks saw it. "Pastor, are you alright?"

"Don't rightly know doc, just a bad stomach I think."

"You look a little pale Pastor, maybe I better get my bag and check you out."

"just to be safe." he added.

"Nah, doc, that won't be necessary. I think it's just a lot of gas. I'll be fine soon as I get to preaching, and get rid of some o this hot air inside me." Jeff managed a weak laugh.

Dr. Parks started to object, but knew he would be wasting his breath. Everyone shook hands with Jeff and Samuel and Becky and Becky Sarah. Dr. Parks carried Jeffrey Joseph in one arm, and Josephine in the other, walking proud as a peacock, with his little daughter in one arm, and his namesake in the other.

Inside the church house, the crowd anxiously waited to surprise Jeff with a big banner hanging over the pulpit, stretching from one wall to the other, with the words, "Happy Birthday Pastor" written on it.

Jeff got all choked up when he saw the big banner. All the youth of the church were standing in rows behind the pulpit. As soon as Jeff entered the door, they all began singing Happy Birthday to him. Jeff had never been one to cry much, but this scene touched him so deeply he just couldn't hold back the tears.

The children ushered him to a big chair in front of the pulpit, as each of them brought him a small gift. Some of those gifts were only letters of thanks, written to a man who had been like a second father to them. As Jeff accepted each gift, he remembered the day each of them had accepted Christ as their Savior, and the day each of them was baptized. One by one, each young person, followed by his or her parents, shook his hand, hugging his neck, saying, "Thank you Pastor Jeff, for being our preacher and our friend."

Just before time for Jeff to preach, the whole congregation stood, as Carolyn Parks sat down behind the piano. Dr. Parks led the congregation in Jeff's favorite hymn, The Old Rugged Cross. As Jeff got up from his chair to step behind the pulpit, Dr. Parks couldn't help but notice the slight wobble in Jeff's walk, and the paleness of his face, and the large beads of sweat on his forehead. He was still a little uneasy about how Jeff had looked when he arrived. In the many years he had known Jeff, he had never seen any sign of physical weakness in him. But now, deep in his gut, he sensed something was wrong, physically wrong with Jeff Townsend. He gently nudged Carolyn, nodding his head toward Jeff, with that questioning look on his face. Carolyn nodded back to Dr. Parks, not saying anything, but silently acknowledging that she had noticed Jeff's appearance also.

Jeff took out his handkerchief, wiping the tears from his eyes, and proceeded,.

"Thank you all so much for all the love and kindness you have shown to me and my family these many years. It is an honor to serve you all, and to call you my friends and family in Christ. And now, if you would all stand once more in reverence to the Word of God, please turn in your Bibles to Matthew, chapter nineteen, verses thirteen and fourteen, where we will read:

"Then were there brought unto him little children, that he should put his hands on them, and pray: and the disciples rebuked them. But Jesus said, Suffer little children, and forbid them not, to come unto me: for of such is the kingdom of hea.....

Before Jeff could finish the word heaven, he suddenly grabbed his chest, and sank to the floor, his chest heaving for breath. The whole congregation gasped. Some turned pale. Others screamed and cried. Samuel, Becky, Becky Sarah and Dr. Parks ran to Jeff's side immediately. He still held his open Bible in his right hand. Becky's eyes were streaming with tears. All she could manage to say was Jeff's name. Now the whole crowd had gathered around the pulpit area, praying for Jeff, and expecting the worst. Dr. Parks asked everyone to move back away from Jeff, as he loosened Jeff's tie and shirt. Rufus was already running down the aisle with Dr. Parks' medical bag. Dr. Parks took out his stethoscope, placing it over Jeff's heart. Tears filled his eyes, as he looked at Becky and Samuel, shaking his head, sobbing.

Before his last breath, Jeff managed a weak smile at Becky, as he barely whispered.

"I love you Bec."

Becky whispered, "I love you Jeff."

He whispered Samuel's name, as Samuel and Becky knelt at his right hand. Jeff looked into Samuel's eyes, then at his Bible, whispering.

"Take it son, it's yours now."

Samuel gently eased the old and well-worn Bible from Jeff's hand, sobbing.

"I love you Papa."

Dr. Parks checked Jeff's pulse again. There was none. He held a small mirror under Jeff's nose. There was no sign of breath from his nostrils. He looked at Becky and Samuel with the saddest expression they had ever seen, as Dr. Parks himself cried openly.

"He's gone folks, our Pastor is gone home."

For a few minutes, it seemed as if time had stood still inside the church house. There was total silence. Every head was bowed. Without anyone saying a word, everyone knew that Pastor Jeff Townsend had done what he was put on Earth to do. His work was done, his race was run, and he had gone to Heaven with a smile.

Samuel quickly scribbled some words on a piece of paper, handing it to Rufus Rutherford. Rufus glanced at the piece of paper, nodded, and he and Claudette left immediately for the little telegraph office just south of the church. The message was for Tom Tillotson in Cleveland Tennessee. It read simply,

"Papa is dead. Come quickly. Samuel."

Tom Tillotson was now sixty-five years old, with snowy white hair, and walked with a cane. His associate Pastor, Michael Stewart, now did most of the preaching at Copper Springs Baptist Church. Tom mostly taught Bible studies on Wednesday nights, and preached occasionally on Sunday evenings. He was planning on turning the pastorate over to Brother Stewart in another month or two. When he received the telegram, his body shook with grief and sorrow, as vivid scenes of the past, one by one, flashed across his mind. He had been sure that Jeff would outlive him, and had actually hoped for that. And now Jeff was gone! The best friend he had ever known.

He and Pearly Mae, Thomas Clark and Erica, Ollie Marie and Sheriff Todd Jackson, Elick and Tracy Michelle, Michael and Mollie, and Carter Puckett, all boarded the train at 2:00 a.m. on Monday morning, April 24th, headed for Bruceton Mills West Virginia.

Becky and Samuel had made plans to meet them when they arrived. Becky wanted to be there for her other three children, it was the hardest thing she would have to do. She had dragged herself out of bed, not wanting to face the days of grief she knew were coming. Her heart screamed with pain for her beloved Jeff.

Visions of his last moments, his last words, his last breath were still imprisoned in her mind. She couldn't shake it no matter how hard she had tried. Even though the house was filled with friends and neighbors, Becky had wandered around, lost, in a complete daze. So many voices talking low still seemed to deafen her. Everyone was trying so hard to be helpful and to give her words of love and encouragement, but all she wanted to do was to climb to the top of the highest mountain and scream. She had cried until there was no more tears. Her insides felt like an empty hole, where, just a short while ago, was a beating heart filled with joy and happiness.

She and Samuel arrived at the train station. Standing there waiting, Becky began to tremble. Samuel held her steady on her feet as she greeted her other three children. They all held onto each other, crying as they grieved for the father and husband that they had lost. There was not a dry eye in the crowd that had gathered around them. Friends, and even total strangers offered a hand as they climbed into the carriages and buggy's that would take them back to the Townsend farm.

Plans for the funeral had to be made. Becky gathered her children close by her side in the big sitting room. They talked for hours about the wonderful man that was no longer with them. They agreed he must have the best, because he had always given them his best. The plans were to keep his body at the church, the church he had loved more than he loved himself. Visitation would be for one night, and the funeral would be the next day at 2:00 pm, with Michael Stewart and Jeff's long time friend Joseph Parks preaching the service. Lilly Murphy and Lucy Collins were to sing their Pastor's favorite hymn, The Old Rugged Cross.

Morning came too quickly for Becky. She dreaded this day worse than any day she could remember in her lifetime. The children kept a constant watch over her, making sure she ate and rested. Despite all the people in and out of the house that day Becky still remained in a daze. Folks dropped in to help with the chores and to bring food, but to Becky it was all just a bad dream. She sat there in that lonely bedroom that she had shared with Jeff for many wonderful years. The smell of his hair was still on the pillow where she buried her face. How she longed for Jeff to be there, and to hold her in his arms, telling her that all would be alright. Again she burst into tears, knowing that he couldn't, and even worse, never again would he be there to comfort her.

There was a knock at the bedroom door. Becky slowly sat up on the bedside, wiping her eyes

"Yes," she stammered in a weak voice.

"Mama, it's time to get ready to go to the church."

It was Ollie Marie on the other side of the door.

"Ok, I will be ready soon," Becky replied.

She knew her children were hurting just as bad as she was, but could only pray that God would give them comfort and peace that she herself was unable to give. She managed to pick out a dress to wear to the church. Looking it over slowly, she remembered it was one of Jeff's favorites, long black, trimmed in pale blue around the hem and sleeves. Slipping into her shoes, she walked out of the bedroom, as Samuel suggested they have a word of prayer before heading out toward the church. They all joined hands and bowed their heads, as they had done many times before as a family, but this time tears of grief flowed from every eye.

Todd prayed for comfort and peace for this dear family that he had learned to love so deeply. Becky could feel the sorrow from each person in that circle. Beside the fact that her own heart was broken for the loss of her beloved Jeff, it seemed that now she was also carrying the sorrow and grief of each of her children. Everyone slowly made their way out the door, with Samuel and Elick on each side of their mother. The ride to the church was much too short for Becky. She did not want to see the cold still body of her husband lying there, but she knew she had to.

The church yard was filled with wagon's and buggy's. A large crowd had gathered beside the church, crying for the loss of their dear pastor and his grieving family. They had left empty spaces for the Townsend family to park near the door. As the boys helped their mother down from the carriage, she was greeted by so many wonderful people, but Becky still seemed to be in a state of shock and denial. She tried to smile through her tear filled eyes. She thanked each of them for their kindness and love they had shown Jeff down through the years.

"We must go in now Mama," Samuel whispered, as he took her by the hand.

With his arm around her waist they entered the door of the church, followed by each of her children. Becky stood over the casket of the only man she had every loved. She felt her legs weakening as she looked down on his handsome face that was once so full of life. Now it was cold and silent. She wept openly, not caring who heard her mournful cries. So many emotions flooded her body and soul.

She screamed inside, "Why, why?"

Samuel and Elick stood there holding onto their mother with tears flowing freely, as their own bodies shook with grief for their father. Ollie and Erica both sat down on the middle pews, crying uncontrollably, unable to walk another step. Todd and Thomas Clark tried to comfort them.

The tears finally ceased for a short period of time, long enough for Becky to instruct Samuel to let Jeff's precious friends come inside. It was a sad sight as they filed in family by family, no dry eyes could be seen. Becky sat there on the front pew and listened as each one told her how much they loved him, and how he had always been there for them. This was what Becky had needed to hear, that her beloved husband had not lived nor died in vain; he had left behind a legacy of faithfulness and love that would never be forgotten. She was so proud of that legacy, and she knew her Jeff would be also.

The church was running over with beautiful flowers, homemade throws and quilts for Becky to take home after the service. A large tent was set up outside, where the women had prepared so much food for all to eat. Becky's heart swelled with pride as she took in her surroundings, thankful for her wonderful friends and neighbors. Becky stayed at the church far into the early morning hours. Her body became so weak she could no longer stand. Samuel insisted that she go home and sleep a few hours before the funeral. He and Elick promised they would not leave their father's side. Todd and Thomas Clark drove Becky and the girls home. The next day, they entered the church house for the final goodbyes to one of the finest men in the county, a man who had led his friends and neighbors through troubled times, hardships, the births, weddings, and deaths of their own families. Every seat in the church house was filled with folks from several counties. Other's were standing, and there were just as many outside as there were inside.

People of both races had come from other counties where Jeff had either held revivals, or preached funerals, or both. Becky was so pleased to see her own father and Sarah there as well as Tom and Pearly Mae. Her father held her in his arms while she cried tears of grief. Sarah wiped her tear-stained face as she planted a kiss on her cheek. Becky now knew somewhat of the sorrow that both her father and Sarah had felt so long ago.

The service began with the beautiful voices of Lilly and Lucy singing in perfect harmony. Michael Stewart read the obituary. Then Dr. Joseph Parks delivered the perfect message, one that Jeff would have been so proud of.

Dr. Parks entitled his eulogy, "Thou good and faithful servant of God."

This was one service which Becky, in one sense did not want to end, but in another sense, wished it could end quickly. She just did not want to say goodbye to her precious Jeff. All too quickly it came to an end, as Carolyn Parks played softly on the old piano. The people marched by the casket with tears streaming down their faces, as they looked at their pastor and friend for the last time. When all from the inside and outside had said farewell, someone closed the door so the family could have some privacy. Becky gathered her small family together, as they all, one by one, said their goodbyes. As Erica and Ollie wept loudly, Becky again felt burdened with double sorrow, for the loss of her husband and for the broken hearts of her children.

The casket was closed and carried by some of the men from the church to the cemetery. Tom Tillotson spoke at the grave side, expressing his great love for Jeff as a brother and friend as well as his pastor. He ended with a short prayer. Samuel and Elick led their mother off the cemetery and helped her into the buggy. Her father Ray, Sarah, Tom and Pearly Mae followed them back to the farm. Carolyn, Lucy and Lilly were already there preparing food for everyone. After the burial Dr. Parks, Michael Stewart and some of the others came in, assuring Becky that all had been taken care of at Jeff's final resting place.

Days turned into weeks, weeks turned into months. Becky's aching heart slowly, little by little, began to hurt less as time went by. The nights were lonely without her Jeff to talk to. Not a day went by that she didn't think of him. She would sit by the pond after supper and cry softly so no one could hear. Sometimes she caught herself speaking to him as though he was sitting there by her side. Walking ever so slowly back to the house, she sat on the big sofa, picked up the old family Bible, turned to the page entitled Deaths, and slowly and carefully recorded the entry.

Jeffrey Townsend, father, born April 26th, 1843, died April 23rd, 1893.

Samuel and Elick were kept busy running the two farms. Ollie had now decided she needed a change, so when the handsome young sheriff Todd Jackson asked her to marry him she accepted immediately. She had fallen head over heels in love with him and he with her. After their wedding they moved to Tennessee, where Todd continued to hold the sheriff's position, and Ollie felt very lucky and blessed that a teaching job was available. Thomas Clark and Erica lived too far apart, and soon their courtship become nothing more than a long distance friendship. Erica now had her eye on a handsome young school teacher, Malachi Thompson, who had ridden in from Clay County Kentucky, with dark hair, blue eyes and a killer smile. Everyone knew that a courtship between those two young people was inevitable, for Malachi couldn't keep his eyes off Erica, and she managed to be near him every chance she got.

One year after her father's death, Erica married the man of her dreams. She had always longed to have her father escort her down the aisle, but she knew he would be happy with the wonderful man she was marrying. Malachi and Erica built a small house on the farm very close to Becky.

With every break he could get from farm work, Elick spent a lot of time at Sheriff Murphy's office, studying all the books he could get his hands on concerning the law. Sheriff Murphy had made him a part time deputy.

Samuel, meanwhile, was trying to fill his father's shoes as the pastor of the church. His first heart-wrenching test as a pastor came in the form of a funeral service for Claudette's brother Burt, who was killed while serving as a missionary in Korea. Samuel had grown up with Burt and his brother Curt, which made it very difficult for him to preach the funeral of someone he had known from childhood.

Another young minister, Stephen Cole, had moved into town, and Samuel was quickly making friends with him. Everyone who met him approved of him immediately. Stephen and Samuel spent many long hours studying and researching the scriptures. After a year at the church, Samuel made Stephen his assistant pastor. Once again the church grew and prospered greatly.

Becky had many gentleman callers, but she would just smile and graciously decline their invitations to dinner. No one could measure up to her beloved Jeff. She watched her family grow and become prosperous young men and women. That, in itself, at least for now, made her happy.

As the evening sun set on the Townsend farm day after day, Becky would kneel by her bedside, fold her hands and bow her head in prayer, thanking God for all His many blessings. Each evening she picked up Jeff's picture from the night stand, placing a gentle kiss on his forehead, whispering.

"Goodnight my love, I will see you in the morning."

The End